Sawyer laced his fingers through hers.

They strolled to the end of a pier and there, under the star-speckled sky and with the gentle breeze playing over her skin, he turned her to him. With a finger, he tipped her chin up.

"You're beautiful, Shannon. Inside and out."

Before Shannon could think of a response, he slid a hand around her and up to rest on the nape of her neck and lowered his head.

With a sigh, she let her eyelids flutter closed as his lips touched hers. The stars overhead paled in comparison to the brilliant lights that burst against her eyelids as she gave herself over to the sensation of Sawyer's kiss.

The touch of his lips was light. Undemanding.

But it stirred feelings in her that made her question everything.

Dear Reader,

Home to Stay is the fourth book in what is now called the San Diego K-9 Unit series!

Those of you who have read the first three books might recall that they were originally intended to be a trilogy. After finishing the third book, *When I Found You*, I was saddened by the prospect of saying goodbye to the K-9 Unit, its heroes and their love interests. It seems that readers weren't prepared to say goodbye, either, as Harlequin contracted me to write a fourth book. I'm thrilled to have had this opportunity to tell the story of rookie K-9 officer Shannon Clemens, her search-and-rescue dog, Darwin, and law professor Sawyer Evans. Thank you for giving me the opportunity to do so.

I hope you'll enjoy Shannon, Sawyer and Darwin's story. I couldn't do what I do without your support. Thank you for choosing my books to spend some time with.

If you would like to use *Home to Stay* for your book club, you can find discussion questions on my website at www.kate-james.com.

As always, I would love to hear from you! Connect with me through my website, Facebook page (www.Facebook.com/katejamesbooks) or Twitter (www.Twitter.com/katejamesbooks), or mail me at PO Box 446, Schomberg, ON, L0G 1T0, Canada.

Happy reading!

Kate

HEARTWARMING

Home to Stay

——

Kate James

HARLEQUIN® HEARTWARMING™

Recycling programs
for this product may
not exist in your area.

ISBN-13: 978-0-373-36843-3

Home to Stay

For questions and comments about the quality of this book, please contact us at CustomerService@Harlequin.com.

Printed in U.S.A.

Kate James spent much of her childhood abroad before attending university in Canada. She built a successful business career, but her passion has always been literature. As a result, Kate turned her energy to her love of the written word. Kate's goal is to entertain her readers with engaging stories featuring strong, likable characters. Kate has been honored with numerous awards for her writing. She and her husband, Ken, enjoy traveling and the outdoors with their beloved Labrador retrievers.

To my husband, Ken, who is an inspiration to me every day.

I never fail to be amazed and impressed by the hard work, dedication, professionalism and sheer brilliance of the Harlequin team working behind the scenes to help make each of my books the very best it can be. I owe special thanks to Victoria Curran, Kathryn Lye and Paula Eykelhof.

When I started down the winding path to becoming published, it never occurred to me that I would realize an enormous side benefit: getting to know so many wonderful authors whose friendship, support and generosity of spirit continue to astonish and inspire me. There isn't enough room on this page to name you all, but I would like to acknowledge two remarkable women in particular. Catherine Lanigan and Loree Lough faced enormous personal challenges over the course of 2016, and they did so with extraordinary grace, dignity and determination. Even so, they never failed to think of others, and freely gave their love and friendship. I consider myself inordinately fortunate to be one of the beneficiaries! Heartfelt thanks to Catherine, Loree and all the other Harlequin Heartwarming authors whose friendship I value more than I can put into words.

CHAPTER ONE

SAWYER EVANS WAS in that languid state of semi-consciousness, waking from a restful sleep. It must have been the insistent chirping of a bird outside that had drawn him from his dreams. The muted glow of the early-morning light filtering in through the tent infused him with a sense of serenity.

As a single father and a professor of law, serenity wasn't something Sawyer experienced frequently. He smiled as he remembered that he'd categorically rejected the idea of a week-long camping trip at Cuyamaca Rancho State Park with his sister, Meghan, and their parents when Meg had first suggested it. He wasn't the rugged, outdoorsy type, not by any stretch of the imagination. He thought of himself as the nerdy academic, more comfortable with his head in a law book than plodding up a mountain trail. He'd felt that way even before he'd left the San Diego County District Attorney's office to teach, which he'd done to give him more time with Dylan after Jeannette abandoned them.

Three days in, and who'd have guessed he'd enjoy the experience so much?

And Dylan? He worried about his son becoming a bookish geek like him, and constantly encouraged him to play sports and spend time outdoors. But the apple hadn't fallen far from the tree with his kid. Dylan had to be the most studious four-year-old on the planet. Yet Dylan *loved* it here. He seemed to be in his element, despite this being his first camping trip. Dylan had been full of energy and enthusiasm ever since they'd arrived. And the exercise was doing him good. The fact that he was sleeping in, and without the nightmares that had plagued him the last couple of years, made Sawyer immensely glad he'd let Meg cajole him—maybe *bully* was a better word— into coming along.

Dylan was his life. He'd do anything for his son.

Sawyer rolled onto his side and tucked an arm under his head. He considered drifting back to sleep for a few more minutes as he listened to the sounds of nature and the gentle flapping of canvas…

Flapping of canvas?

That wasn't right.

He bolted up and stared at the tent flap, un-zipped and fluttering in the light breeze. He immediately shifted his gaze to Dylan's cot. From this angle, and with Dylan's form as slight as it was, he couldn't tell if his son was in his sleeping bag. Sawyer wasn't taking any chances. He scrambled out of his own bedroll and hurried over to Dylan's.

The adrenaline rush had him gasping for air.

The sleeping bag was empty.

Sawyer burst out of the tent and glanced frantically around.

No Dylan. Anywhere.

It must have been just past dawn. The sky was tinged with the first weak rays of sunlight, and a hazy mist shimmered across the water's surface. Meg and his mom, both early risers, weren't up yet.

Where was Dylan?

Sawyer's heart pounded so hard, he was sur-priscd it didn't slam right through his rib cage.

"Dylaaan!" he bellowed. "Dylaaan!"

His gaze was drawn to the small lake that their campsite edged, and his heart stopped.

"No. Please God...no," he mumbled as he ran toward the water. He'd been teaching Dylan to swim, but that didn't mean he couldn't have wandered into the lake and... *No!* He wouldn't think about that.

"Dylan!" Sawyer shouted again as he waded in.

A hand latched on to his arm and tugged him back. Too big a hand to be Dylan's.

He turned and stared into Meg's huge eyes.

"Sawyer, what are you doing? Where's Dylan?"

"I...I don't know where he is." He noticed his parents standing a few feet back at the edge of the lake. "Dylan wasn't in his sleeping bag..." His voice cracked, and he willed himself to stay calm.

"Dad, dial 911!" Meg, obviously thinking more coherently than Sawyer, called to their father. "And the park ranger."

As his father hurried to his parents' tent, Sawyer shook off Meg's grasp and took a few more unsteady steps into the lake. Other than the ripples he and Meg had created, the water's surface was smooth as glass. No disturbance...no air bubbles. He turned and brushed by Meg, hurrying toward his mother. She, too, was looking anxiously about, concern furrowing her brow.

Sawyer yelled Dylan's name several more times, then he, his mother and Meg stood motionless and quiet, hoping for a response. Only birdsong filled the silence until his father returned. "The park ranger's on his way. The

San Diego Police Department is also sending someone," he said.

"Okay. Okay," Sawyer murmured, trying desperately to think coherently. "Mom, you stay here. Wait for the ranger and the cops. I'm going over there." He gestured vaguely toward the left. He pointed again. "Meg, you look in that direction. Dad, can you search back there, behind the camp?"

Not waiting for replies, Sawyer raced back to his tent, pulled on his running shoes, then took off at a run.

He had to find Dylan. The thought of his son alone in the woods, frightened, maybe injured, terrified him. He didn't know how long Dylan had been gone.

Animals, including coyotes and mountain lions, inhabited the forest. He remembered reading in the guide book that the California mountain king snake lived in the park, too. He couldn't recall if the book said the snake was venomous.

"Dylaaan!"

His voice was hoarse from shouting his son's name. Occasionally, he heard Meg or his father calling out, too, but without response.

Never a response.

They *had* to find Dylan.

Tripping over an exposed tree root, Sawyer landed hard on his hands and knees. He pushed back up to his feet, absently brushed at the grime and the blood, and moved on.

He hadn't bothered with his watch when he left, and he had no idea how long he'd been stumbling around in the forest. He was barely aware of the cuts and scrapes he'd sustained running through dense growth and falling a couple of more times.

An incongruous sound caught his attention. Was it a rustling in the brush?

He paused to listen and began to wonder if he'd imagined it.

Then he heard it again. It was his name.

His mother was calling him. Her voice was faint but distinct.

Elation surged through him. Dylan must've found his way back to the campsite.

"I'm coming, Mom!" he shouted and thrashed through the forest, running as fast as he could.

The thorns and branches clawing at his arms and legs didn't slow him. He ran full speed in the direction of his mother's voice. His muscles screamed and each breath was agony, but the thought of Dylan, safe and sound in his mother's arms, propelled him forward.

What seemed like an eternity later, he hurtled through the brushwood bordering their campsite.

His energy gone, he bent over. Panting, trying to control his nausea, his eyes landed on his mother sitting at a picnic table. He swept his gaze around, searching for Dylan.

He saw his father and Meg talking to a couple of park rangers, but he didn't see his son. Limping over to his mother, his voice gravelly, he asked, "Where's Dylan?" But he knew the answer. Her tear-streaked face, swollen eyes and red nose said it all.

Dylan hadn't returned.

His mother rose, took a couple of halting steps toward him and collapsed in his arms. He held her while she wept.

When had his mother become so frail? Bird bones, he thought, as she shuddered in his embrace. Over the top of her head, Sawyer met his father's eyes. The torment in them was a reflection of what he felt himself.

One of the park rangers walked over. "Mr. Evans, we need to speak with you."

SHANNON CLEMENS'S DREAM had finally come true. She was now officially a member of the San Diego Police Department's K-9 Unit. Not on probation anymore, but a full-fledged K-9 officer, with her own specialization. It hadn't come easy. She'd worked diligently for it.

The K-9 Unit was one of the toughest in the department to get into.

And she'd done it! For the last few months, she'd been conferring with the unit's captain, Logan O'Connor, to identify the appropriate specialization for her and her police-service dog, Darwin. Well, now she was formally assigned to do search and rescue. She'd thought she might want to do explosives detection, but the incident at the San Diego International Airport half a year ago had helped her decide against it. Search and rescue presented its own challenges for her, but maybe it was destined that was where she'd end up.

She shifted her head on the pillow and watched the beautiful brown-and-black German shepherd lying on his own bed in a corner of her room. Darwin was only two years old, and was already showing exemplary skills and high detection accuracy. He was born in the Czech Republic, bred to be a service dog and had joined the SDPD K-9 Unit about the same time Shannon had. He was trained in tracking, building and area searches, article search, suspect apprehension and, like all dogs in the unit, handler protection and obedience. She was proud of Darwin, not just because she loved him, but because she'd been instrumental in his training.

Darwin moaned in his sleep and curled into a tighter ball. Shannon grinned at the way he'd tucked his snout under his tail.

She couldn't believe that Darwin was assigned to her and she had her dream job. Here they were…partners!

When her cell phone rang, Darwin immediately looked up. Shannon glanced at her bedside clock as she reached for the phone on her nightstand. It was just after six.

"Clemens," she said.

"Officer Clemens, this is Dispatch. I'm sorry to call you on your day off, but we have an incident at Cuyamaca Rancho State Park. Usually we'd send Officer Palmer and Scout for this, but he's not available at present."

Shannon swung her legs over the edge of the bed and sat up. Since Darwin had strolled over, she rubbed him behind the ears. She knew that Cal Palmer, the only other SDPD K-9–Unit officer who specialized in search and rescue, was enjoying a well-deserved vacation. He and his wife, Jessica, were due to have a baby soon, and they'd decided to take their two girls on a Disney cruise before the arrival of their new addition. They were on a ship, and there was no way to summon Cal back, even if the SDPD had wanted to.

"No problem," Shannon said. "What's the situation?"

"We have a missing child. Four years old. He reportedly wandered away from his family's campsite. We don't know how long he's been gone, but the State Park Rangers don't want to take any chances. They've asked for our assistance in finding the boy. They need all the help they can get to cover the twenty-six thousand acres of forest, should it come to that."

Shannon was familiar with the park, roughly forty miles east of San Diego in the Laguna Mountains. She'd frequented it with her family and her childhood friend, Kenny, when she was younger, and now she liked to go hiking there. In fact, she'd run training exercises in the park with Darwin.

But a missing child…that was *not* what she would've wanted for her first solo search assignment.

She tried to ignore the cold dread that slithered along her spine and wrote down the particulars.

The missing boy was four-year-old Dylan Evans. His father, a professor at Thomas Jefferson School of Law. Shannon's heart went out to the man. She was certain the last thing he would've expected when he went camping with his family was that he'd wake up in the early hours of the morning to discover that his son had somehow gotten out of their tent and disappeared. Dylan was potentially alone in a wilderness that was home to mountain lions and other creatures that posed a threat to a young boy's survival.

Oh, she was well aware of the hazards a child could face in the park on his own. Time was very much of the essence.

"I'm on it," she said and glanced at her clock again. "I should be there in under an hour."

She didn't bother to shower. While Darwin ate his breakfast, she had a toasted bagel, then dressed quickly. To get her chin-length blond hair in some semblance of order, she ran a wet brush through it. She retrieved her equipment duffel from the bottom of her closet and rushed down the stairs.

Ten minutes after she'd received the call from Dispatch, she and Darwin were in her SDPD-issue Ford Explorer heading to Cuyamaca Park. The adrenaline was pumping, a good thing, since it was blocking out the dread.

She could do this. She *would* do this.

A child's life depended on it.

As she merged onto I-5 San Diego Freeway South, a moment of guilt had her wondering if she should've told her captain about Charlie. Would that have made a difference? Would it have kept Logan from assigning her to search and rescue? It was too late for second-guessing. She'd simply have to do the best she could.

When her phone rang, she answered it.

"Shannon, it's Logan."

Speak of the devil. "I'm on my way," she assured her captain.

"Good. I knew you would be. I wanted to tell you that you're up for this. You're skilled and so is Darwin. Two of the best rookies I've worked with."

She could hear the sincerity in his voice. The pep talk bolstered her confidence. "Thanks, Jagger," she said, calling Logan by his alias. "I appreciate your belief in me."

"It's earned. Give me an update when you have something."

"Roger that."

She focused on her driving and soon she was passing through the entrance to the park. She checked in at the ranger station and was escorted to the Evanses' campground.

Her stomach tensed as the site came into view.

A tall, rangy man, dressed in plaid shorts,

a white T-shirt and wearing black-and-white high-top running shoes, sat at a picnic table. He had his elbows on his knees and his head cradled in his hands. She couldn't see his face, but his dark brown hair was standing on end. His arms and legs were scraped and bleeding in places, and his T-shirt had a long tear on one side.

A woman, roughly the same age and with nearly the same color hair, sat huddled against him, an arm around his shoulders. Shannon wondered, as she climbed out of her SUV and released Darwin, why his wife—assuming that was who the woman was—seemed to be holding up much better than the man.

Shannon turned her attention to the elderly couple on the other side of the table. The man was holding the woman, who was crying silently. Obviously the grandparents. Shannon waved to a ranger when he noticed her arrival. He walked briskly toward her and quickly briefed her on the situation. They'd been searching for over an hour, and had found no trace of the boy.

Shannon knew—and not just because of her police training—that wasn't good news.

The ranger pointed out the boy's father and signaled for her to follow him.

"Mr. Evans?" Shannon said softly when

they'd reached the picnic table. The woman looked up but the man didn't. "Mr. Evans," she repeated, more loudly this time.

When his head jerked up, his forest green eyes—an unusual blend of green and brown— bored into hers. Their intensity triggered an involuntary urge to step back.

He had a strong jaw, straight nose. Good features. He might've been attractive under normal circumstances. But right now, his skin was splotchy, his hair even more disheveled from this angle, his eyes red-rimmed and his lips compressed so firmly they were edged with white. He had an angry scratch on his left cheek, just below his eye. The desperation she saw in his eyes evoked memories of Charlie and nearly destroyed her composure.

Everyone's attention was now on her and she had to maintain control.

"Mr. Evans, I'm Officer Shannon Clemens with the San Diego Police Department. I'm here to help find Dylan." She had to give him hope. She could see he was barely hanging on. "We'll locate him," she promised. She prayed they could.

Because it was too disconcerting to keep looking into his tormented eyes, she shifted her gaze to the woman. "Mrs. Evans, your son—"

"It's Ms.," the woman corrected her. "I'm Meghan. Dylan's aunt."

"Okay." Uncertainty formed a hard, tight knot in her stomach. She wished Cal hadn't taken *this* particular week off—and that her first solo search and rescue assignment didn't involve a boy nearly the same age as Charlie had been…

Shannon forced herself to stay focused, stay sharp. "Darwin." She pointed to her dog. "He's trained in search and rescue. Darwin and I will do everything we can to find Dylan. Before we start, I need your help."

The father straightened. "Of course. Whatever you need."

She took a deep breath to brace herself. "I require something that's Dylan's and has his scent on it, to get Darwin familiar with it. The more recent, the better."

He lurched to his feet. "Yeah. Sure. His sleeping bag. He was in it before he disappeared."

"Good, but I also need something smaller. Something I can take with me to refresh Darwin's memory, if necessary. An article of clothing Dylan slept in perhaps?"

He clenched his hands, the knuckles turning white. "He… He's wearing the clothes he slept in."

Twelve years later, she still remembered that all-consuming, devastating feeling of having a loved one go missing. Maybe it was wrong, but Shannon touched his arm. "Let's see what there is in the tent that we can use," she said gently.

She settled on a pair of socks that had been stuffed into Dylan's sneakers. When the father said that was the only pair of shoes he'd brought for Dylan, she made a mental note to consider how far the boy could've wandered without shoes.

To be on the safe side, Shannon also took the T-shirt Dylan had worn the evening before and a picture the father had in his wallet.

Again she laid an encouraging hand on his arm. "I promise we'll do everything we can to find your son."

CHAPTER TWO

SHANNON CLIPPED A leash to Darwin's collar. She let the dog smell both articles of clothing before storing them in her pouch, and instructed him to "find."

Based on the information she'd been given, she estimated that Dylan had been missing for about three hours. That was a considerable time for a young boy to be alone in a forest.

But not so long that Darwin couldn't pick up his trail. The dog's behavior confirmed Shannon's assessment of the elapsed time. The boy's scent had dissipated sufficiently that Darwin was sniffing the air rather than the ground. They entered the forest at a run. Shannon said silent thanks for the hours she spent at the gym. Not wanting to break Darwin's concentration, she matched her speed to his.

She dodged branches, leaped over fallen logs and, when she couldn't avoid it, crashed through undergrowth to keep up with him. Once or twice when Darwin slowed, she pulled Dylan's picture out of her pocket. Each

time she looked at the image of the smiling
little boy, she thought of Charlie. Her remorse
over Charlie's death, and the possibility that
she might not be able to find and return Dylan
safely to his father caused a constriction in her
chest that made it hard to inhale.

Distracted, she nearly tripped over Darwin
when he paused at a fork in the trail. He turned
in circles, uncertain which way to go. Shannon let him scent Dylan's clothing again. With
a short bark, he was off once more.

Shannon was breathless by the time they
reached a narrow gravel lane that appeared to
be a service road. Darwin stopped and looked
to Shannon for direction. When she held out
the sock for him and urged him to "find," he
started down the road, but Shannon called him
back.

It seemed that Darwin had lost the trail and
was going to run down the road, probably because it was the path of least resistance.

She placed her hands on her knees and
leaned forward to catch her breath.

She'd failed Charlie and now she was failing
Dylan, too. The thought of that turned the constriction into a roiling, greasy mess in her gut.

No longer able to contain it, she bent over
the bushes and lost the contents of her stomach.

Feeling steadier, she forced herself to concentrate on her task. A little boy's life depended on it, and she wouldn't risk his life by not doing her job to the best of her ability.

Shannon tried one more time with Darwin, but he kept wanting to run down the road. Dylan couldn't have walked down that road barefoot. That thought had her considering the good two miles that she and Darwin had run. How likely was it that a four-year-old could've walked that far, and without shoes?

Had she made a mistake? Had Darwin? Had they gone the wrong way at the fork in the trail?

The park rangers had dogs and handlers searching, too. If she and Darwin couldn't find the boy, maybe one of them would. But she knew the rangers' dogs were multipurpose, while she and Darwin specialized in searches. Because of that, they were considered Dylan's best chance.

Dejected, Shannon led Darwin back to the campsite at a brisk jog. Along the way, she called Logan and provided him with an update. He said he was en route and would see her at the site.

It was hard telling her boss that she'd failed. She didn't know how she was going to break the news to the boy's father. How could she confess to him that her best hadn't been good enough?

She hadn't been able to find his son.

The pain of losing Charlie all those years ago seemed as intense at that moment as it had back then. She remembered the police officer who'd broken the news to her parents that he'd found her little brother. But by then it had been too late.

She remembered how it had felt not to know if Charlie was dead or alive…and if he was alive, to worry about him suffering. The officer back then had brought closure for Shannon and her parents. Not the way they'd hoped, but it was closure nonetheless.

There would be no closure for Sawyer Evans, at least not that morning.

The bile had left a bitter taste in her mouth. She popped a breath mint as she neared the campsite. It would be challenging not to let Dylan's father see her emotions when she spoke with him; he didn't need to know she'd lost her breakfast.

She saw him standing at the edge of the small lake, his back to her, legs spread, hands in the pockets of his shorts. A quick scan of the area told her that he was alone. She assumed his family was inside one of the tents. A ranger's pickup was parked by the roadway, the ranger sitting behind the wheel and talking on his phone.

She gave Darwin the hand signal to "downstay" next to her Explorer, poured some water in his bowl and walked quietly toward the father.

"Mr. Evans?"

His head snapped around, and she nearly cringed at the desperate hope she saw in his features and his bloodshot eyes. As the hope transformed into desolation, she understood that he already knew the outcome, because she'd returned without Dylan. His whole body sagged as if the air had been sucked out of him, and he looked so bereft, she wanted to wrap her arms around him. Instead, she shoved her hands in her own pockets, her stance mirroring his.

"I'm sorry. We didn't find Dylan."

Another emotion flitted across his face. Uncertainty? Relief that at least they hadn't found him dead?

She realized he might have feared the worst, but… She couldn't even finish the thought. "We followed his trail to a service road," she explained. "Without shoes, I don't think he'd have walked along a gravel road…"

"Then where did he go?"

Shannon shook her head. "I'm sorry, but I don't know."

"The rangers haven't found him either." He gestured toward the pickup. "They said you and your dog would find Dylan. You said it, too."

He took a step toward her. It was the look in his eyes that told her his temper was brewing. That was okay with her. Anger was better than misery, if it helped pull him out of the depths of despair.

"What now? You're not giving up, are you?"

"No…of course not."

She heard a vehicle approach and glanced back. With mixed relief and trepidation, she watched Logan bring his Explorer to a stop next to hers. "Ah, excuse me a minute," she said. "That's the captain of our unit."

Logan climbed out, took one look at Shannon as she strode over to him and guided her to the other side of his vehicle, where they had some privacy. "Is there a new development?" he asked in a hushed whisper.

"No, um, I told you on the phone…" She choked back a sob, and angled away so she wouldn't embarrass herself further by crying.

She felt his hand on her shoulder. "Shannon, talk to me."

"I…I…"

He turned her to face him.

When tears filled her eyes and threatened to overflow, she struggled to suppress them. She was not a crier as a rule, and she would *not* cry in front of her boss—or worse, the father of the missing boy.

"I know this isn't easy. Shannon... I never want you *not* to care, but now's not the time to fall apart. We don't know that the boy's come to any harm."

"It's not just the boy."

At Logan's raised eyebrows, she took a deep breath. "When I was fourteen, my brother died. Charlie... He'd wandered into a forest. When the police found him, it was too late."

Logan took a step back. "Why didn't you consider that relevant information to share with me?" he demanded.

Shannon could see he was annoyed, and with good reason, she thought.

"If not when we were discussing your specialization, then you should've told me when we spoke on your way here."

Shannon didn't know what to say. Logan was right. Of course, he was right. She'd failed him. She'd failed Sawyer Evans. She'd failed Dylan. And if it came down to it...she'd failed herself, too.

She wouldn't be surprised if her captain decided to fire her over this. He expected truth and integrity from all his officers. She raised her hands. Dropped them again.

Logan let out an aggravated breath and ran a hand over the top of his head. "I'm sorry about your brother. I can't imagine how I'd feel if I lost Becca," he said, referring to his younger sister. "But you should've confided in me."

Shannon's mouth fell open, but before she could formulate any words, he continued. "We'll talk about it later," he said firmly. "Right now, our focus is on finding Dylan Evans."

When Shannon's eyes misted again, he looked at her sternly. "Shannon, if you can't do this, say so, and I'll have someone else work with Darwin. I don't mean to be insensitive, but the missing boy *is* our priority."

Shannon forced thoughts of Charlie to the back of her mind and nodded. "I can do it."

Logan watched her for a moment, then nodded, too. "Okay. I brought Scout with me," he said as he walked to the back of his SUV and let Cal Palmer's search-and-rescue dog out of the back. "I don't doubt Darwin...or you, but two dogs are better than one in this case. The park has a lot of ground to cover. Not that I think a four-year-old could've gotten far from the camp."

She'd had the same thought earlier when she and Darwin had reached the service road. But if Dylan had been snatched by a mountain lion or a coyote… No. She'd stay positive. If she couldn't, how was Dylan's father supposed to?

She called Darwin over as Logan clipped a leash to Scout's collar. "Let's move and you can fill me in on the details as we go."

She glanced over to where the father had taken a seat at a picnic table, his head in his hands again. His sister and parents had emerged from their tents and were clustered nearby, but she got the sense that he wasn't aware of their presence, isolated in his own world of grief and anxiety.

"Sure. Just give me a minute, please."

Shannon handed Darwin's leash to Logan. She jogged to the picnic table and sat down next to Sawyer. "Mr. Evans…" She waited until he looked up at her with tortured eyes. The tightness in her chest was immediate and acute, but she didn't flinch or avert her gaze. "We're not giving up on finding Dylan. You have my word."

"You said before…that you'd bring him back."

His anguished comment intensified Shannon's sense of failure.

Before she could respond, he held out a

shaky hand and took hers. "I'm sorry. That was unwarranted. I know you're doing your best. *Please* find him."

"The captain of our unit brought another search-and-rescue dog with him. We'll go now."

"Okay. Good."

She released his hand and rose.

Rejoining Logan, they gave both dogs Dylan's scent and let them lead the way into the forest.

"This is the same trail Darwin and I took earlier," Shannon confirmed a few minutes later.

Logan nodded but kept his eyes on Scout. If the dog lost the scent or picked up any conflicting smells, she knew Logan didn't want to miss it.

Because of that, Logan signaled to her when Scout paused at a clump of elderberry. They both crouched down to investigate. There was a small damp patch of soil at the base of a bush. Logan bent lower. "Urine," he said. "I'm betting Dylan relieved himself here."

She looked around. "Yeah. Darwin and I stopped here, too. I missed the urine," she said apologetically.

"The important thing is that we're on the

right trail," he assured her as he placed a marker by the spot. "Let's keep going."

The next time they stopped was at the end of the service road where Shannon had abandoned the search. The dogs were about to bolt down the drive when Logan ordered them back.

Shannon shook her head in frustration. "The boy couldn't have walked there. He wasn't wearing shoes. I don't even know how he could've gotten this far, but he certainly didn't walk across the gravel in bare feet."

"No, he didn't."

"Then what?" she asked in a subdued voice. "Darwin and I weren't wrong about the trail. Scout brought us here, too."

"No, you weren't wrong."

"I don't understand."

"Watch the dogs. Remember, search-and-rescue dogs can follow scents even if those scents are in a vehicle. See the way they're behaving?"

Shannon nodded.

"My bet is Dylan got into a vehicle here… or was put in one. Hold on a minute," Logan said, pulling his cell phone out of its holster.

Shannon squatted down by the road, trying to make sense of the various tire tracks in the gravel. How would a small boy who'd wandered away from his family's campsite end up in a vehicle? She couldn't see anything that enlightened her. Then she noticed a small pool of engine oil. It looked fresh. She glanced up at Logan. He was still talking on his phone.

Thinking optimistically, she supposed that someone working in the park could have come across Dylan. But if that was the case, Dylan would've been taken to the rangers' station and would have been reunited with his family by now.

Since they hadn't heard anything yet, that scenario was unlikely.

The alternatives unnerved her.

Could someone have happened upon Dylan and simply taken him? If not…was it possible that Dylan hadn't walked away from his campsite at all?

"You're thinking that Dylan didn't wander away from the campsite?" she asked as soon as Logan was off the phone. "That he was *abducted*?"

"Yeah. That's what I think. No one has contacted the rangers' station or the division about finding a boy." He looked around. "This is where one trail ends and another—in a vehicle—begins."

"There's fresh engine oil on the gravel."

Shannon gestured toward the spot. "If the dogs have the scent, should we follow it?"

Logan frowned. "No. The ranger I spoke with said the service road is at least four or five miles and it connects to a main arterial. If we're correct that Dylan was put in a vehicle here, that vehicle had no place to go except down this road. At the arterial, the scent will be much too faint for the dogs to determine which direction it took, let alone follow it from there."

As they made their way back to the campsite, Logan called the division to get additional resources. The Special Response Team would lead the search, and the FBI would be brought in to assist, which was normal procedure for suspected abductions. All Shannon could think of was how shattered Sawyer had looked and the small glimmer of hope that had flickered in his eyes when she'd said they weren't giving up.

How could she explain that they thought his son had been abducted?

And why?

"What sort of salary would a professor of law earn?" she asked Logan.

"If you're thinking of money as a motive, I'd bet he has enough. We ran him. He was an assistant DA before he switched to teaching."

Shannon mulled that over. She checked her watch. It must've been at least five hours since Dylan had disappeared. "If it is kidnapping, shouldn't there have been contact by now? A call or a ransom demand?"

Logan shrugged. "Odds are, but not necessarily. And money isn't always the goal. As an assistant DA, he impacted a lot of people's lives. Those he sent to jail. Their loved ones."

When they reached the campsite, Shannon immediately noticed that Sawyer wasn't at the table with his family. Again, he was alone. This time, he was sitting in the sand on the shore of the lake. His knees were bent, arms wrapped around them.

"Do you want me to tell him?" Logan asked.

Shannon wasn't going to shirk her responsibilities, regardless of how difficult it would be for her. She knew Logan had more calls to make to coordinate the next steps. "Thanks for the offer, but I'll do it."

She handed Darwin's leash to Logan, drew a deep breath and walked slowly to where Sawyer was.

"Mr. Evans… Sawyer?" she said softly as she approached him.

He gazed up at her as if he'd just come out of a trance and scrambled to his feet. His eyes were wild as he glanced about.

"We didn't find him," she said.

He seemed to close in on himself and collapsed back onto the ground, elbows on his knees and his forehead in his hands. "What now?" he asked in a barely audible voice.

She lowered herself to the sand beside him. "We need to ask you some questions."

He didn't move. Didn't look at her. "You and the others have already asked me all the questions imaginable."

Shannon understood his frustration, but the questions so far had focused on the possibility of a child wandering away. She had to tell him what their hypothesis was and that it required a whole new set of questions to be explored—including those that would probe whether he or another member of his family could've had anything to do with it. "No, we haven't," she responded. "We suspect that Dylan didn't wander away."

Sawyer lifted his head and stared at her as if she'd suddenly grown horns. "What? If he didn't wander away, then where is he? One of us has been here at the camp since I discovered he was gone."

As painful as it had been when she'd learned that Charlie was missing—and all because he'd wanted to be with her—it would be far worse for Sawyer once she explained the situ-

ation to him. She wished there was something
she could say or do to soften the blow, but the
cold, hard truth had to be said.

WHEN THE POLICE officer didn't answer his
question right away, Sawyer scrabbled around
to face her and grasped her upper arms. "What
do you mean Dylan didn't wander away?"

Her eyebrows furrowed and she glanced
down to where he was gripping her.

Only then did he realize he was holding her
and not gently. He immediately released her.
Seeing the distinct marks left by his fingers
below the short sleeves of her uniform shirt,
he was dismayed. "I'm sorry. I'm so sorry…
Officer," he mumbled.

She rubbed a hand over the spot on her arm.
"It's okay. And it's Clemens. Shannon Clemens. We followed a trail to a service road. We
think he was put in a vehicle there."

Sawyer slumped back on his heels. "Someone found him? Have you checked to see if
anyone's reported finding him? To the rangers or the police?"

"Yes. Neither the park rangers nor the SDPD
have received any report of a young boy being
found."

"But you think someone put him in a vehicle and…*took him*?" Sawyer couldn't believe

what he was hearing. If someone had found Dylan, lost and alone, surely that person would have taken him to the rangers' office or the police by now. And if not? As he realized what she was saying, the horror of it threatened to overwhelm him. "You think he's been...*kidnapped*?" he asked, his voice raw.

"We think someone took Dylan. The distance he would've had to travel to the service road, especially in bare feet, is too far. He was probably carried, if not all the way, then part of it." Shannon nodded to her captain, who'd just joined them, before continuing. "Based on the behavior of the dogs, we suspect a person or persons put him in a vehicle at that location."

Sawyer staggered to his feet. Turning his back on the cops, he dragged the fingers of both hands through his hair.

He was fairly certain this was what losing one's mind felt like. His son was missing—might have been abducted—and there wasn't a thing he could do about it. After Jeannette had left them, he'd sworn he'd protect Dylan and give him enough love for two parents.

He stumbled to the edge of the water and stared off into the distance.

Was this some incomprehensibly cruel joke the powers that be were playing on him? Three years ago his wife went missing and now his son? Jeannette might be lost to him, but he *had* to get Dylan back. Whatever it took. If not, he really would go insane.

If Dylan had been abducted, who would've done it?

"Mr. Evans?"

A male voice, so the captain, not the officer. Sawyer spun around.

"It might be advisable for you and your family to go home. We'll need to ask you some more questions, but we can do it there."

Sawyer looked around and noticed that the campsite was now being treated as a crime scene. There were more cops present and yellow do-not-cross tape had been used to cordon off the area.

"Dylan..." he whispered and turned imploring eyes on Shannon.

"There's nothing more you can do for him here," she said softly. "If he *was* abducted, you should be home near your phone."

He nodded. "I...I have to tell my parents and Meg."

"Okay. Then we'll have someone drive you home. You can get your vehicle some other time. It'll be fine here until then."

"Sure. Yeah." Didn't they understand that he didn't care about his damn car?

All he cared about was getting Dylan back.

CHAPTER THREE

THE AUTHORITIES WERE convinced that the young boy, Dylan Evans, had been abducted. Despite there being no ransom demand. No contact. At least not yet.

When the possibility had first occurred to Shannon, dread had washed over her. Telling the father, Sawyer Evans, what they suspected had broken her heart.

Afterward, she'd gone to Sawyer's home with Logan, and then back to the division for the briefing of the Special Response Team. Richard Bigelow was the lead detective assigned to the case, and she was glad of it. She didn't know him well, but he was said to be the best on his team.

The SDPD had called in the FBI to assist, standard operating procedure with children presumed to have been abducted. The FBI had assigned a special agent in charge to work with the SDPD, Gavin Leary, and another special agent, Anne Wilson, to assist.

Shannon didn't know if her help would be

required again, but took comfort in the fact that they had the top resources available on the case.

Back at her desk, she scooped kibble into Darwin's bowl. She watched him scarf down his food. Shannon might not be hungry, but the events of the day didn't seem to have hurt her dog's appetite.

After he finished his meal, he ambled over and rested his head on her lap. She stroked him as she thought back to the meeting.

They'd considered all the possibilities and narrowed it down to two. Either Dylan had wandered off and someone had seized him opportunistically, or it had been planned and he'd been taken from the campsite and to the vehicle.

Everyone present had agreed that the second scenario was more probable, since the former would've been too coincidental and highly improbable in the middle of the night. Also, as Shannon had concluded, it would've been too long and arduous a trek for Dylan to walk from the campsite to the service road on his own.

But how could someone have gotten Dylan out of the tent without waking his father? The only plausible scenario they could come up with was that the boy had gone outside to relieve himself and been taken then. But that would've meant someone had been watching and waiting, possibly all night, for Dylan to appear. She returned to the fact that it had been hours and there was still no ransom demand.

Shannon got her laptop, put her feet up on a chair and opened a picture of Charlie.

She was fourteen when her little brother died and the events that had led up to it still haunted her.

All through her childhood, people had called her a tomboy. When she'd first heard the term, she hadn't known what it meant. Curious, she'd looked it up online, where it said something about how the way she was didn't follow the "female gender norm." That hadn't bothered her. She'd seen it as fact. When other girls her age were playing with dolls or going to tea parties, she'd been engaged in sports or building mechanical things.

Her best friend since the first grade was a boy. Kenny had been her only friend for most of her life. When her parents had another child and that child turned out to be a boy, she'd been relieved. Shannon would've loved her sibling no matter what, but she'd secretly worried about how she'd handle having a sister. She was okay with being a tomboy, maybe even pleased by it, but what sort of influence would she have been on a little sister? So, she'd been glad when her mother had given birth to Charlie.

There was a ten-year age gap between them, but she'd loved Charlie completely and unreservedly.

And Charlie had loved her unconditionally in return. Their mother had said he idolized her. That put a lot of pressure on Shannon to be a good role model. Charlie wanted to do everything Shannon did; in fact, their father called him her shadow. As Charlie had grown, he'd also developed an open adoration for Kenny. Shannon had worried about how Kenny would respond to a young child hanging around them. She'd been delighted when Kenny, an only child, treated Charlie as if he was his kid brother, too.

Shannon's parents started calling them the Three Musketeers. Shannon had Googled that, and she liked the sound of it. Yeah, the three of them against the world!

Shortly after Shannon turned fourteen, something had changed between her and Kenny. At first it was subtle; with time, it became more pronounced. She couldn't put her finger on it, but their relationship just wasn't the same. She worried that because Kenny was sixteen, two years older than her, he now thought of *her* as a kid. Her idea was reinforced when he'd insisted that she—and everyone else—start calling him Ken. He considered himself too old to be called Kenny. But she concluded she couldn't have been correct about how he felt because they still saw each other as much as they used to, if not more. Then she'd fretted that it was Charlie, since Ken no longer wanted to have him around.

Shannon's mother had sat her down and had a talk with her about Ken and their relationship now that they were teenagers, but Shannon had assured her that Kenny—Ken—was just a friend.

When Ken had asked Shannon to go for a hike in Torrey Pines State Reserve north of San Diego, Charlie had wanted desperately accompany them. Kenny had insisted that it would be a long hike, too strenuous for Charlie. Tears had coursed down her brother's cheeks when she'd told him he couldn't come with them.

If only Charlie had listened...

SHANNON CLOSED HER eyes and the memories came rushing back.

It was shortly after Kenny had gotten his driver's license and he was so proud to be able to drive them to the park in his mother's car.

As they walked side by side along a forest path, Kenny bumped Shannon's shoulder. Shannon had been watching the shifting patchwork of light and shade on the sun-dappled forest floor, her thoughts so focused on how to broach the subject of what had caused the change between them, that the movement made her lose her footing.

He caught her with one hand on her arm, the other at her waist.

"Thanks, Kenny." Noting his annoyance, she quickly amended her words. "Sorry... Ken." Steady on her feet again, she tried to step away, but he kept an arm around her waist. "Um... I'm okay now. Thanks."

Instead of releasing her, he closed the gap between them. Shannon saw his mouth open and his eyes close as he lowered his head toward hers. With an appalled jolt, she understood that he intended to kiss her. Letting out a squeal that sounded girlish to her own ears, she placed her palms on his chest and shoved. She must've taken him by surprise because he staggered and landed ingloriously on his butt.

"What did you do that for?" he demanded, his irritation obvious.

"You...you were going to *kiss* me!" Shannon swiped her forearm across her mouth, almost as if he'd managed to accomplish what he'd set out to do.

Leaning back, he continued to stare up at her. "Yeah. What's wrong with that?"

"What's *wrong* with it?" she heard herself sputter. "You're my friend. You're like a brother."

He rose and dusted off his jeans. "Is that so? Is that how you think of me?"

"Well, yeah. How else?"

She and Kenny—Ken—couldn't reach any kind of agreement, but at least she had her answer to the question she'd been grappling with.

Something *had* changed between them.

Kenny no longer thought of her as a friend or a sister. He confessed that he wanted her as his *girlfriend*.

Shannon couldn't think of him that way. Her mother's warning, and how readily she'd dismissed it, came to mind.

Kenny suggested she take some time to decide. She knew she didn't need time, since her feelings for Kenny weren't going to change.

Kenny drove her home. He didn't bother to get out of the car. They said a terse goodbye and, with a heavy heart, she walked into her house.

When Shannon entered the kitchen, her mother glanced over her shoulder from where she was standing in front of the stove, stirring a pot. "Oh, thank goodness you're back," Victoria said. "Your father has a charter booked to go fishing and wants to take Charlie with him."

"Charlie?" Maybe it was because Shannon was still in a daze from what had happened with Kenny, but she didn't understand what her mother was talking about.

"Yes, Charlie." Victoria turned, a wooden spoon in her hand. "Where is he?"

Shannon felt cold tentacles of dread slithering through her. "Why are you asking me? I was with Kenny. Charlie wasn't with us."

The spoon slipped out of Victoria's hand and clattered to the tile floor. "Then where is he? When we couldn't find him, we…we assumed he must've gone with you."

The tentacles were constricting, and she imagined her ribs would snap at any moment. It was nearly impossible for her to breathe. "No…" Shannon's voice was a disembodied whisper. "He wasn't with us."

Victoria rushed to the hallway. "Paul! Paul… Charlie wasn't with Shannon!"

The rest of the day was a nightmare for Shannon.

The police were in and out of their home as if it had a revolving door. They visited Kenny and found Charlie's stuffed dog on the floor of his car. They'd speculated that Charlie had followed Shannon out of the house and that while she and Kenny had gone into the garage to get her hiking boots, he'd hidden on the floor in the backseat of the car and sneaked after them when they went on their hike.

A police officer and his search-and-rescue dog were brought in to find Charlie.

They discovered his body the next day.

He must've gotten lost in the forest and had drowned in a creek. The K-9 officer had tears in his eyes when he told them. Shannon hadn't blamed the police. She could tell they'd done everything possible to find Charlie. The K-9 officer had just been brought in too late, as he'd been deployed on another assignment. She'd concluded that if there were more police officers with dogs, they could've found Charlie in time. She knew her parents felt the same way, because they made a donation in Charlie's memory to the San Diego Police Department Foundation to acquire and train a police service dog in search and rescue. Shannon had asked that the dog be named after Charlie. The foundation had agreed.

It was back then that Shannon had resolved to become a police officer working in the K-9 Unit. If she could save one little boy like Charlie, dedicating her life to policing would all be worth it…

Now, here she was, and she'd had that chance. And she'd failed.

IT WAS WELL past eight when Logan finished the last of his paperwork and turned off his computer. He said silent thanks that Ariana was so understanding about the odd hours he had to work. He smiled, thinking that she'd soon be his wife. Logan wouldn't have imagined it six months ago, when he'd first met the cool and competent head of security and loss prevention for San Diego International Airport.

Logan retrieved his duffel, whistled for Boomer, his explosives-detection dog, and left his office.

He'd thought that he'd been alone in the squad room, but he was wrong. Shannon was leaning back in her chair, her feet propped up on another one, her legs crossed at the ankles. She had her laptop on her lap, but she was completely still. He couldn't tell if she'd dozed off or not, but the computer screen was dark. He knew she'd been working long hours since Cal had left on vacation, and this should've been her day off.

"Hey, Shannon," he said quietly as he approached her.

She dropped her feet to the floor and nearly

knocked the laptop off her thighs as she bolted up. The jostling had the screen coming out of hibernation. "Logan. Sorry, I didn't hear you."

He smiled. "Obviously."

She hurriedly shut down her laptop, but not before he saw the smiling, freckle-faced kid's picture.

He pulled the chair she'd had her feet on forward and sat. What would another fifteen or twenty minutes matter when he suspected he knew what was going on. He signaled for Boomer to lie down. The beautiful near-black Dutch Malinois/shepherd mix did, right next to Darwin.

"Shannon, the boy in that picture is your brother?" He searched his memory for the child's name. "It's Charlie?"

Shannon nodded.

"You want to talk about it?"

She took a deep breath, then blew it out. "I just relived it in my mind. I'd prefer not to go through it again. At least not now." She placed a finger on her touch pad, fiddled with it a bit and clicked. She turned the screen toward Logan. "And that's Dylan."

Logan noted the similarities in age, coloring and the wide, gap-toothed grins.

"I don't want what happened to Charlie to happen to Dylan." She raised her hand. "Oh, I know the situations are entirely different, but I don't want a cop—me or someone else—to have to tell Sawyer Evans that his little boy is…is gone. I don't want Sawyer to have to go through what my parents did. To live with having lost a child." She reached down and stroked the top of Darwin's head, then shook her own. "No parent should have to endure that. I know what it felt like to lose my brother and to carry the blame—"

Logan's eyes narrowed. "Blame?"

With a resigned sigh, she gave him the highlights.

"You're *not* to blame," Logan said vehemently when she'd finished, but he understood her better now.

"Maybe not. However, it doesn't mean I don't still carry the guilt. Reason is one thing. Emotion, something else altogether." She paused for a long moment. "Is it worse knowing someone *took* him? That it wasn't an accident?"

Logan understood that the question was rhetorical, but irrespective, he didn't have the answer. He and Ariana had discussed having children, and the idea of anything like that happening to one of them petrified him. "At least we have a chance of getting Dylan back safe and sound," he said gently.

Logan still had to address with Shannon the fact that she'd withheld material information about herself, information that could've impacted the specialization he'd assigned her. Especially considering the particulars she'd just shared. But looking at her and how fragile she seemed he knew that now was not the appropriate time.

As for the abduction, if they talked it through, they might come up with something they'd missed. If not, it would at least serve to get her mind off her own loss. "Okay, let's go over what we have." Logan looked up when he heard the squad room door open. Seeing Ariana stride in—with her confident, no-nonsense gait, and carrying a large bag of Chinese takeout—he appreciated again how fortunate he was to have her in his life. The more he got to know her, the more he respected her intelligence and agile mind. He couldn't ignore her beauty, either, with all that long, dark hair and her exotic features.

She dealt with many significant issues in her job. Having her perspective on this situation could help.

"I guess we won't be going hungry while we do it," Logan added. "Let's move this into the conference room," he said as he rose to give Ariana a kiss.

CHAPTER FOUR

SHANNON WAS BACK in the squad room early the next morning. She watched the flurry of activity around her and knew most of it had to do with Dylan Evans.

The boy was still missing.

She, Logan and Ariana hadn't come up with any great revelations the evening before. Judging by the bustle around her, neither had the investigative team.

She recognized the two FBI special agents who'd been assigned to the case—Leary and Wilson. Bigelow from the Special Response Team was there too, and she knew most of the other officers, who were from the SDPD. They were filing into the conference room.

When she saw Logan enter the squad room, she hurried over to him.

"I know I'm not needed actively on the case right now, but is it okay if I sit in on the briefing?"

He looked at her sympathetically. "You have

a heavy workload with Cal gone. Are you sure you have the time?"

"It matters," she said softly.

Logan held her gaze, then slowly nodded. "Okay. Good training for you," he said, making her feel less awkward about her personal interest in the case.

She started toward the conference room, but he forestalled her with a hand on her arm.

"If you need to leave anytime during the briefing, there's nothing wrong with that."

She felt his comment was a discreet reference to her emotional state the evening before. It told Shannon that Logan realized she wanted in, not just because of Dylan but also because of Charlie. She was fortunate to have such an understanding boss. "Thanks," she said with a grateful smile.

She took a seat along the back wall, near the door rather than at the table. She was an observer, not a participant. And it would make for an unobtrusive exit should she need to leave.

"First, to recap," Bigelow began. "The missing boy is four-year-old Dylan Evans. Dylan's been missing for over a day, and there's been no ransom demand. No contact with his family or the police. Dylan's father, Sawyer Evans, is a former high-profile prosecutor with the San

Diego County District Attorney's office and
is now a professor at Thomas Jefferson School
of Law. Evans says he stopped practicing law
and became a professor shortly after a challenging case involving a young man, Stewart
Rankin, from a rich and privileged family."
He swept his gaze around the room. "Many
of you will remember that Rankin killed five
people in a motor-vehicle accident while driving under the influence."

A hand went up and Bigelow pointed at the
uniform.

"That's the guy who'd been out partying
with his buddies. A stag before his wedding.
Drove a high-end Porsche Carrera, right?"

Bigelow nodded. "Yeah, that's Rankin.
Evans was the prosecutor. He won the case.
Rankin was sentenced to twelve years in
prison. His family has money and they threw
a considerable amount at his defense team.
Evans says the trial was brutal and his in-
volvement, the effort and energy required,
took a toll on his personal life. His wife, Jeannette Evans, left him and their one-year-old
son shortly afterward, without discussion or
warning. She didn't return home from her fitness club one day. His workload had been an
issue between them ever since Dylan's arrival.
Although the case was technically still open,

since there was no indication of foul play, the assumption was that she'd had enough and left. There was some speculation that post-partum depression might have been a factor, but nothing conclusive was known in that regard."

That was news to Shannon. Sawyer must have been heartbroken and reeling from his wife's desertion. She raised her hand. "Is Jeannette a possible suspect?" she asked when Bigelow signaled to her to speak.

"I was just getting to that. I checked the case file. She simply disappeared. Vanished without a trace. Her car was in the club's parking lot. There was nothing captured on the facility's security cameras. Subsequent to her disappearance, there was no use of credit cards, accessing of bank accounts or contact with anyone she'd known. Ultimately and on that basis, the detectives concluded she was more than likely deceased. This is where the question of post-partum depression arose. As I said, the case remains open, but since there was no evidence of a struggle or any indication to the contrary, foul play was ruled out."

He got up to walk around the room. "I spoke to the detective who had the lead. She said Evans hired a private investigator to look for his wife. It was his call, although the detective had cautioned that it was highly unlikely

the PI would find anything we hadn't. She said
Evans was highly distraught. Understandably.
He had a new kid and had lost his wife. Said
they'd been together since high school." He
shrugged. "As expected, the PI didn't turn up
anything new. There were no clues as to where
she'd gone or what had happened to her.

"The only thing that kept Evans function-
ing, according to the detective, was his kid.
His son's welfare became Evans's priority. He
changed jobs to be able to spend as much time
with the kid as possible. As is standard procedure in cases like this, Evans was looked at as
a possible suspect but cleared."

Bigelow was known to be a tough cop, but
Shannon could see that even he was moved.

"How could the guy have foreseen that taking his son on a family vacation would turn
into a parent's worst nightmare?" He shook his
head. "Speaking of nightmares, Evans said his
kid had them from the time his mother left,
and only now are they becoming less frequent.
Let's get this kid back to his father as soon as
we can. Special Agent Leary will cover what
we've got so far."

Bigelow switched places with Leary. "Sadly,
not much," Leary began. "Yesterday we went
over all the possibilities with Evans. His acquaintances and neighbors, his current and

past colleagues and, going further back to his tenure as an assistant district attorney, any and all people he'd prosecuted. The DA's office is reviewing their files, too. We haven't hit on anything, but the most likely suspects— operating on the assumption that he or she is known to Evans—are people he'd prosecuted as an assistant DA."

Leary held up his hands when murmurs broke out across the room. "I know that takes us back three years or more, but we can't ignore it. We're paying particular attention to the people who'd been convicted. Especially those who received long sentences, as well as their family members. We also looked at associates—in and out of prison—where applicable. Anyone who'd been recently released. Five made it to the top of our list. First up is Stewart Rankin, whom Detective Bigelow just mentioned. He's serving twelve years in the George F. Bailey Detention Facility. Next is Donna Thompson, convicted of being a drug mule for one of the Mexican cartels, serving a seven-year sentence. With her, there could be a cartel angle, depending on how integrated she was with the organization."

"You should talk to Rick Vasquez about that," Logan interjected. "Rick and his narcotics-detection dog, Sniff, were instrumental in taking her down. Rumor had it she was personally involved with one of the Sinaloa cartel's lieutenants. Although we didn't get any of the cartel's key operatives, the takedown was significant because of the size of the seizure and, perhaps more importantly, the closing down of one of their most lucrative smuggling routes."

Leary nodded. "If it impacted the cartel and/or there was a personal relationship, that moves her up the list. We'll talk to Vasquez."

Shannon glanced over at Logan, but his expression was inscrutable. If the Sinaloa cartel had anything to do with Dylan's abduction, that was bad news. They wouldn't have done it for financial gain.

"But before we get too concerned about the cartel," Leary said, "my opinion is that if it *was* them, we would've heard by now—one way or another. They wouldn't have taken the kid for money."

That confirmed Shannon's belief.

"To them, whatever Evans could pay would be a drop in the bucket. If they took the kid, it would've been for revenge. And in Thompson's case, we're going back nearly four years. I doubt the cartel bosses would've been this patient if they wanted retribution.

"Third on our list is Colin Jansen, serving life for killing a man in a barroom brawl when he hit him on the back of the head with a pool cue. Jansen reportedly has anger issues, and he has associates on the outside. Number four is Nadine Crosby. She was twenty-three at the time she was convicted of the attempted murder of her mother and her mother's then-boyfriend. Diagnosed as a psychopath, she fits the profile, and the fact that she was released a few months ago moved her up our list to fourth position. However, she's solidly alibied for the time of the abduction. Rounding out the top five, we have Norman Blackstone, a fifty-six-year-old father of four who defrauded his employer of nearly a million dollars. Evans sent him to prison for five years. That covers the probables."

Leary nodded at Bigelow. "Anything you want to add?"

Bigelow shook his head. "No, other than to say that the DA's office is continuing to go through all of Evans's case files. Anything else?" he asked the room in general.

A hand shot up. "What are the chances that Evans might be behind it?"

Bigelow inclined his head. "That's a good question. As usual, we're taking an in-depth look at the family. We haven't gotten a red flag in our discussions with Evans. We've interviewed the other campers in the area and got nothing from them, either." He scanned the room. "A complexity in this case is that the boy is the second member of Evans's immediate family to disappear. That's too coincidental for my liking and warrants closer scrutiny. It would answer the question we've been grappling with of why the father didn't wake up if the boy was abducted from the tent."

"Is it worth looking at the missing wife again?" someone else asked.

"Yes. We'll review Jeannette Evans's file, although as I said, the investigation into her disappearance had ruled out the possibility that Evans played any role in it." Bigelow frowned at his notes. "On the other hand, if it *is* Evans, if he *was* involved in her case, where's the body? And if he's responsible for his son's disappearance, where would he have taken the boy?"

There was murmuring in the room, but Bigelow ignored it and continued.

"We brought in the air support unit with infrared capabilities," he continued. "Their lack of results, combined with what our search-and-rescue dogs have indicated, leads us to conclude the boy was no longer in the park when Evans sounded the alert. But we know he didn't leave the place until we escorted him home."

Shannon realized it was standard procedure to look at family members in child-abduction cases, yet hearing that Sawyer was a possible suspect made her feel defensive. She couldn't believe it. Yes, she was going on a gut feel, but a lot of good police work depended on well-honed instincts. She'd been the first cop on the scene, the first to speak to Sawyer. He couldn't have faked the raw grief and distress she'd seen.

"Evans's parents are retired, and we've found no reason to suspect them. The sister, Meghan Evans, is single and a marine biologist working for the Scripps Institution of Oceanography in their Marine Biology Research Division. We don't suspect her, either," Bigelow said.

When the briefing was concluded and all the questions answered, Shannon left the conference room, along with everyone else. She didn't know if the others felt as dejected as she did. Yeah, cops hoped they'd never get so callous that they didn't feel for the victims, but Shannon had to wonder if she'd be able to deal with this sort of thing on a regular basis.

She focused on her work and got some satisfaction when she and Darwin were called out and located an Alzheimer's patient who'd wandered away from Ocean Crest Hospital;

they were able to return him unharmed to his family. They also helped apprehend a man who'd crashed a stolen vehicle, injuring an elderly woman, and had fled the scene. He blew well over the legal limit and, right now, was warming a bench in a holding cell.

But her thoughts kept drifting back to Sawyer Evans and his son, Dylan. How could she not be emotionally engaged when a child's well-being was at stake? And it wasn't only about the boy. It was the father, too.

There was something about Sawyer... He stirred up feelings in her that were unprecedented in her experience, and she couldn't set them aside. Was it empathy she felt because of Charlie?

She tried to take comfort in the fact that the investigation was a top priority. The assistance from the FBI added much-appreciated resources.

But no new information had emerged. The time factor associated with when Sawyer had left the DA's office made it less likely that one of the people he'd prosecuted was responsible for the abduction, but the investigative team could not ignore it, as they had no other leads.

Shannon knew the SDPD and FBI couldn't discount a random, opportunistic abduction either, improbable as it seemed. In addition to tapping their combined manpower, they were appealing to the public for help.

Missing-child posters went up across San Diego County. She'd heard that Sawyer had used his own resources to broaden the distribution. It wasn't just because Shannon was focused on the case that she saw Dylan's smiling face everywhere she went.

Shannon knew that as more time passed, concerns about the boy's safety intensified. The first twenty-four hours were crucial, and they'd pulled out all the stops in their search.

But those critical early hours had now passed.

Sawyer had come into the division midday. His eyes had been vacant until they met hers. He'd paused, and she'd felt a brief connection before he moved on to catch up with Bigelow.

Sawyer must've been going out of his mind. For Shannon and her parents, it had been a little over a day until they learned Charlie's fate. She remembered vividly those excruciating hours of not knowing.

Long after Sawyer left, the raw pain she'd seen on his face haunted her. She knew it was contrary to department policy, but she *had* to contact him. Offer him whatever comfort she could.

She hoped that if this turned out to be a second transgression, it wouldn't end her career with the K-9 Unit when it had barely begun.

She thought about going to Sawyer's home at the end of her shift. She knew the address. She'd been there with Logan on the day of the abduction.

Even if she was to step over the line and contact Sawyer, going to his home uninvited was decidedly wrong. She'd stop by his office instead. She debated staying in uniform and decided to go in civilian clothes. After all, it wasn't official police business. She didn't want to create any false expectations.

She'd worked the seven-to-three shift. If she changed quickly, she could be at the Thomas Jefferson School of Law by four, a time she assumed was within the normal hours of a professor. She wouldn't call first, since she couldn't explain over the phone why she wanted to see him. She didn't entirely understand it herself.

She'd take her chances. If he was giving a lecture, so be it. Then she'd leave a message.

At the school, she got Darwin settled in the climate-controlled comfort of her Explorer and followed the signs to the faculty offices.

Sitting behind the reception counter was a slim young woman with a pretty face and a mass of wavy auburn hair falling nearly to her waist. The name plaque on her desk said Miranda Smith.

Shannon absently ran her hand through her own short hair. The word *tomboy* flitted through her mind. The presence of this beautiful, feminine woman made her feel self-conscious.

Miranda glanced up and smiled, revealing perfect, even white teeth. "May I help you?"

Well, at least Shannon had nice teeth, too. The braces she'd worn for the better part of two years as a teen had ensured that. She smiled back and walked to the counter. "I'd like to see Mr., ah, Professor Evans, please, if he's available."

Miranda's smile faded immediately and her eyes clouded. "I'm sorry, but Professor Evans isn't here. He's taking some time off..." Of course he wouldn't be at work while his son was missing! Shannon should've thought of that. She was obviously more affected than she'd realized. "Yes. Thank you," she murmured. She pulled out a business card and a pen. Jotting her personal cell phone number on the back, she handed it to Miranda. "I'd appreciate if you'd ask him to call me...when he gets a chance."

The receptionist accepted the card and glanced at it. Her eyes rounded. "You're with the police? Is there news?" she asked hope-fully. "I can try to reach him at home right now."

Shannon shook her head. "I'm sorry, no." She suddenly wanted to take the card back and leave. This was a bad idea, but it was too late to undo what she'd done. "Please just have him call me. There's no urgency." She thanked the receptionist and quickly left.

Inside her Explorer, she grasped the steering wheel with both hands and rested her forehead on it. How dumb was *that*? she asked herself.

CHAPTER FIVE

SAWYER SAT ON his sofa, head back, eyes shut.
He'd closed the shades. He didn't want to see
sunshine, nor did he care what time of day it
was.

He'd never felt so helpless, or so distraught,
in his life.

He wanted to rage. He wanted to lash out.

He wanted to give in and break down.

But his lethargy prevented all of it. And
what purpose would any of those reactions
serve?

They wouldn't bring his son home.

Not knowing where Dylan was… Maybe
injured…

No, he refused to think about that.

As a father, he'd sense if harm had befallen
his son. Wouldn't he?

His parents. Meghan. They'd all wanted to
stay with him.

He couldn't handle company. He couldn't
bear their pain. The weight of his own was
intolerable.

He just wanted to be alone.

And he *hated* being alone, in his own head, with his own thoughts. It was a dangerous place for him right now.

He wanted to be with Dylan, but that was impossible.

The sudden jangle of his phone startled him.

He kept his cell phone within reach at all times. Wishing. Praying. Hoping beyond hope that it would be the police. Calling to say they'd found Dylan. Safe and unharmed.

But whenever the phone had rung, it'd been his mother or father, his sister or a friend.

He picked it up and checked the call display. It was his office.

He couldn't imagine what they'd want. He'd advised the dean he'd be off until further notice. When he'd told her why, there'd been no further questions.

So why was Miranda calling?

He nearly put the phone back down, but curiosity got the better of him.

"Sawyer, how are you?" Miranda asked as soon as he answered.

Sawyer leaned his head back and stared up at the ceiling. How did she think he was, with his son missing for almost two days?

"I'm sorry," she whispered. "That was a stupid question."

There was nothing to be gained by making Miranda feel bad. She was a smart, well-intentioned young woman. He understood why no one knew what to say to him. "It's okay, Miranda. Why are you calling?"

"I have a message for you that I thought you'd want."

"Yeah?" He had no interest in messages. Unless it had to do with Dylan. "Who's it from?"

"San Diego Police Officer Shannon Clemens."

Sawyer leaped off the sofa. "When did she call? What did she want?"

"Um…"

He softened his tone. "Sorry, Miranda. Go ahead."

"Uh, she didn't call. She stopped by. She left her cell phone number."

Sawyer wrote it down. "Thanks, Miranda. I appreciate you letting me know."

"Sawyer, I'm so very sorry. We're all thinking of you and praying for Dylan's safe return."

"Thanks."

Sawyer hung up almost before she'd finished. Shannon Clemens was the officer with the dog. He'd immediately trusted her. She seemed to truly care. She'd given him hope…

With unsteady fingers, he dialed the number Miranda had provided.

Please, God...please, God, he chanted in his head as the phone rang once. Twice.

On the third ring, she answered.

"Ah, Officer. It's Sawyer Evans returning your call."

"Oh, Mr. Evans... Sawyer, um, thank you for calling me back."

"Yeah. Sure. Do you have news about Dylan?" He recognized the sound of desperation in his own voice but couldn't help it.

"No... I'm sorry, I don't."

"But...but..." Now he was stammering. If she didn't have information, why had she contacted him? "I don't understand."

"I wanted to tell you how sorry I am about Dylan, and that I couldn't find him for you."

Sawyer brought back the image of the police officer. Youngish. Twenty-eight or nine. She was maybe five-five or five-six, slim, and she'd looked competent and steady. She had short blond hair in an edgy cut that, under different circumstances, he might've thought of as sexy. Well-defined features and a full, expressive mouth. And her eyes had caught him. They were a vivid sky blue, he remembered, and they'd had an intensity. Her eyes had told him that what she did was more than a job to her. And when she'd promised she'd do her best, the sincerity in those eyes had made him believe it. But even her best hadn't been enough to bring Dylan back to him. "You're calling to apologize?" He realized he hadn't been getting any sleep and his mind was a mess, but her call made no sense to him.

"Well, yes."

Her voice was soft. Somehow it dulled the sharpest edges of his despair.

"The department is doing everything possible. The FBI is involved, as you know. I wanted to tell you that I understand what you're going through and—"

"You *understand*?" Sawyer tightened his grip on the phone until his knuckles ached. "How can you *possibly* understand what it's like to have your child go missing?"

"Not my child. No. But my brother went missing. He was the same age then as Dylan is now. I saw what my parents went through. I was very close to my brother," she added.

Sawyer squeezed his eyes shut. He'd been harsh and was sorry about it. He couldn't imagine anyone understanding what he was experiencing, but she probably could, more than most people. "How much time had passed before your brother was found?"

"A day."

Dylan had been missing for over a day. Going on two. As a former prosecutor, he knew the statistics about missing children. "What happened to him? To your brother?"

He heard her inhale sharply.

"Charlie got lost. In Torrey Pines State Park."

Also a forested area with wildlife. Yeah, there were similarities. Sitting back down on the sofa, he took a long drink of the beer that had gone warm. "I'm sorry. I didn't mean to jump down your throat." He laughed bleakly. "I'm not myself right now."

"How could you be?"

Again, her voice soothed him. "The police found Charlie?"

"Yes."

The tone of her voice said more than the single word. "Was he hurt?" Sawyer wasn't sure he was prepared for the answer, but he had to ask.

"Charlie... He drowned in a creek."

Sawyer pressed a hand over his eyes. He remembered the terror he'd felt standing at the edge of the lake by their campground, and praying that nothing like that had happened to Dylan. "I'm very sorry."

"It was a long time ago..."

Her voice was sorrowful. Maybe this wasn't the same, but here *finally* was someone who could understand what he was going through, without amplifying his personal pain. Being a police officer, she might be able to give him details he needed. Maybe she could keep him from going completely crazy. All of a sudden, Sawyer wanted to talk to her.

He glanced at his watch. No, not today. "Officer Clemens…"

"Shannon," she corrected him.

"Shannon, can I buy you a coffee? Tomorrow sometime, if you're free?"

There was a brief hesitation. "It's my day off. I could meet you anytime."

"Good. How about the Starbucks on East Harbor Drive? Do you know where it is?"

"Yes."

"Two thirty?"

"That works for me."

SHANNON ARRIVED AT the coffee shop ten minutes early. She ordered a latte and sat at a table with a clear view of the entrance.

Since she'd spoken to Sawyer, she'd incessantly questioned the wisdom of what she was doing. Why was she having coffee with a man whose son was missing? What could it lead to, if not heartache? He expected information from her; she was bound to disappoint him. He'd know as much or more from Detective

Bigelow and FBI Special Agent Leary than she did from Logan and the departmental briefings.

The last thing Sawyer needed was another complication.

The last thing *she* needed was another complication.

Sawyer hadn't been cleared yet as a possible suspect in his son's abduction, although she was certain he would be, in due course.

And his wife's? She knew that Bigelow and Leary were taking another look at that. But she didn't believe he would've done anything to harm his wife, either. Still, seeing him today was a bad idea and maybe she should leave before he showed up.

Too late for that. Shannon noticed Sawyer the moment he walked in.

He wore faded jeans. Not the designer type a lot of men were wearing these days. He'd paired the jeans with a blue-and-white striped button-down, the sleeves rolled halfway up his forearms. His hair, a deep brown with chestnut streaks, looked only slightly more orderly than it had the day his son went missing. She was struck again by the strength of character evident in his face. The strong jawline, straight nose and sensitive eyes made him very appealing.

He'd lost weight. Was it possible to lose

enough weight in two days for it to be notice-able? He was tall, but his build was lanky. He couldn't afford to lose much more.

She knew him to be thirty-six. She'd read the file. He'd looked his age when she'd first met him. Today? He appeared older than his years. There were deep lines etched across his forehead and bracketing the sides of his mouth. His eye sockets were hollow and had dark cir-cles beneath them, but his eyes warmed briefly as they connected with hers.

No, he didn't seem like a man who'd harm his own son. Departmental procedures or not, if she could help ease his pain or be a sounding board for him to release some of it...

He raised an arm in a halfhearted greeting and walked toward her. She rose and held out her hand.

His grip conveyed hesitation, despite its strength.

"Can I get you a coffee?" she offered.

"No. No, that's fine. I'll buy my own."

He was back a few minutes later and slid onto the chair opposite her.

"I'd like to clear up one thing, if that's okay?" Sawyer asked.

Her nerves hummed. "Sure."

"You're not here on police business, are you?"

She felt like squirming in her seat, but re-sisted. She shook her head slowly. "No, I'm not."

He nodded. "I just want to be clear on that. Can I call you Shannon?"

"Yes. Of course."

He closed his eyes. With an unsteady hand, he rubbed his forehead. "This is all surreal. I have moments when I convince myself that it's a nightmare and I'll wake up any minute. Then I realize I *am* awake, and Dylan isn't with me."

He opened his eyes, and what she saw in their depths tore at her heart.

"I don't know how to cope. How I can go on one more minute, never mind an hour. But then I don't have a choice, do I?"

Shannon could see by the tensing of his jaw and the pulse jumping at his temples that the effort to contain his emotions was costing him.

"Is there anything at all that you can tell me that I haven't already heard?"

She wished… Oh, God, she wished there was. Anything that would in any way ease his pain. "I'm sorry. I'm not involved in the investigation."

"Okay." He looked away abruptly. Even in profile, she could see the sheen of his eyes, the tension in his features. When he glanced back at her, he seemed more controlled. "I want to ask why you contacted me, but I can't help thinking that would be rude. So, I'll ask you another question, if that's okay."

She nodded once more.

"How are your parents?"

"Excuse me?" She didn't understand the relevance of the question.

"If you don't mind me asking, how did your parents deal with the loss of a child?"

Shannon went with her instincts. She placed her hand on top of Sawyer's. "You can't think about that." Maybe there was something she could say to ease his mind. "We—the SDPD and the FBI—have no evidence to suggest that any harm has come to Dylan. You have to stay positive."

She saw him swallow, then clear his throat. "I'm grateful to hear that. Thank you." He groped for his coffee mug and took a drink. "I suppose you know about my wife?"

"Yes. It was mentioned in a briefing."

"Dylan hadn't celebrated his first birthday when she went missing. For the police it's a cold case, but under the circumstances, they think she died…as do I." He rubbed the bottom of his nose with a finger. "You probably know all this, but in law, there's an assumption that a person is alive until there's reason to believe otherwise. Seven years is the usual amount of time. Then, legally, she'll be presumed dead, but for all intents and purposes, the evidence—or lack thereof—points to her having died.

"I've lived with it. Never knowing with one hundred percent certainty if she was still living or not. Hoping month after month, then year after year that the police were wrong. That one day she'd come back to us. But she never did…"

"It must have been dreadful for you to live with that uncertainty," Shannon responded. "How did Dylan take it?"

Sawyer seemed surprised by the question. "Oh, he was so young. A psychologist I consulted advised me to keep things as normal as possible for him. I told Dylan that Mommy had to go away. He seemed to accept it, but then the nightmares started." Sawyer turned away and shook his head. "I suppose even at that age he knew. A few months after the police told me they presumed Jeannette to be…gone, on the recommendation of the psychologist, my mother and sister helped me pack up her belongings. Having everything around probably kept her alive in Dylan's memory…and made it harder on me.

"At first, I insisted that we keep everything in storage, just in case… I ended up donating all her belongings to charity." He turned back to her. "I'm sorry. That was probably more information than you wanted."

"No. That's okay," she told him, her own voice not quite steady.

"The police looked at me as a suspect in her disappearance," he said.

Shannon could see in his eyes—more brown than green now—the torment that still caused him.

"I know they're looking at me now in Dylan's disappearance, too." He made a sound of frustration. "Maybe I'm even the prime suspect because it's the second time a member of my family disappeared."

Shannon opened her mouth but had no response, because his assumption was correct.

He held up a hand. "You don't have to say anything. Intellectually, I know the odds and I can't argue with it. Emotionally? It's a different matter. Most importantly, they're spending valuable resources eliminating me as a suspect. I'd like them to get on with it and clear me, so they can focus all their energies on finding Dylan and determining who *is* responsible." His voice faltered and he lowered his gaze.

"You can't give up hope," Shannon said, more sharply than she'd intended.

Sawyer's eyes, when he raised them, were dark and gleaming. "My question about your parents. When they did hear… How does a parent handle that? I…I don't know if I could."

His voice faltered on the final words. It was more than Shannon could tolerate. She rose and sat on the chair next to him and laid her hands on his shoulders. "You have to stay positive," she implored.

He stiffened for a moment, then lowered his forehead against hers.

Not knowing what else to do, she closed her eyes and rubbed his back, much as she would to comfort a child. She felt a connection to him, but it was so fleeting she wondered if she'd imagined it.

He straightened and raked his hair back, while Shannon returned to her own side of the table.

"I'm sorry about dumping all of that on you." He seemed to take in his surroundings, as if he'd only now recognized that he was sitting in a public place. His gaze returned to Shannon and she felt that link with him again.

A moment later, he broke eye contact. "Listen, I appreciate what you're doing." His eyes softened. "I really do." He stood and regarded her with sad eyes. "My life is shambles right now. I don't know how to do something normal like have coffee and a conversation. I'm sorry, but I have to go."

CHAPTER SIX

SHANNON FELT BAFFLED and unsettled as she drove away from the coffee shop. With the resources available to the SDPD, combined with the expertise of the FBI, they *had* to be able to find Dylan and return him to his father. What was the point of being a police officer, if you couldn't help in situations like this?

She checked her rearview mirror, signaled and made a quick U-turn. It was her day off, but she wanted to see Logan.

There had to be *something* she could do.

"Do you have a minute?" Shannon asked from the doorway of Logan's office.

His surprise at seeing her was evident, but he gestured for her to enter and have a seat. "What're you doing here today?" he asked.

Shannon noticed a loose thread at the hem of her shirt and fidgeted with it. When she glanced up, Logan was watching her intently. She wondered if she'd made two colossal mistakes in the same day, but there was no taking back her meeting with Sawyer and no avoiding her discussion with Logan. "I know I'm not on the Dylan Evans case, but I was wondering if there's anything new with the search."

"Nothing of substance. Are you asking because of Charlie?"

"No," she whispered.

Logan pushed back in his chair and rested one ankle on the opposite knee. "We've already established that the missing boy hits close to home for you. You need to be honest with me."

"This isn't about Charlie," she asserted. "Or not entirely. I… I'm concerned about Dylan. He's been missing for over two days. That's not a good sign."

Logan tapped his fingers on his thigh. "You're right. It's not. But we're doing everything we can to find him."

She nodded. "If Darwin and I had gotten there faster, maybe…"

Logan rose, moved around his desk and sat down in the chair beside Shannon's. "You know better than that. You've been here long enough and you've had enough training to appreciate that based on Darwin's reaction, whoever took the boy was at least an hour and a half ahead of you."

She felt the tears stinging her eyes and was horrified to think that she'd embarrass herself by crying in front of her captain again. She lowered her gaze. "I can't help feeling I failed."

Logan leaned forward and rested his forearms on his knees, forcing her to make eye contact. "You did everything by the book."

By the book maybe, but could she have done more? She was afraid to say anything, since her emotions were a maelstrom, rioting just under the surface and threatening to break free. She pressed her lips together and glanced away.

"Shannon, I need you to be the very best officer you can be. It would be counterproductive for me to tell you that you did well if that wasn't the case. Look at me," he instructed, drawing her attention back to him.

"I'm deeply sorry about what happened to your brother. This is the last time I'll say this, but you should've told me about him. I want you to understand why. No one would be unaffected by a child's disappearance. For you, those feelings are compounded and could—I'm not saying they did—but they *could* impact your performance. Don't keep salient facts from me again. Are we clear?"

"Yes. So noted," she managed. "Is there anything wrong with me monitoring what's happening with the case?"

"Not from the department's perspective."

Logan sighed. "On a personal basis, I can't see that it's good for you. I'll leave it to your judgment."

"Thank you."

Logan got to his feet. "Go home. Try to put it aside." He placed a gentle hand on her shoulder before moving behind his desk again.

Shannon walked out of Logan's office, knowing that what he asked of her would be impossible. And she knew there was no way Sawyer could put it aside for even a heartbeat.

SHANNON HAD JUST returned from a long walk with Darwin when her personal cell phone rang. It was Sawyer.

"I'm sorry I left you at the coffee shop the way I did," he said. "Especially after you were kind enough to get in touch with me. I can't seem to say or do anything right these days."

"That's okay." Nobody could expect him to think clearly with what he was going through.

"I just want you to know that it matters to me that you care," Sawyer continued. "It gives me hope that it's not just you, but that everyone who's looking for Dylan cares, too."

"They all do. I can promise you that."

"And thank you for telling me about your brother. I wish you'd never had to go through that, but knowing you did… Talking to you helped me, because you understand in a way that not many people could. I just want to tell you how much I appreciate that."

She felt a tightness in her chest. "I'm glad it helped. If you want to talk, feel free to call anytime."

After they said their goodbyes, Shannon got a Coke from the fridge and took Darwin out to the back patio. As the first stars blinked awake in the darkening sky, she hoped that wherever Dylan was, he was safe and would soon be home with his father.

She hadn't known what to expect when she'd encouraged Sawyer to call her, but he took her up on her offer.

During the next week, she and Sawyer spoke every day and sometimes more than once. She knew he was receiving official updates from the department, but she tried to fill in as many of the details for him as she could—without going too far.

And provide support, to the extent that she was able to.

She felt him gradually opening up to her in his sorrow, and she despaired that she couldn't provide him relief from the agony he was living with, since the investigation kept coming up empty.

Each day that passed, she struggled with the

ethical dilemma of developing a relationship with him. There wasn't any plausible reason to suspect he had anything to do with his son's disappearance, but in the absence of evidence pointing to anyone else, he hadn't been completely eliminated.

Shannon tried to tell herself that she wasn't attracted to Sawyer. How wrong would that be, to fall for a man under these circumstances? She berated herself for taking advantage of his weakened state. Would he be talking to her, if not for her connection to his son and the bond—as tenuous as it might be—because of Charlie? She kept reminding herself that she *should* maintain an emotional detachment.

But she was incapable of doing it. She was drawn to Sawyer in a way she couldn't remember being drawn to any other man.

Layered over the question of ethics was the self-reproach of not telling Logan what she was doing. Yes, he'd okayed her sitting in on the briefings and keeping herself up-to-date on the investigation, but what would he say if he knew she had feelings for Sawyer Evans?

She took a sip of her beer and eyed Logan on the other side of the table. It was the K-9 Unit's monthly Friday night get-together at The Runway, a bar close to San Diego International Airport. Logan's girlfriend—fiancée now—

worked as chief of security and loss prevention at the airport. Shannon remembered how intimidated she'd felt by the highly competent, drop-dead gorgeous Ariana Atkins when she'd first met her during a police investigation at the airport six months ago. No question she respected Ariana. Was probably a little awed by her. But since Ariana and Logan had gotten together, she'd had a chance to know her on a personal level. Now she considered her a friend.

Shannon watched as Logan slid his arm around Ariana's shoulders and whispered something in her ear that had Ariana blushing. Who would've thought that the professional, *unflappable* Ariana—who'd helped them bust a major smuggling ring operating at the airport—would blush? Then again, who would've thought the tough and emotionally reserved Jagger would fall so hard?

Maybe she was just a little envious of the obvious love Ariana and Logan shared. What they had was the love of a lifetime. She glanced around the table. She could say the same about Rick and Madison, and Cal and Jessica. Cal and Jess had just gotten back from their vacation. They still had that honeymoon glow about them, and it had nothing to do with the light tans they'd acquired aboard the cruise ship.

Although Shannon had been in relationships before, she could safely say she'd never been in love. With a certain wistfulness, she turned her attention back to the interplay between Ariana and Logan.

"Is everything okay?"

Shannon jerked slightly and turned to her left. Madison Vasquez, the veterinarian responsible for the SDPD's canines—and K-9 Unit sergeant Rick Vasquez's wife—was watching her with concern.

"Yes." She took another sip of her beer. "Why do you ask?"

Madison's eyes were probing. "I've known you since you joined the K-9 Unit. What is that now? Eight months?"

"That's about right."

"You've always struck me as focused, with a laser-sharp mind and a terrific attitude."

Shannon felt heat rise to her cheeks. "Um, thanks. That's high praise coming from you."

"Don't thank me yet. You look distracted tonight. Unhappy."

She exhaled heavily. "It shows?"

Madison squeezed Shannon's arm and nodded. "Do you want to talk about what's bothering you?"

Shannon cast a furtive glance at Logan. When she looked back at Madison, she realized her tactical error.

"Work-related problem, then?"

"Yeah. No. Not really." Her eyes shifted to Logan again. He was laughing at something he, Ariana and Cal had been talking about. "It's nothing. I can handle it."

"Uh-huh. I hope you know you have friends here."

When Logan's phone rang, they all fell silent. He had a brief conversation, obviously with Dispatch.

"Yeah. Got it. We're on it." He sent an apologetic look around the table. "Sorry to cut our evening short, but Rick and I have to go."

"Aw, man," Rick complained halfheartedly.

"Sorry, pal. The Vice Squad got a tip that one of the drug cartels has something big going down across the San Ysidro border tonight. The rest of you enjoy the night out."

Jessica grinned at her husband. "How nice! You can stay with us for girl talk."

Cal shot his wife a pained expression. "You sure you don't need me to come in on whatever's going down, Jagger? Scout and I can track any fleeing suspects," he suggested hopefully.

"No. You and Shannon can stay." Logan

chuckled. "Not up to the company of four beautiful women?"

Cal grimaced. "I think I just remembered something I need to do."

"What?" Jessica asked with a skeptical look on her face.

Cal grinned sheepishly. "I'm sure something will come to me on the drive home. Will you be okay getting back on your own, Jess?"

Jessica laid a hand on her protruding stomach. "I think I'll manage. I'm also happy to be the designated driver if anyone needs a ride, since I'm not drinking."

"Okay, but if you feel anything, even a twinge, you promise to call me?"

"Yes, I promise." She smiled at him. "I'm a doctor. You can rest easy. I'll know when it's time."

"Glad that's settled." Rick pushed his beer away, rose and kissed Madison in a way that Shannon was certain would've made her toes curl if she'd been on the receiving end.

"Is it okay if…?" Madison asked Rick.

He touched his lips to her forehead, then tenderly ran his hand down the length of her curly red hair. "Sure."

"What was that all about?" Ariana asked after the men had left.

"Well, this isn't exactly how we'd planned

to announce it," Madison said, her face glowing as she pressed a hand to her flat stomach. "We're expecting a baby!"

"You guys didn't waste any time!" Ariana remarked, and was the first to hug her.

With a chorus of squeals and excited congratulations, Jessica and Shannon hugged Madison, too. Madison smiled widely at Jessica. "You aren't going to be the only designated driver in the foreseeable future. Rick and I think it's wonderful that our kids will be so close in age."

"To Madison, Rick and their soon-to-be new addition," Shannon said, and they all raised their glasses in a toast.

The usual questions were asked about Madison's due date, if they knew whether they were having a boy or a girl and how she was feeling. When the pregnancy topic was exhausted, Madison turned to Shannon with an appraising look. "So, is there something you'd like to discuss, while it's just us girls?"

Shannon's mouth dropped open and she snapped it shut again. Everyone's attention was now on her. She thought about denying it, but she knew there wasn't any point. "I met someone I like."

"You're seeing someone? That's terrific!" Madison said excitedly.

"Not really *seeing*. Just…sort of."

Ariana leaned forward. "You're seeing someone 'sort of,' but you don't look happy about it. We're all good listeners, if you want to share. Lord knows, we've each had ups and downs with our guys."

That elicited nods and chuckles from Madison and Jessica.

Feeling uneasy, Shannon took a sip of her beer. "First of all, like I said, I'm not actually *seeing* him. And I don't think he's interested in me…in that way."

Ariana gave her head a little shake. "He'd be crazy not to be, but what makes you say that?"

Shannon felt warmth seep through her at the words of support. "It's…complicated."

"I'm sure that whatever it is, it's not insurmountable, if you're interested in him," Madison said.

Shannon considered the wisdom of opening up to her captain's fiancée, the unit sergeant's wife, and her colleague and trainer's wife. How much more exposed could she be?

But she valued and respected each of the women around the table. Their reaction would be a good indicator of what it might be like to have a conversation with Logan about this.

If it came to that.

She took a fortifying breath. "The man I'm seeing is Sawyer Evans."

Judging by the looks on the other women's faces, Shannon knew she'd shocked them.

"The man whose son was abducted?" Ariana finally asked.

Shannon nodded.

Ariana blew her bangs out of her eyes. "That *is* complicated. Does Logan know?"

"No," Shannon replied. "Let me explain. I—"

"I'm sorry, but I have to say this," Jessica interrupted. "Blame it on the hormones that I'm being this direct, but what kind of father would start a relationship while his son is missing?"

Shannon regretted starting the whole discussion. Good judgement seemed to have deserted her lately. "It's not like that. It's not as if we're having a *relationship*. And…it's probably one-sided. As I said, I don't believe he thinks of me like that. We just…talk. He knows I can—in a way—relate to what he's going through."

In response to the three pairs of questioning eyes focused on her, Shannon gave them an abbreviated version of what had happened to Charlie.

"I'm so sorry, Shannon," Madison said and gave her a hug. "What a terrible thing for you and your family."

"I can see what you mean about being able to understand. Are you sure your interest in him isn't because of your brother?" Ariana asked.

Shannon shook her head slowly. "Believe me, I've been around that block more times than I can count. He's a good man and by all accounts a good father. I like him. His values. His integrity. His obvious love for his son." She tucked her hair behind her ears. "I can't believe I'm even thinking about this! How can *I* contemplate a relationship with him when his entire focus is—and has to be—his son?" She locked eyes with Ariana. "Your job is the closest to policing there is, and you know Logan best. Am I crossing a line here?"

"I wouldn't say you're crossing it, but you're certainly stretching it."

"Do you think Logan would see it that way?"

"Shannon…" Jessica interjected. "I'm not worried about what Logan will think. My concern is for you. I know how Cal felt when he couldn't see his daughter, back when we first met, and that wasn't nearly the same. He knew that Haley was safe and fine with her mother. I can't imagine how much Sawyer Evans is suffering, not knowing if his son is—I'm sorry, but it must go through his mind—dead or alive." She rubbed a hand over her belly. "Be careful with your heart, Shannon. This long without a ransom demand or a clue as to the child's whereabouts is very concerning. Even I'm aware of that. You don't know how it'll turn out or how the father will handle it."

And that was the crux of her dilemma, Shannon thought as she drove home later that night. She'd developed feelings for Sawyer, but was uncertain how he felt about her. And the guilt of being interested in him at a time like this weighed heavily on her. Jessica had suggested not so subtly that people did strange things during a crisis and didn't always react in the manner they normally would. Was she experiencing a weird projection and trying to make some form of restitution for her role in Charlie's death?

No, she decided. She was sufficiently self-aware to know what she was feeling.

When Shannon got home, she took Darwin for a long walk, then called her mother.

"Your father and I have been thinking about you," Victoria said.

Just the sound of her mother's voice helped settle Shannon's anxiety. She'd purposely avoided calling her parents since Dylan had gone missing. Time might have lessened the pain for her parents, but it hadn't healed the wound entirely. "I'm sorry I haven't called, Mom."

"No need to apologize. That poor boy still hasn't been found, has he?"

Shannon should've realized that not calling wouldn't have spared her parents the heartache. There'd been too much media coverage. "No, Mom."

"Are you involved in the case?"

"I was initially. Not now, though. The FBI has been called in, too."

"This whole thing—it's hard on you, honey," Victoria observed.

"Yeah. But not as hard as it is on the boy's father."

There was a pause. "Yes, that's true."

"Mom, you and Dad got through losing Charlie. How did you manage it?"

Shannon heard her mother's deep sigh. "I don't have the answer to that question, other than to say we'll never be over it. We live with it every day," she said softly. "But your father and I had each other, and that made a world of difference. The missing boy doesn't have a mother, does he?"

"No."

"The news reports said she disappeared three years ago."

"She's presumed dead, Mom."

"Oh?"

Shannon didn't want to get into the details about Sawyer's wife.

"It's unfortunate that the man's going through this on his own," Victoria continued when Shannon remained silent.

"He has parents and a sister. They seem close."

"Good. That's good. Although I don't think it's the same. I don't know how I would've survived without Paul." Shannon could hear the emotion in her mother's voice. "That boy's father needs all the support he can get."

"I speak to him regularly and I do what I can."

"As part of the job?" Victoria asked, sounding surprised.

"No. He's...he's become a friend."

"Oh..." This time there was a long silence. "How did that happen?"

Shannon shrugged even though her mother couldn't see it. "It just did. I've talked to him about Charlie. It seems to help him."

Her mother made a noncommittal sound.

"He's asked me how you and Dad dealt with losing Charlie."

"It's very personal and I imagine different for everyone who goes through it. A lot of marriages don't survive that sort of loss."

"You and Dad made it and are stronger for it, aren't you?"

"Yes. We're blessed in that regard. If you're that man's friend…what's his first name again?"

"Sawyer."

"Well, if you're Sawyer's friend, he's fortunate to have your help. But, Shannon, honey, you still carry scars, too. Please be careful and don't take on more than you can manage."

"I won't. I promise."

When Shannon hung up, she wondered if that, too, was a promise she wouldn't be able to keep.

CHAPTER SEVEN

"SHANNON! COME IN HERE!" Logan called from his office doorway.

Shannon got out of her chair and hurried over.

"There's been a break in the Evans case," he said.

"What is it?"

"There's been a reported sighting of Dylan Evans near Marina del Rey."

"That's the first real lead since Dylan disappeared."

"Correct. I thought you'd want to know."

"Has Sawyer—Mr. Evans—been told?"

"Yeah. Bigelow notified him just before he called me."

Shannon lowered herself into a chair. "The local police have been alerted?"

"Yeah, they're investigating the lead. Bigelow and Leary are on their way."

"Does the local police department have tracking capabilities? Canines?"

"Marina del Rey is served by the LAPD.

They have a K-9 Unit, all right. Three times the size of ours."

"But they don't know Dylan."

"Shannon, if you're going where I think you're going with this, neither do you."

"No. But Darwin searched for him. Sawyer—Mr. Evans wouldn't have anything with a recent scent of Dylan on it. That'll make it harder. Darwin might have sensory memory. It's possible," she insisted, when Logan looked at her doubtfully. "He might be able to do a better job."

"Better than experienced LAPD K-9 officers?"

Shannon understood Logan's skepticism. She sounded foolish to her own ears. But she *needed* to help, if she could. "Maybe not, but an additional resource wouldn't hurt. Logan, could you lend me to the Marina del Rey Sheriff's Department to take part in the search? This is a child we're dealing with. Surely any help would be of value. If you explained the situation to the sheriff, he wouldn't object, would he?"

She watched Logan as he considered her request. Not telling Logan now that she had a personal relationship with Sawyer—whatever that relationship was—would be another transgression. Regardless, she couldn't bring herself to do it. He obviously wasn't enthusiastic about her getting involved, and she didn't want to say anything that would tip the scales against it. She wanted to be part of the search team.

For Dylan. For Charlie. For Sawyer.

"Are you sure you're up for this?" he finally asked.

Not trusting herself to speak, she nodded.

"I'll make the call. Get ready to move."

She rose. "Thank you, Logan. I appreciate it."

She went back to her desk, packed up her duffel and waited for word from Logan. She could see him on the phone through the window of his office. It wasn't a quick conversation and he looked grim. When he finally hung up, she prepared herself for bad news.

He leaned out of his doorway and gave her a thumbs-up. "I'll text you the coordinates. Report to Sergeant Brian Anson of the Marina del Rey Sheriff's Department."

She shot to her feet. "I'm on it. Thank you."

"Go make a difference," she heard him say as she jogged out of the squad room.

As a former prosecutor with the DA's office, Sawyer knew the statistics about abducted children and that the likelihood of finding them unharmed decreased exponentially with time. The more time that passed, the more pessimistic he became. The more despondent.

His parents and sister had done everything they could to lift his spirits, but they were grieving, too, and their grief only compounded his. So—rightly or wrongly—he'd avoided them.

His one saving grace had been Shannon. She was a steady, calming influence, and had managed to give him hope when he'd felt there was none left. And she really did seem to understand because of her brother, and her job.

Sawyer had been worried about his own mental state. His moods veered dramatically from rage, wanting to lash out at the Fates, to depression so severe he doubted he could drag himself out of bed.

And through it all, when he felt he could no longer go on, there she was. Shannon seemed to know just when he needed her the most, and what he needed to hear to get him through to the next hour or day.

But now…there finally *was* hope.

Detective Bigelow had called to inform him that they'd had a credible sighting of Dylan. Shortly after, Shannon phoned.

"You believe it could be Dylan? That this could lead the cops to him?" Sawyer asked.

He knew she wouldn't have any more information than Bigelow, but her opinion mattered.

"Yes, I do. After the tip, local police checked security camera footage and we've seen the image." Her voice was filled with emotion. "I think it's him. And if it is, he's okay, Sawyer. He's unharmed."

Sawyer closed his eyes, and let the hope and relief surge through him. "Can I... Can I see it? The picture?"

"Did Detective Bigelow offer to show it to you?"

"No."

"Sawyer, normally you wouldn't have been told about this. We keep family members out of investigations for good reason. We don't want you to have expectations only to be disappointed. In this case, Bigelow made an exception, respecting your background. I can't give you more than he already has."

He wanted to push, but knew it wouldn't get him anywhere. And it wouldn't be fair to her. "Okay," he said grudgingly.

"I'll be going to Marina del Rey. Logan's arranged for me to be part of the search team."

"That means a lot to me." His voice sounded stronger.

"I'd like to stop by, if that's okay. Pick up some more items that belong to Dylan. For

Darwin to use, and also the search-and-rescue dogs the LAPD is deploying."

"Yes. Of course. Whatever you need."

"Any of his clothing you haven't washed yet. If not, a special stuffed animal perhaps."

"Laundry hasn't been high on my list of priorities." He smiled weakly. The first smile he could remember since Dylan had disappeared. "I have clothing. I'll have it ready for you. And some toys, too, if it helps."

As soon as he hung up, he grabbed a small gym bag and went to Dylan's room. Every time he walked in there, it was like a hard punch to the gut. To see the room exactly the way it had been the day they'd left for their camping trip...

But without Dylan.

He gathered the items for Shannon, then stopped abruptly.

He glanced around the room, yanked open the closet door and looked inside. He then turned around slowly, searching the room again.

"Where's Joey?" he murmured, perplexed.

He jammed a few more things into the bag and rushed back into the living room to call his parents. "Mom, the police think they might have a lead. Someone reported seeing Dylan."

"Oh..."

He could hear his mother's soft crying, followed by murmurs, and it helped him understand why the police didn't usually inform family members about unsubstantiated leads.

"Sawyer?" His father's voice was on the line. "What's happening?"

"The police have a lead—"

"Finally! What have they got?"

"I'll tell you, but first I have to get some things ready for the police. Dad, did you and Mom take Joey home with you from the campground?"

"Joey? You mean the stuffed kangaroo?"

"Yes. Do you have it?"

"No. Why would we?"

"Just checking. I'll call as soon as I hear anything further. Talk to you later, Dad."

Dylan had had the stuffed kangaroo with him on the camping trip. There was no question about that. He wouldn't have gone without Joey. With everything else on Sawyer's mind, he'd only now realized that Joey wasn't in the house. He called Meg, too, but she hadn't taken the toy home, either. When Shannon arrived, he swung the door open before she had a chance to knock. "Hi," he said, surprised that he was able to smile again.

He smiled even more widely when he pulled

Shannon into a hug. She smelled of something soft and floral, which he found comforting.

He stepped back. He hadn't seen her in uniform since the day they'd met. He noticed her eyes were a deep blue. How could he have missed that? He supposed he'd been seeing the world through a filter of hazy gray since Dylan had disappeared.

Picking up the bag of clothing and toys, he handed it to her.

"Thanks. Um, I need to go now."

"Yeah... Oh, I don't know if this matters, but I noticed today that Dylan's favorite toy is missing. It's a stuffed kangaroo, about this big." He indicated with his hands. "He must've had it with him when he was...taken."

Shannon looked at him thoughtfully. "We didn't find it along the trail, so there's a chance he might still have it. I appreciate you telling me."

She started to walk away, paused and turned back. Reaching for his hand, she squeezed it. "We'll do everything we can to find Dylan. I'll bring him back home to you, if I can."

Sawyer nodded, wanting to believe her. *Needing* to believe that she'd do it, this time.

He continued to stare down the road long after Shannon's Explorer was gone. The reported sighting gave him renewed optimism.

He hoped it wasn't a mistake. He didn't know how he'd survive if it was.

The fact that Shannon was going to be involved in the search for Dylan eased his anxiety. He'd asked Bigelow about driving to Marina del Rey; he wanted to be there in case they found Dylan. Bigelow had told him it wasn't possible. If they found Dylan, they'd get his son home as soon as they could. In the meantime, Sawyer trusted Shannon to do what was needed.

Sawyer hoped Dylan did have Joey with him. It helped to think he hadn't been alone all this time without anything familiar.

Sawyer's parents and Meg had said they'd come over when he'd spoken to them earlier. They arrived within minutes of each other.

Although he'd wanted to keep to himself over the past few days, now he realized how much he appreciated their being with him. He would've lost his mind waiting there without them. They were all tense, anxious, and they needed each other. That was family. That was what he wanted for Dylan, if only he'd come back home again.

And they waited for the phone to ring.

SERGEANT ANSON DIDN'T seem particularly pleased to have Shannon involved. But she didn't let that bother her. She had authorization to be here. At least the three LAPD K-9 officers were more welcoming. Yes, she'd been a little intimidated seeing them and—based on their ages—realized they had far more experience than she did. So be it. She wanted to help find Dylan. It mattered to her professionally and personally.

Shannon watched the security camera footage, showing the boy holding the hand of a dark-haired woman. She appeared to be of Hispanic descent. They left a playground, stopped to purchase ice cream, then crossed the street and headed south on Walgrove Avenue.

Shannon's heart thudded heavily. She was certain the boy was Dylan. They'd checked the woman's image against the possible suspects they were considering from Sawyer's days as a prosecutor and there wasn't a match. They tried facial recognition, on social media and in police files, and nothing popped. The woman was not known to police.

The ice-cream vendor was gone when they got to the playground, but the local police were tracking him down. Shannon allowed herself a moment of satisfaction that it was Darwin who'd picked up Dylan's scent from where the cart had been.

Despite the passage of time—more than

four hours—and the dozens of kids and adults who must have traversed the area, Darwin recognized and isolated Dylan's scent. Two local officers were instructed to accompany them. They jogged along the perimeter of the park, until Darwin turned sharp left toward a densely-treed area. Focused on Darwin, Shannon didn't notice the low-hanging branch. She certainly felt the sting when it slapped her in the face. Without slowing, she touched a hand to the sore spot. The tips of her fingers came away damp with blood.

She'd worry about it later.

They left the park and crossed a street. Unerringly, Darwin led them to a low-rise apartment building. They assumed Dylan was inside the building, but they didn't know which floor. They'd have to check each corridor. Another unknown was whether the woman was alone with Dylan or not.

They needed a game plan so as not to alert whoever was with Dylan. If she felt trapped, they didn't want her lashing out at the boy and possibly hurting him. There were no security cameras for the building that they could discern. One of the locals, Officer Robbins, contacted the resident building manager.

"I don't make a habit of watching the comings and goings of the building occupants," he declared. "I don't know if this helps, but we have a new short-term sublet for apartment 108."

They'd check the unit. If Darwin could follow the scent, he'd provide probable cause for entry.

While Robbins called in an update to Anson, she and the other officer discussed how best to proceed. As thcy spoke, he handed her a handkerchief to wipe off the now mostly dry blood from her cheek.

"Thanks," she said and dabbed at the scratch.

Concluding his call, Robbins rejoined them. "Anson, Bigelow and Special Agent Leary are on their way. We've got authorization to proceed."

Shannon instructed Darwin to "find" and he nearly pulled her off her feet. Rather than entering the building through the front door as she'd expected, he streaked off to the right. He followed the chain-link fence surrounding a grassy area adjacent to the building. When he reached a gate, he repeatedly jumped up against it. Shannon directed Darwin to settle and turned to the uniformed officer who'd accompanied her.

"Dylan is either back there or he recently passed through this gate. Could you hold Darwin for a minute?" she asked.

"Sure," he said, but with a bit of apprehension.

"You'll be fine. Stay," she instructed Darwin as she handed off his leash.

She moved cautiously along the fence until she could see the back patios of the units, separated by wooden partitions. She peered around the corner and her heart rate spiked.

A young boy was sitting cross-legged on the grass, a stuffed brown kangaroo in front of him. It had to be Dylan.

There was no one else on the patio. A sliding glass door was open, sheers billowing out in the breeze. She heard the clatter of pots and pans inside.

She moved quickly back to where the other officer was waiting. She had Darwin "down-stay" near a lamppost and looped his lead around its base. Robbins radioed that he was in position at the inside entrance to the apartment. Robbins was going in through the front door; Shannon's job was to get Dylan and keep him safe. The officer accompanying her would prevent anyone from escaping through the patio door.

Shannon gave the go-ahead, opened the gate and ran straight to Dylan, the other officer right behind her.

"Dylan, don't be afraid. I'm with the police and I'm taking you home to your father."

She saw wide-eyed surprise and confusion, but thankfully no tears as she gathered the boy in her arms.

"Joey," he squealed and pointed to his stuffed kangaroo. "Joey!"

"Okay, okay," she reassured him, and bent down to pick up the toy.

Hearing the commotion inside, she held the boy tight against her and sprinted toward the gate.

CHAPTER EIGHT

SHANNON WAS BARELY through the gate when she saw two police cars pull up at the curb. Sergeant Anson was the first one out of the cruiser, followed by FBI Special Agent Gavin Leary. Bigelow got out of his own SDPD vehicle and started toward Shannon.

When Dylan began to whimper, she put him down. Holding up a hand to keep Bigelow from approaching, she crouched in front of Dylan.

"Is this Joey?" she murmured, trying to distract him.

"Uh-huh," he said with a sniffle.

"I bet Joey is a little scared, huh?"

Dylan nodded.

"Do you know what I think would help Joey?"

"Uh-uh?"

"Because he loves you so much, I bet it would help if you showed him how brave you are, and told him you'll both be seeing your dad in a couple of hours."

Dylan raised his eyes, huge and round, to meet Shannon's.

"Can you do that? Show Joey how brave you are?"

His lips trembled, but he whispered, "Yes." When Shannon saw Bigelow advancing toward them again, she gave him a steely look and a slight shake of her head. Bigelow changed direction and joined the officer standing close to Darwin. Her gaze resting on Darwin, Shannon had an idea.

"Dylan, do you like dogs?"

He nodded again and held his stuffed toy out toward her. "Joey's a kangaroo. I like kangaroos, too."

"I can see that. Would you like to meet my dog?" she asked, pointing at Darwin.

"'Kay." He took a moment to assess the dog. "He's big."

"Yes, he is, but he's gentle, too."

"He's pretty." Dylan's eyes rounded. "Is he a police dog?"

"Yes, he is," she repeated. "Would you like to say hello?"

He nodded with more enthusiasm this time.

She rose and held out her hand for him. She felt an odd flutter when he placed his small one in hers and clung tight.

She led Dylan over to Darwin, introduced

him to Bigelow and the officer, and then to her dog.

"Can you and Joey stay here for a minute with Darwin and Officer Martin?"

Dylan looked up at the officer and hugged Joey tighter. ""Kay."

As she and Bigelow walked to where Anson and Leary stood, she sent a quick text to Sawyer, telling him that Dylan was with her, safe and unharmed. He'd hear soon enough through the proper police channels, but if she could save him a single minute of worry, it was worth it.

His reply was immediate.

Thank God.
Thank you for letting me know.

All Shannon wanted to do now was get Dylan home to his father with as little additional trauma as possible. She had a brief discussion with Bigelow, Leary and Anson. They agreed it was best if she traveled with the boy. They'd take her Explorer, and Robbins would drive so she could stay with the boy. Martin would follow in another cruiser to bring Robbins back.

Once they settled on the logistics, she hurried back to Dylan. He was squatting in front of Darwin, stroking him.

She bent down beside them. "Ready to go home?"

"To Daddy?" he asked in a subdued voice.

"Yes."

His lower lip quivered and Shannon sensed he was about to start crying. "You'll get to ride in a police car, and Darwin and I will be right there with you. Is that okay?"

He nodded, and her heart melted when he wrapped his arms around her neck, Joey dangling from one hand. She lifted him up. Unhooking Darwin's lead from around the lamppost, she signaled for him to "heel," and carried Dylan to her Explorer. When they reached her vehicle, she tried to put Dylan down, but he refused to let go. With the boy still in her arms, she opened the hatch and instructed Darwin to hop in.

That made Dylan smile. "He jumped so high!"

Robbins headed for the driver's side of the Explorer while she placed Dylan in the backseat. Climbing in after him, she fastened his seat belt.

She tried to do everything she could to distract him and keep him happy during the drive to San Diego.

As they sped along I-405 South, she pointed out landmarks and scenic areas, but she was careful to avoid any discussion of where he'd been and who he'd been with. Victim Services cautioned officers not to get into any of the details with victims of abduction until they'd been professionally assessed. The fear was that it could bring back all the bad memories and trigger post-traumatic stress. "How's Joey doing?" she asked instead, hoping to get an indication of how Dylan himself was holding up.

"He's okay, I guess." Dylan seemed preoccupied with his toy for a few minutes. "See, Joey has a pouch and everything!" he exclaimed suddenly, pointing to the pocket on the toy's belly. "That's where the mama kangaroos keep their babies," he informed her solemnly.

At one point, he touched her face. "You're hurt," he said softly, concern clouding his eyes.

"I'm okay," she assured him, and wished she'd thought to put a bandage on her scratch.

As Dylan fell silent again, Shannon watched him out of the corner of her eye. The only outward sign of his distress was how tightly he clutched his stuffed toy, and—when she wasn't distracting him—the way he rocked back and forth. Eventually, Shannon let Dylan set the tone to talk or not, as he wished. He asked about his father, but he also asked about the woman who'd been in the apartment with him. Shannon made a mental note to tell Biglow and Leary that he called her "*tía*," Spanish for aunt.

Dylan didn't say much about what had happened to him, but he did clear up the question of how he'd been taken. He'd gone outside the tent to pee, and a woman had grabbed him before he could do anything. The woman had immediately covered his mouth so he couldn't call out.

During the entire trip home, he didn't let go of his toy.

After nearly two and a half hours, they finally turned onto Sawyer's street. Sawyer and his family were sitting outside on his front porch. As soon as he noticed the police vehicles, he rushed toward the road and was waiting by the curb as they pulled up.

Dylan cried out when he saw his father, and Shannon had to hold him back from trying to jump out until the vehicle had come to a full stop. For the first time, he released Joey, abandoning the toy on the seat next to Shannon.

Shannon could feel the sting of tears in her

eyes as she watched Dylan fling himself into his father's outstretched arms.

"Thank God. Thank God you're okay," Sawyer muttered.

With his head resting on top of Dylan's, Sawyer took deep, gulping breaths. When he eased back, he framed Dylan's face with his hands and scrutinized every detail.

"What happened? Where have you—" Sawyer stopped midsentence.

Shannon assumed that Victim Services had advised him, too, to not question Dylan.

"Never mind. Never mind any of that. I'm just so happy you're here," Sawyer said with a laugh, engulfing Dylan in another hug. "You're home. That's all that matters."

His parents and his sister had clustered around them, and they held on to each other.

"It's days like this that make the job worthwhile," said Robbins, a thirty-year-veteran of the force, in a gruff voice. "Not all of them turn out this way, but when one does..." He smiled down at her. "Well, that's what the job's all about."

Although his eyes were dry, the tone of his voice had betrayed his emotions. Shannon tried to keep her own composure, as she held out a hand to Robbins. "Thank you for driving us. And please thank your sergeant for letting me be part of this."

"I will, and we're glad you were. Who knows if we would've had the same outcome without you." He gave her a little salute before he walked back to the LAPD unit that had accompanied them and the waiting officer.

Shannon turned her attention back to the family and wondered again what was between her and Sawyer. When he'd glanced up, he'd given her a crooked smile. After that it seemed she might as well not exist.

She shut that selfish thought down quickly. Who could blame him?

He had his son back. That was the most important thing in the world, and of course his focus.

She pushed away from the side of her vehicle. She'd let the family have their reunion. Tomorrow or the next day would be soon enough to see if she and Sawyer had anything between them, or if their…relationship had been contingent on the search for Dylan.

Shannon waved goodbye to the other officers as they drove away. Pulling Joey out of the backseat, she placed him on the grass and was climbing into her Explorer when Sawyer called her name.

She turned to see him gently handing Dylan to his mother, then he jogged over to her.

"You said you'd find Dylan. And you did. I'll never forget this. Never."

"Um… I'd better get going. Leave you to Dylan and your family." She bent down to grab Joey and handed the toy to Sawyer.

He tucked Joey under his arm. "Go?" He sounded shocked. "Can't you stay and celebrate with us?"

"I… Thanks for the invitation, but I have to return to the division. There's a debrief and there'll be reports to write."

He touched her forearm. "Will you come back? Tonight? When you're done?"

She gazed into his eyes, fascinated by the light she saw glowing in their depths. A light that she hadn't seen before.

A thrill of anticipation flowed through her, and she felt her lips curve in a smile. "I'll see what I can do. It depends on how long we'll be. I'll send you a text."

His eyes scanned her face. Rested on her cheek. He brushed his fingers over the abrasion.

"How did this happen?"

She shrugged dismissively. "I wasn't paying attention and ran into a branch. It's nothing."

He skimmed the pad of his thumb across the

spot. Then, taking her by complete surprise, he touched his lips to it and drew her briefly into his arms. "I'm sorry you were hurt," he murmured. "Come back if possible."

She nodded. "Go be with Dylan. I'll see you later, if I can."

As she walked back to her Explorer, she raised her own hand to the tender spot on her cheek. Instead of the dull ache that had persisted, she felt a pleasant tingling where his lips had touched.

THE DEBRIEF WAS underway by the time Shannon arrived at the division. Dylan was home, but they had many unanswered questions.

"The LAPD apprehended two people in the apartment where the boy had been kept," Bigelow said. "Yet it got us no closer to determining who'd abducted him."

"How can that be?" Shannon asked, in disbelief.

"Because we don't bclicvc they're responsible for the abduction. Juanita Sanchez—the woman who was with Dylan—claims she'd been hired as a caregiver for the child. She said she was given the apartment and paid in cash to take care of the boy. She was contacted through an ad she'd placed in the local paper, seeking employment. She'd been a nurse in

Mexico and said she wanted to work with children, as a nanny."

Shannon shook her head. "I'm sorry, but I don't understand. What about the person who contacted her? That must be the woman who abducted Dylan. Am I wrong?"

Bigelow's frustration was palpable. "You'd think. Sanchez was contacted by a woman who'd said she was calling on behalf of her employer. She said she was his executive assistant. According to her, he'd been indefinitely detained on business out of the country. He needed someone to take care of his child until he returned. When Sanchez asked about the child's mother, she was told the mother had died."

"How could someone fall for that?" Shannon didn't understand. How on earth did someone not question being asked to take care of a child without expecting to see at least one of the parents? But that was a moot point. "She's got to know more than she's saying."

Logan caught her attention. "Let Richard finish," he said quietly.

"Sanchez was distraught but she held up during questioning." Bigelow picked up the flow again. "Regardless of how many times we asked the same questions and how many different ways. I'm convinced she was telling the truth. Having been in the country for a few months with a legal work permit but without employment or any other source of income, she'd been feeling the pressure. Feeling desperate."

"And how did she end up with the boy?" someone else asked. "When and where did this woman hand him over?"

"Sanchez met her at a coffee shop. No video cameras," Bigelow added. "We showed her a picture of Jeannette Evans. Sanchez claimed there was no resemblance to the woman she met. She was given an envelope with the security deposit and first month's rent on the sublet, and another envelope with her payment in it, along with what she was told was extra money to buy the boy clothes, incidentals and food. She was told the building manager would have the key.

"We verified that with the manager. He also had signed papers for the apartment, which were sent electronically. The email address is bogus and the IP address led us to a public-use workstation at a library. The woman's name is, as expected, fake, too."

"Sanchez was paid generously and considered herself fortunate to have the job." Leary spoke for the first time. "Desperate people can do desperate things. When we challenged her during interrogation—asking if the whole situation hadn't seemed questionable to her—she admitted she'd had qualms. But she'd convinced herself that it was legitimate, since she needed the money."

"Sanchez was genuinely horrified to discover that Dylan had been abducted, and terrified of the consequences, including possible jail time or deportation," Bigelow added. "The call she received was from a prepaid cell phone. She'd said that according to the woman, the father had indicated he'd pick up his son—Dylan—in another week. The locals are keeping an eye on the apartment to see if anyone shows, but we suspect it won't come to anything. We've cautioned Sanchez that if she receives another call, to pretend all is well and to contact Special Agent Leary right away."

"And the man who was staying in the apartment? Who is he and what did he have to say?" someone else wanted to know.

"Nothing there, either. He's a distant cousin of Sanchez's and had no knowledge about Dylan or what had happened to him. He'd just been happy to have a place to stay. Unlike Sanchez, who seemed genuine and sincere, the man struck me as having fewer scruples. We came down hard on him in interrogation, but he held up, as well.

"He, too, was afraid of the possible consequences," Bigelow went on. "He was of no help, other than to corroborate Sanchez's story, to the extent that he was aware of the facts. There was no reason to suspect he'd been involved in the abduction in any way," he concluded. He got out of his chair and strode to a window.

"If you're sure they're not responsible, why can't they lead us to the person or persons who *did* abduct Dylan?" Shannon knew she was probably out of line challenging those with higher rank and more seniority, but there *had* to be something that would help them identify the kidnapper.

"We had Sanchez work with a sketch artist to get a likeness of the woman who brought Dylan to her. We knew that unless she had a criminal record or is one of the people we've looked at, it wouldn't help us much, and it didn't. The effort didn't produce anything worthwhile."

"What about the boy? According to what you've said, he was in public places. Why didn't he run or cry?" another SDPD officer asked.

"Victim Services has seen cases like this before," Bigelow responded, but Shannon could tell that his patience was wearing thin. "We suspect Stockholm syndrome. Sanchez said that Dylan asked about his father, but she'd reassured him that he was away on business and would be back to get him soon—just as she'd been told by the woman who'd contacted her."

All very strange and improbable, Shannon thought. "It makes no sense. I've never heard of anything like this before."

"Nor have we," Leary agreed. "We'll keep at it, though, and we *will* find the person or persons responsible."

They had no choice but to resume their efforts from a blank slate, Shannon realized. They had no viable leads.

The debrief was lengthy. After that, there was report writing, complicated by the fact that it had been a multijurisdictional effort, which meant more paperwork.

Shannon had sent a quick text to Sawyer when she'd left the conference room during a break, letting him know she wouldn't be able to make it. She didn't have a chance to check for messages again until well after ten.

She grinned at the picture he'd attached of Dylan sleeping peacefully in his bed, one arm securely around Joey, the thumb of his other hand in his mouth.

Her heart did a little skip when she read Sawyer's message.

I'm eternally grateful to you.
We're blessed that you came into our lives.
Will you have dinner with me next week?

She bit her lower lip as she typed the reply.

Yes!

CHAPTER NINE

SHANNON WAS EXCITED and nervous at the same time. She had a date with Sawyer!

She respected him for wanting to wait a week before leaving Dylan with his sister, but the passage of time had only added to her nervousness about the date.

At least she *hoped* it was a date, rather than a "thank you for returning my son to me" expression of gratitude. Whatever his feelings toward her, Shannon's were becoming clearer to her now. She was attracted to Sawyer. More than attracted...

Well, for better or worse, it was a first step—and an important one—to discovering what, if anything, could be between them.

Although she was immensely glad that Sawyer had his son back, the cop in her couldn't avoid a lingering sense of unease about the fact that they still didn't know who'd abducted Dylan. But she kept her thoughts to herself. There was no point in worrying Sawyer, when his elation over having his son home safe and sound was obvious and so understandable. Besides, the SDPD and FBI continued to work cooperatively, and she was certain they'd get to the bottom of it soon.

At the moment, her primary concern was deciding what to wear for dinner with Sawyer.

She skimmed a hand along the clothes hanging in her closet, mostly jeans and khakis, with a variety of casual shirts and sweaters. The word *tomboy* echoed through her mind. She groaned. *Once a tomboy, always a tomboy*, she thought. She could count the number of dresses she owned on one hand. Then her gaze landed on a garment bag tucked away at the back of her closet.

"Wait a minute!" she exclaimed.

Darwin scrambled over to her, making her laugh. She scratched him behind the ears. "Everything's okay. Go lie down."

Darwin leaned against her for a final rub before trotting back to his bed.

Shannon took the bag into her room and placed it on the bed. Unzipping it, she pulled out a silver-blue silk pantsuit. When she'd been invited to Jessica Palmer's Jack-and-Jill baby shower a couple of months ago—being new in the unit and wanting to make a good impression—she'd decided to splurge on an outfit. The pants were slim-fitting and hemmed to wear with high heels. The sleeve-less tunic top showed off her arms—well-toned because she worked darn hard at it. A thick belt, a slightly darker shade of blue, cinched the top, highlighting her waist.

She clipped on pearl earrings and fastened a matching strand around her neck. She fingered the necklace and smiled. Her parents had given her the set for her twenty-fifth birthday. She slipped her feet into a pair of off-white stiletto pumps she'd worn only a couple of times, and hoped she wouldn't break an ankle. Examining herself critically in the bathroom mirror, she had to admit she looked good, her slim shape appearing curvier than she usually gave her-self credit for.

"How about that, Darwin?" she said, as she walked into the bedroom and smiled. "I can look girly when I want to."

The dog tilted his head and made a noise that sounded very much like "huh."

She chuckled as she let Darwin out. She'd just fed him when the doorbell rang. Taking a final glance in her hallway mirror, she quickly fluffed her hair, then opened the door.

Shannon knew as soon as she saw Sawyer standing in the doorway that all her primping had been worth it. He stood there, staring at her, holding a bouquet of flowers in one hand.

When he stepped toward her, he tripped on the door stoop.

"Sorry," he said. "I just didn't expect… wow!"

Before she could respond, Darwin rushed over to greet Sawyer, and he obliged by squatting down and rubbing the dog's head. Standing up again, he reached into his jacket pocket and pulled out a package of gourmet dog treats. "Is it okay for him to have these?" he asked. "I wanted to thank him for his part in bringing Dylan home."

"Sure." With a grin she couldn't suppress, she looked meaningfully at the huge bunch of flowers in his hand. "And are those for him, too?"

"What? Oh…" He glanced down. "These?" He lifted the bouquet and presented it to her. "They're for you. A small token of my appreciation."

"They're beautiful." Raising them to her nose, she inhaled deeply. "They smell wonderful." Emboldened, she leaned forward and placed a kiss on his cheek. "Thank you." She stood back from the doorway. "Come inside so I can put these in water and you can give Darwin a treat."

"Great. Yeah."

He seemed a little nervous, maybe uncertain, and that just added to Shannon's giddiness.

"Can I get you a drink?" she asked over her shoulder as she led him toward her kitchen.

"No, thanks. Nice place."

"I like it, and it's convenient for work. It's on the small side, but it made it affordable for me. It has a good-size yard for Darwin, and I've been fixing it up gradually. How's Dylan?" she asked as she got a vase from a bottom cupboard and filled it with water.

"Good. Good. I arranged for a therapist—a child-trauma specialist—to see him. I'll tell you about it over dinner," he said.

She looked up at him while she arranged the flowers in the vase, trying to gauge whether his comment was an indication that this dinner was more about Dylan than them. She'd know soon enough.

Putting the vase on the kitchen table, she stood back to admire the flowers. She didn't consider herself the type of woman men bought flowers for. They were much more likely to take her to a ball game. She *liked* flowers, and was touched that Sawyer had thought to bring her some. Even if it was just to thank her.

"Oh, I almost forgot," Sawyer said, patting his jacket, then reaching into the inside pocket. He handed her an envelope with her name printed on it in blue crayon. She raised her eyebrows as she accepted it from him.

"Go ahead and open it," he said with a wide smile.

She did, and pulled out a hand-drawn card, obviously made by Dylan. It showed an uncanny likeness of her and Darwin. On the bottom he'd drawn a big red heart and in bold, capital letters, his name.

"It was his idea," Sawyer explained.

Shannon was touched by the thoughtful gesture. She propped the card up against the vase. "It's beautiful," she said to Sawyer. "Please thank Dylan for me."

"I hope you'll have a chance to thank him yourself," he said, as he offered an ecstatic Darwin one more treat before sealing up the pack and placing it on the table, too.

Sawyer held the door for Shannon as she climbed into his Range Rover. His treatment added to her warm glow and made her feel special.

He hadn't told her where they were going, and she turned to him in surprise when he pulled up in front of the restaurant.

"You're taking me to La Petite France?" she asked with a small laugh.

"Is that a problem?"

"No. Just a little intimidating, since it's one of the top restaurants in San Diego."

Sawyer put the vehicle in Park. "Have you been here before?"

She laughed again. "No."

"Well, then, mission accomplished," he said with a grin. "I wanted something different."

He got out and opened the door for her again, before she had a chance to do it herself. Passing his keys, along with a twenty-dollar bill, to the valet, he set one hand lightly on her lower back and guided her toward the entrance.

Unobtrusively, he passed another bill to the maître d' and they were seated at an outside table next to the railing.

The waiter handed them menus, recited the specials and asked if they wanted a cocktail. They both declined. Instead, Sawyer asked for the wine list. After consulting Shannon, he ordered a bottle of 2006 Bourgogne Chardonnay.

Once their wine had been served and their orders taken, Sawyer raised his glass. "To you and how beautiful you are," he said, clinking his glass against hers.

Shannon took a sip, then made her own toast. "And to Dylan being home."

He touched his glass to hers again, but a shadow settled across his eyes.

"You said Dylan was okay," she said with immediate concern.

"Oh, yes. But not unaffected." He shook his head and stared out across the water. "How can a child *not* be affected by something like that?"

"I'm sorry..." Shannon murmured, feeling ineffectual. "You said he's seeing a therapist."

Sawyer exhaled. "Yeah. Outwardly, Dylan is behaving as if nothing happened. Much as he did after Jeannette disappeared. But he asks about '*tía*,' the woman who was with him, and I can't get him to let Joey—his stuffed kangaroo—out of his sight. Sometimes he rocks himself and he's also started sucking his thumb again. Something he hasn't done since he was nine months old." Sawyer let out another long breath. "The therapist working with him says he wasn't abused or mistreated, but she diagnosed him with Stockholm syndrome." He glanced at Shannon.

She nodded. "That's when a—" She was going to say "victim" but caught herself, realizing it would've been an insensitive way to refer to Dylan. "It's when a person develops feelings of trust or affection toward a captor."

"Yes. That's why the therapist thinks the trauma might have long-term consequences."

"I'm so very sorry." There wasn't anything else Shannon could say.

"On the plus side, she feels that getting Dylan treatment early will help. But look," Sawyer said with a hesitant smile. "That's not why we're here. I wanted this to be a celebration. Yes, there are issues we'll have to work through, but the outcome could've been a lot worse."

Shannon thought of Charlie and had to agree, but kept her opinion to herself.

"I appreciate everything you've done. Especially bringing Dylan back to me. So let's put that aside for now. I'd like to enjoy a meal with a fascinating, beautiful woman."

The evening passed much too quickly. As they shared tiramisu and lingered over coffee, Shannon couldn't remember enjoying a man's company as much as she did Sawyer's. It was as if she was getting to know him all over again. He'd been filled with fear, rage and angst while Dylan was missing. The anger was still there, but now she was discovering a lighthearted, humorous, intelligent man. He made the butterflies flutter in her belly just by smiling at her.

"Would you like to go for a walk along the water's edge?" he asked once they were standing in front of the restaurant.

She was caught up in the romance of the evening and wasn't ready to say good-night

to him yet. "I'd like that very much," she said,
hoping she wouldn't twist an ankle in her high
heels.

He took her hand and laced his fingers
through hers. They strolled to the end of a
pier and there, under the star-speckled sky and
with the gentle breeze playing over her skin,
he turned her to face him.

"You're truly beautiful, Shannon. Inside and
out."

He slid his hand around her shoulder and
up to the nape of her neck. Then he lowered
his head.

With a sigh, she let her eyes close as his
lips touched hers. The stars overhead paled
in comparison to the brilliant lights that burst
against her eyelids as she gave herself over to
the sensation of Sawyer's kiss.

The touch of his lips was light. Undemanding.

But it stirred feelings in her that endured
long after the kiss had cnded.

When she opened her eyes again, the ten-
derness in his and the warm smile on his lips
set a thousand more butterflies aflutter in her
stomach.

He brushed his fingers across her cheek, and
placed another light kiss on her nearly healed
abrasion. Then he took her hand in his as they
strolled back to his vehicle.

At Shannon's house, Sawyer walked her to the front door. "Thank you for a wonderful evening," he said. Framing her face with his palms, he kissed her again.

He waited until she was inside before getting into his SUV. She watched from the living room window as he backed out of her driveway.

She was falling for Sawyer Evans. With a giddy sense of joy, she thought she knew how he felt about her now. This hadn't been a simple thank-you dinner. He was interested in her as more than a friend.

SAWYER PULLED INTO his garage and shut off the engine.

He thought back over his evening with Shannon. Who would've guessed he'd fall for a cop? He'd dealt with enough of them while he was assistant DA, but he'd never met one quite like Shannon. He'd grown closer and closer to her while Dylan was missing, but he'd believed it was only because she was a link to the police and the investigation to find his son. He'd rationalized that his emotions were overactive because of the turmoil he was feeling over Dylan.

It was more than that.

Yeah, he'd taken her out tonight to thank her

for everything she'd done. Supporting him. Keeping him informed. Keeping him *sane*. And most important of all, bringing Dylan back home.

But tonight had proved something to him.

He had *feelings* for Shannon.

And that surprised him. What surprised him even more was that he'd wanted to kiss her.

He'd dated a few women since Jeannette's disappearance, mostly at the urging of his family.

But none of them had stirred his emotions the way Shannon did. Nor had he expected anyone to do so.

Sawyer had met Jeannette in high school. She'd been his first and only love. She'd been his soul mate—something a lot of people never found in their lifetime. Her loss had left a void that he'd accepted would never be filled.

And yet, Shannon roused emotions deep inside him.

He hadn't been able to resist touching her. Kissing her. Sure, he'd kissed her once before, but that was on the spur of the moment, part of the excitement of having Dylan back.

Tonight was different.

He rested his head against the back of the seat. He needed to pull himself together before he went inside or Meghan would see right through him.

And he wasn't prepared to discuss his feelings for Shannon with her or anyone at this point.

Yes, he was drawn to Shannon, but his feelings for her came with guilt.

Over the three years Jeannette had been gone, he'd never really stopped thinking of himself as married. Three years after her disappearance, he still couldn't bring himself to accept that she was dead.

Even though his feelings for Jeannette now seemed to be a mere shadow of what they'd once been, did his new feelings for another woman make him unfaithful to her?

And was it fair to Shannon if his heart, now and possibly forever, belonged to someone else?

Dejected, Sawyer removed his wallet from his pocket and took out the worn picture of Jeannette and him on their wedding day.

They'd been so young and hopeful when they got married. He hadn't had a single doubt.

With a resigned sigh, he replaced the picture.

Maybe he was a one-woman man, not capable of falling so deeply in love again.

He got out of the vehicle, and forced what

he hoped was a casual smile as he unlocked the door leading from the garage into the mudroom. He steeled himself to face Meg—and more than likely the prospect of a solitary life.

CHAPTER TEN

SAWYER HUNCHED OVER the table in the interrogation room at SDPD headquarters. With him were Detective Richard Bigelow and Special Agent Gavin Leary. Sawyer had wondered if he'd see Shannon, but a casual question to Bigelow had informed him that she was out in the field. He'd avoided calling her since their dinner together while he tried to sort out his scrambled thoughts about her—and Jeannette. When Shannon had texted to thank him for dinner and offered to return the favor, he'd made some feeble excuse about being busy.

It was hard trying to keep his mind off her without being in the place where she worked.

And being there just annoyed the hell out of him.Sawyer was as anxious as anyone to have the person or persons responsible for Dylan's abduction caught, but his nerves were frayed by the incessant questions. He'd been a prosecutor; he knew how the system worked. But he was getting tired of going over his past, having the FBI special agents and the SDPD officers digging into details about his friends and acquaintances, business associates and the people he'd prosecuted and sent to jail.

No, he didn't have any idea who'd abducted Dylan.

No, he couldn't think of anyone who might have such a serious grudge against him.

Dylan was home and seemed to be getting better day by day.

Couldn't well enough be left alone?

No, he answered his own question. He wanted—*needed*—justice to be served. Whoever was responsible had to be held to account. Wasn't that what he'd dedicated the early part of his career to?

If not for wanting to be available for Dylan, he'd still be working in the DA's office. And a lot of good changing jobs had done for his son!

At least Dylan's therapist was pleased with his progress. The Stockholm syndrome diagnosis had explained why he hadn't tried to run away. The therapist clarified that in Dylan's case, the situation was exacerbated by the fact that he'd been—no offense meant, she'd said—deprived of a mother figure in his life. The woman who'd been taking care of him in Marina del Rey had briefly filled that void. This information ripped open all the wounds Sawyer had been struggling with, leaving them raw and festering. Dylan's nightmares, which had started soon after Jeannette left, were recurring.

On the positive side, the therapist was giving Sawyer encouraging reports about how resilient Dylan was. She was also giving him hope that they might, after all, escape any long-term consequences. He prayed that would be the case.

But he couldn't ignore the facts.

Someone had abducted his son.

That person—or persons—had to be caught, had to pay for this crime. There would be no justice without it.

So he continued to meet with the FBI and the SDPD, and kept answering their questions. Over and over.

They'd also gotten all the relevant files from the DA's office, so Sawyer had a hard time understanding what additional value he could provide.

Well, at least they'd cleared him. That was something. They'd told him first thing today when he'd sat down with them. They said they'd found no reason to suspect that he or any member of his family had anything to do with Dylan's disappearance.

"Are you with us, Mr. Evans?" Bigelow's voice broke through Sawyer's musings.

"What? Oh, yeah. Can we get on with it?"

"Okay. Of the people you prosecuted, the most likely possibilities remain Stewart Rankin in first place. He killed an entire family while driving under the influence of alcohol. Next is Donna Thompson, convicted of being a drug mule for one of the Mexican cartels, serving a seven-year sentence. We moved Nadine Crosby up to third place, based on her psychological profile. Last but by no means least is Colin Jansen, serving time for killing another man in a bar brawl.

"Let's start with the most recent conviction first and work our way back, if that suits you," Bigelow suggested.

"Number one, Stewart Rankin, is from a wealthy family," Sawyer began, as he dragged his fingers through his hair. "You know all this already," he said, not hiding his annoyance.

"Yes, we have the facts," Leary responded. "But we'd appreciate you taking us through it again. We're particularly interested in any impressions or hunches. Keep in mind," he added, his tone placating, "we have the same goal here."

Sawyer planted his elbows on the table and fisted his hands. He wished none of this had ever happened. But since it had, he wanted it all behind him.

He raised his head and his eyes were drawn to the one-way mirror. He could've sworn he felt Shannon watching him from the other side. Reminding himself of the role she'd played in returning Dylan safely to him, his determination to avoid her wavered.

Forcing his thoughts back to the question, he got his emotions—and temper—under control.

"All right. Here we go again. So, the twenty-seven-year-old son of the Rankin construction dynasty had gotten behind the wheel of his Porsche Carrera 911, inebriated after his bachelor party, and killed five members of a family. With his money and resources, you'd have thought he'd be smart enough to arrange for a driver. No, he didn't. He was convicted and sent to prison over three years ago." Sawyer heaved a sigh of frustration. "If it's him, why now? He's still in prison. You've looked at his father and other members of his family, too, and eliminated them all. And if it is one of them, why now?" he repeated. "Why *three years* after he went to jail?"

"Sometimes a situation can chafe for a long time," Leary said. "Did Rankin or any member of his family make threats against you?"

"No."

"Did you ever feel intimidated by any of them?"

"No. In fact, to me, Rankin seems to have shown high levels of remorse, and I got the sense that his father was disappointed in him, so not in a frame of mind to avenge him."

"All right, Mr. Evans. Let's move on to Donna Thompson."

Sawyer tried not to roll his eyes. "In Donna's case, you have all the information I do and probably more, since your Sergeant Vasquez was instrumental in apprehending her and bringing her to justice." He glanced at the mirror. "One of the best examples I've seen of a clear-cut case with solid documentary evidence. Sergeant Vasquez made my job easy."

"Rick is one of our very finest," Bigelow acknowledged. "Let me remind you, we're looking for impressions, which only you can provide. Do you remember anything about her family or loved ones?"

"The name wasn't the one she was born with. Her heritage is Mexican. She'd changed it when she moved here. She had no family in the US at the time." He paused. "But she did have an unpleasant boyfriend. A high-ranking cartel operative. He probably moved on quickly and I can't see him holding a grudge for..." He thought back to when she'd been convicted. "For nearly four years."

Bigelow closed the file in front of him and opened the next. "How about Nadine Crosby?"

"Crosby was twenty-three when she was charged with the attempted murder of her mother and her mother's then-boyfriend. She'd claimed self-defense because of sexual abuse by the boyfriend. There was no evidence to substantiate her allegations. A psychologist diagnosed her as emotionally unstable and motivated by jealousy rather than abuse. Crosby had made similar allegations against a couple of her mother's former boyfriends, and those were deemed to have been false, as well."

"Crosby fits the profile of someone wanting revenge against you," Leary stated. "She and Thompson are the only two females we're looking at. The fact that she'd been recently released contributed to moving her up to number three on our list."

"Yes, but she'd never shown any hostility or resentment against me," Sawyer said.

"She's also alibied for the time of the abduction," Bigelow added. "If the alibi holds, she's off our list."

They ran through Colin Jansen in a similar fashion, but nothing about him seemed to resonate. He'd lost his temper in a big way in that barroom, but it hadn't been premeditated and he hadn't intended to kill anyone.

"We haven't got much further with Blackstone. Seems like a dead end. Should we keep digging?" Bigelow asked Leary.

Leary glanced at Sawyer. "No harm in it, if Mr. Evans doesn't mind, since we don't have any clear winners at this point."

Sawyer shrugged, but his eyes were drawn to the mirror.

"So, Blackstone was fifty-six at the time, and a father of four who defrauded his company of nearly a million dollars," Bigelow said, flipping to the next file.

Sawyer ran a hand over his face. "If I've ever regretted sending someone to jail, it would've been him. His wife quit her job after their fourth child was diagnosed with autism. When their oldest child developed muscular dystrophy, Blackstone's income was insufficient to care for their children. I don't believe the man had an evil bone in his body. He acted out of desperation to provide for his family and take care of two children with serious disabilities."

Leary scratched his chin. "Tell us about the wife," he said. "If we hypothesize that the abductor acted alone, then it's reasonable to conclude we're looking for a female, since it was a female who took Dylan from that campsite, and a female who contacted and retained Sanchez—and is there anything more you can tell us about Blackstone's wife?"

Sawyer searched his memory. "She was... broken." It was the best word he could come up with. "Even so, it was clear that her priority was her children."

"How would you characterize her, other than broken?"

"Tenacious. Committed. I sensed she was all about family and those kids."

Leary nodded. "I wonder if the fact that there were kids involved is a consideration. You sent her husband to jail, depriving them of their source of income and the kids of their father. Might she have wanted to get back at you through your son?"

Sawyer shook his head. "No. If there was anger, it was directed at her husband for having done something illegal and placing them in the predicament they were in."

Leary and Bigelow asked Sawyer a few more questions, but there was nothing Sawyer could think of that might help.

The police had no answers. Still, the meeting took far longer than Sawyer had expected, and he wanted to get home to Dylan. He wanted to spend as much time with him as he could before he went back to work in a few days.

As Sawyer hurried out of the conference room, he almost collided with someone coming around the corner. He reached out to steady her and wasn't entirely surprised that it was Shannon. His instincts had been correct. She must have been watching the interview.

"Sawyer. Hi."

Whatever slight resistance he still had to seeing her again dissipated at the sight of her. She looked so fresh and beautiful, even in uniform. "Uh, I'm sorry I've been...busy," he stammered. He didn't want her walking away. "Do you have time for a coffee?"

"When?"

"Now?"

"No, not right now. I'm on duty."

Her eyes were like a clear summer sky. He wouldn't have been able to look away if he'd wanted to. He didn't give himself time to think. "If you don't have plans, why don't you come over to my place when you finish your shift? I'll throw a couple of steaks on the barbecue. You could see Dylan. He's been asking about you...and your dog. You two made quite an impression on him. Bring Darwin," he rushed on. "If that's okay for police dogs."

Shannon laughed. "Darwin might have an important job, but he's still a dog. When he's not working, he's like any other dog. And he loves kids. Dylan seemed to be fascinated by him when they met."

"So you'll come over?" Suddenly, it felt as if his life hung in the balance. He didn't want her to say no. "You'll come and bring Darwin?"

"Sure. Why not?" she said, making it possible for Sawyer to breathe again.

WHEN SHANNON HEARD that Sawyer was coming into the division that afternoon to meet with Bigelow and Leary, she hadn't been able to resist watching the interview.

Or was it more about seeing him?

She'd planned to head out into the field again before he left the interrogation room. She hadn't expected him to rush out as quickly as he had.

Sawyer had been polite enough in his texts since the night they'd had dinner, but she felt he'd been making excuses not to see her, although it was hard to judge on the basis of texts alone. And the fact that those texts were all that had passed between them since their dinner added to her concern that she might have misread his feelings. But then those kisses would come to mind, and just the thought of them heated her skin. She might have intended to avoid him, but sometimes things happened for a reason. Half an hour after the end of her shift, she was changing into the civilian clothes she kept in her locker at the division. She was looking forward to seeing Sawyer again and Dylan, too. She was a little nervous about spending time with Dylan—for the obvious reason that he was Sawyer's son. She didn't want to say or do anything that might remind Dylan of his ordeal or cause him to associate her with what had happened to him.

Checking her watch, she realized she was later than she'd hoped. She called Sawyer as she was leaving the division to let him know.

"That's okay," he assured her. "Dylan and I are in the backyard. I'll start the barbecue and get the potatoes going, but I'll wait until you arrive before I put the steaks on."

"Thanks! Sorry, again, for running late."

"Don't worry about it. When you get here, come around the back. There's a side gate."

"See you in about forty-five minutes."

Shannon's house was on the way, and she stopped there to switch her police vehicle for her personal car. As an afterthought, she also picked up the ingredients for an appetizer.

At Sawyer's place, she grabbed her purse and the cooler bag from the passenger seat. Letting Darwin hop out of the back, she fastened his leash to his collar.

The side gate was shut but unlatched. It opened silently when she nudged it.

There was smoke drifting lazily from the barbecue. Dylan sat on the grass, building what looked like some sort of castle out of plastic blocks. But it was Sawyer who drew Shannon's attention, and her buoyant mood dulled.

He was sitting in a patio chair, one ankle resting on the other knee, a condensation-coated bottle of soda balanced on the armrest. He was dressed in khaki shorts, a royal blue polo shirt and Top-Siders. She should've seen it as a comfortable, relaxed pose. A man enjoying a cool drink in the late-afternoon sunshine, while his son played.

But that wasn't the sense she got. There was tension emanating from him, and his posture was rigid.

He was staring, trancelike, at the child's playset in the corner of the yard.

"Sawyer," she called softly, as she took a few hesitant steps toward him.

He turned to face her, his eyes dark and unblinking.

He gave his head a small shake and his eyes cleared. "Shannon!" he said, and the single word conveyed his pleasure at seeing her and made her feel welcome. He rose, toppling the bottle. With quick reflexes, he managed to catch and right it, hardly spilling a drop.

"Look, Dad. The officer and the police dog are here!" Dylan said and ran toward them.

"Dylan!" Sawyer called, a little more firmly than Shannon thought was warranted. "You know the rules about dogs. You don't go near them unless the owner says it's okay."

Dylan stopped in his tracks. Sawyer, catching up to his son, placed a hand on his shoulder.

Shannon kept Darwin on a tight leash, not because the dog needed it but to keep Sawyer from worrying. She could understand why he might be more protective of his son these days. "Hello, Dylan," she said.

"Hi, Officer Clem…" Dylan linked his hands behind his back and gazed up at his father, his brows drawn together.

"Officer Clemens," he supplied.

"Hi, Officer Clemens."

"You can call me Shannon, if that's okay with your father."

Sawyer nodded.

"What's in the bag?" Dylan asked.

"I'm going to make an appetizer." She turned to Sawyer. "Neither of you have any food allergies?"

"You didn't have to do that, and no, we don't

have allergies. Here, let me take that from you," he said, reaching for the cooler bag.

Shannon passed it to him and set her purse on the edge of the raised patio.

"Can I say hi to Darwin now?" Dylan asked.

"Before you do that, would you please put the things Shannon brought in the kitchen?"

"'Kay." Dylan looked up at his father. "But can I say hi to Darwin after?"

"Ah… Put the bag inside first."

Sawyer gave his son's shoulder a gentle squeeze. "I'm sorry I snapped at you."

Dylan wrapped his arms around Sawyer's legs. "It's okay, Dad."

Sawyer handed him the bag. "It's not too heavy for you, is it, champ?" Sawyer asked.

"Uh-uh."

When Dylan slid the patio door closed behind him, Sawyer sighed. "I can't believe I did that. It's the last thing the kid needs. I can't seem to help it. I worry that he'll shatter at any minute." He sighed again and shook his head. "It's great to see you," he said, changing the subject, and touched his lips to hers. He bent down and held his hand out to Darwin, letting him sniff it. "Is it okay if I pet him?"

"Sure." She watched as Sawyer crouched down and rubbed Darwin behind his ears, causing the dog to thump his tail against the ground. "Do you want to tell me what's wrong?"

He glanced up at her with a pained expression. "I didn't mean to be harsh with Dylan." He resumed stroking Darwin. "I know I can't keep him in a bubble, but I feel an overwhelming need to protect him from everything."

Shannon held his gaze as he stood up. "Darwin's going to be fine with him. I promise. Dylan met him before, remember? But that's not what I meant. When I got here, you seemed… preoccupied."

"Did I?" He sounded genuinely surprised.

"Yes, you did."

He nodded slowly. "Hmm. Maybe I was. Don't take this the wrong way, but you'll be a welcome distraction for both of us—although I might not be the greatest company right now."

"We can't always be at our best. Don't worry about it."

He reached out and tucked her hair behind her ear.

That simple gesture started the butterflies fluttering in her belly again, and she nearly forgot what she'd been saying. "Is everything okay with Dylan?" she persisted.

"We had an appointment with his therapist today," Sawyer began. "She's worried about

Dylan withdrawing. Also, Dylan's been asking about the Sanchez woman again—about '*tía*.'" He glanced toward the house just as Dylan was opening the patio door. "You're sure Darwin will be okay with him?" he asked hurriedly. "I can't have anything else happen to him."

"Positive," Shannon replied and turned her attention to the boy, as he approached them. "Hey, Dylan, would you like to see Darwin show off some of his skills?" When Dylan nodded, she ran Darwin through a couple of drills, which he executed flawlessly. "For his final trick, I need something that belongs to you," she said to Dylan.

He looked down at himself.

"Use your sneaker," Sawyer suggested.

Dylan sat down on the grass to pull off a shoe.

"I just need one," Shannon explained when he was about to remove the second sneaker.

Dylan rose and brought her the shoe.

She signaled for Darwin to sniff it, but didn't take it from Dylan. "Darwin and I are going to go through the gate. I want you to hide the sneaker somewhere in the backyard so we can't see it. Walk around a bit before you hide it."

"Okay, but what will he do?"

"When you're done, you'll call us back, and Darwin will find your sneaker."

"No way!"

"Yup. You'll see."

Shannon led Darwin through the gate, and waited until Sawyer called them. She latched the gate behind her and was about to take Darwin off lead but paused. "Is it okay if I let him loose?" she asked Sawyer.

"I trust you," he said, and held out his hand for Dylan to join him. That trust, where it concerned his son, meant a great deal to her. She unclipped Darwin's leash and instructed him to find the shoe. Darwin did a quick zigzag, ending up at the playset Sawyer had been staring at when she arrived.

"Go get it," Shannon encouraged the dog. Darwin scaled the three-foot-high plastic ladder leading to a small tree-fort type of enclosure.

"Darwin can climb!" Dylan exclaimed.

A moment later Darwin leaped out with Dylan's shoe in his mouth.

To the sound of Dylan's excited giggles, Darwin streaked over to Shannon, plopped down in front of her and dropped the shoe at her feet. "Great job, Darwin. Take a bow," she said and had the dog stretching his front paws forward, lowering his head to the ground, his rear end in the air.

Shannon gave Darwin a hand signal and he rolled over, ending in a down position. "Look sorry," she told him.

Darwin stretched out his front legs, rested his head on the grass between his paws and looked up at her with eyes that could melt anyone's heart.

She crouched down, and stroked his head as she glanced up at Sawyer.

He had a smile on his face. "That's some repertoire."

"Would you like to say hi to Darwin now?" she asked Dylan.

"Uh-huh," he said, tugging his hand away from Sawyer's.

Although Darwin didn't need it, Shannon gave him a signal to reinforce the stay command. Then she held one hand out for Dylan's. The feel of his little hand in hers made everything inside her go soft and warm, as she showed him how to let Darwin become familiar with his scent. "Would you like to pet him now?" she asked.

Dylan nodded, smiling as he stroked Darwin's head. "He's so soft!"

Basking in the attention, Darwin nuzzled Dylan.

"It tickles!" Dylan said amid another fit of giggles. As the dog kisses slowed, Dylan wrapped his arms around Darwin's neck and hugged him.

Shannon rose and walked over to Sawyer. She thought back to the comment he'd made about Dylan. At that moment, she couldn't detect any reservation in the boy. He seemed happy. Joyful. "You said you were worried about Dylan withdrawing," she said quietly. "I'm not a therapist, but I don't see it."

"This is the most animated I've seen him since you brought him home," he said. "You have no idea how much it means to me, to hear him laugh in such a carefree way." He touched Shannon's arm. "Thank you for this."

"I'd like to take credit, but it has more to do with Darwin than me."

As if to prove her point, Dylan and Darwin collapsed to the ground together in what appeared to be a little lovefest, with the eighty-pound dog trying to climb onto the boy's lap. Sawyer chuckled as Dylan reversed their positions, tumbled over the dog and squealed in delight.

Shannon considered her own comment about Dylan's mood having to do with Darwin. Dogs could be miracle-workers, therapists, friends and companions all in one furry package.

She glanced at Sawyer again. "Has Dylan ever had a dog?"

"What? No. Dylan and I talked about it, but it was too much after..."

Shannon knew he meant after his wife had disappeared, and nodded her understanding.

She looked back at boy and dog as they wrestled on the grass. She saw how Darwin was being with Dylan, instinctively aware that he had to be careful. He seemed to be doing wonders for the boy.

"We should get dinner started," Sawyer said, interrupting her thoughts. "I don't want to keep Dylan up too long past his bedtime."

Sawyer put the steaks on the grill and added a burger for Dylan. He offered Shannon a drink and she chose a glass of wine. Sawyer left her in the kitchen while he went back outside to check on the steaks.

Taking a sip of her wine, she gathered the fixings for her spinach dip from her cooler bag, which Dylan had placed on the counter. Humming, she cut the broccoli and cauliflower into bite-size chunks. She popped a cherry tomato in her mouth as she arranged the vegetables on a serving platter she'd found in a cupboard. She mixed the dip and tested it with a baby carrot. Mmm…

She made an excellent dip, even if she did say so herself. She hunted up a serving dish, filled it with the dip and positioned it in the center of the platter.

Pleased with the arrangement, she picked up the platter and turned around.

Seeing Sawyer standing in the open doorway, his shoulder resting against the doorjamb, she nearly let the platter slip out of her hands.

It wasn't that he'd startled her.

At least not *just* that.

He had the whole lanky, casually sexy thing going for him, but there was something… indefinable about him that made her heart race.

Sawyer pushed away from the doorjamb. "Here, let me help you with that."

She took a couple of deep breaths and followed him out to the patio.

They ate the veggies and dip, and once Dylan had enough he ran off to play with Darwin. While the meat cooked, Sawyer poured himself a glass of wine. Shannon declined a top-up, since she was driving.

When they were almost ready to eat, Sawyer called Dylan, telling him to wash his hands.

With only a mild complaint that he couldn't keep playing with Darwin, he did as he was told.

The steak was delicious, and Shannon had no trouble finishing it all. After the dishes were cleared, Sawyer turned to her. "Will you wait until I help Dylan get ready for bed?"

She smiled. "Sure."

Dylan hugged both her and Darwin before going inside with his father.

Shannon sat at the patio table, sipping the last of her wine, watching fireflies twinkle and listening to the cicadas hum. She smiled again when she heard Sawyer's murmur, followed by Dylan's laughter, drifting down from the open bedroom window above her. She reached over to stroke Darwin, who was stretched out beside her.

She was in a dreamy, contented state when Sawyer returned, carrying a tray with two cups of coffee, a small pitcher of milk and a sugar bowl. He'd brought matches, too, and lit the fat candle that sat in the middle of the table.

Under the black-velvet sky, in the flickering candlelight, with music—something soft and romantic—drifting through another open window, and the sweet scent of gardenia and frangipani all around her, she watched him.

He pulled up a chair next to her and took her hand.

"I'm glad you're here. Dylan enjoyed himself, too. Sorry for taking so long to get him settled, but it's your fault." He gave her a rueful smile. "He wouldn't stop talking about you and Darwin."

"He's a terrific kid."

"Yes, he is." At Sawyer's soft laugh, Darwin scrambled up to a sitting position. "I can't believe the difference in him tonight."

Shannon leaned back, stroking Darwin's head, and focused on the bright pinpricks of stars for a few minutes. Sawyer's last comment had sounded solemn. It brought back the way he'd been when she first arrived. "Dylan seemed happy. Not withdrawn at all."

Sawyer shifted his body toward her. Lowering his gaze to their joined hands, he ran his thumb across her knuckles. "He did, didn't he? Like I said, that's the most…cheerful I've seen him since…" The words trailed off.

"But that's a good sign, isn't it?" she asked, not wanting him to slip into a melancholy mood again. "An indication that he's healing?"

"It's nice to see that he still has the capacity for joy and playfulness." Sawyer stared up at the sky. "But I don't know how much of it is healing and how much of it is Darwin bringing out the young boy in him."

"Dogs are wonderful for therapy." Shannon really did believe in the power of dogs. "They're often used to help post-traumatic stress disorder patients. I'm sure you know they're even used in courtrooms to help children who are testifying feel more at ease."

Sawyer nodded.

"Why not get him a dog?" she asked suddenly. "If a dog would make him happy, perhaps take his mind off things, why not?"

"I don't think—" He took a deep breath. Lifted his face up to the star-speckled sky again. "Maybe that's not a bad idea." He turned back to Shannon. "If after sober second thought I decide to do it, would you come with us? Help us get the right dog for Dylan?"

She smiled. "I'd be happy to, on one condition."

He raised an eyebrow and waited.

"The dog has to be a rescue."

"A rescue it is. It has to be small, though. And not shed…too much."

Shannon shrugged, but had her own notions. "We'll see about the rest," she said cryptically.

"We'll see," he echoed and leaned slowly toward her.

Shannon closed her eyes and a tingling sensation flowed over her skin as Sawyer's lips touched hers.

CHAPTER ELEVEN

"HI, DAD," DYLAN greeted Sawyer, as he walked into the kitchen, Joey tucked under one arm.

"Hey, champ. Did you sleep well?" Sawyer hoped so; at least, he hadn't heard him tossing with nightmares.

"Uh-huh."

Sawyer bent down to receive the hug Dylan offered.

"Did you have a good time last night? With Shannon and Darwin?"

"Yeah! I like Darwin...and Shannon. They're nice."

Sawyer was delighted that the liveliness and joy Dylan had shown the evening before seemed to have carried through to morning. "You and Joey ready for breakfast?" he asked, reaching for his coffee.

"Yeah. Joey wants Froot Loops. Please."

"Okay. Have a seat."

Sawyer turned to pull out a stool for Dylan...and the breath clogged in his throat.

He blinked a couple of times, to be certain he hadn't imagined it.

"What's that you've got there, champ?"

"Huh?" Dylan asked, as he scrambled up onto the stool by the kitchen island.

"That." Sawyer pointed to the chain Dylan clutched in his hand.

"Oh." Dylan held up the chain, the all-too-familiar locket dangling from it. "Joey had it in his pouch."

"Dylan," Sawyer said in as controlled a voice as he could manage. "Do you remember the talk we had about always telling the truth?"

"Uh-huh." Dylan's bright smile dimmed and Sawyer was sorry about it, but he was more concerned about where Dylan had gotten the locket.

"Well, then?"

"I *am* telling the truth, Daddy!"

Dylan looked genuinely confused, but Sawyer couldn't let this go.

"Dylan?"

"It was in Joey's pouch, Daddy." Dylan shoved his fist clutching the chain, toward his father.

Sawyer went over to Dylan, every step a struggle, as if he was wading through molasses. He'd thought he would never lay eyes on that locket again. "May I see it?" he asked.

"Uh-huh."

Sawyer gently took the locket from his son's hand and opened it with infinite care.

And there it was. Nestled inside the heart-shaped sterling-silver locket.

The picture of Jeannette, Dylan and him. Taken the day Dylan was born. Nearly a year before Jeannette disappeared.

Sawyer had expected to see the picture, since he'd recognized the locket, but the shock of it still shocked him to the core. Keeping his gaze on the photograph, he felt as if he'd aged a lifetime in the span of a heartbeat.

His wife…his high-school sweetheart, *the love of his life*…stared back at him from the heart-shaped locket.

There was a raging tornado inside him, his thoughts and emotions caught in its eye.

He paced the length of the kitchen and back. He squatted down in front of his son.

"Where did you find this, Dylan?"

Dylan touched the locket with a finger. "It's pretty," he said.

Sawyer took his son's hand to keep him from clasping the necklace again. "Yes, it is, but where did you get it?"

"It was in Joey," he said. "I forgot I put it in his pouch. I remembered this morning!"

How on earth would he have gotten it? Jeannette had never taken that locket off from the day he'd given it to her. He assumed she'd been wearing it when she disappeared, because he hadn't seen it since. Was it possible that she'd removed it? Or it had fallen off somewhere in the house and Dylan had found it?

"I want it, Daddy," Dylan insisted.

"Please," Sawyer corrected automatically. "How about if I keep it for now? Would that be okay?"

Dylan's lips formed a pout. "But the lady gave it to *me*."

"What lady?" Sawyer hadn't intended to raise his voice, and he immediately clamped down on his emotions. "Sorry, champ. What lady gave it to you?"

"Tía."

"The lady in the apartment with you? Juanita?"

"Nuh-uh. The *other* lady."

Sawyer's blood ran cold. *"What* other lady?"

"The one who took me to *tía*," Dylan repeated.

Not Juanita Sanchez, then, but the woman who brought Dylan to her. The woman who'd abducted him?

Sawyer's mind was racing. The fact that it was a woman didn't surprise him. They knew that. It was a woman who'd contacted Sanchez, and Dylan had confirmed that it was a woman who'd taken him to her. He'd described her to the best of his ability to the police. But how could that woman have had Jeannette's locket? What was the connection? Sawyer wasn't inclined to start interrogating Dylan right now. Especially after the positive mood he'd been in the night before.

But the police had to know about this. Then he felt an ice-cold chill. Was it possible that the locket had never left Jeannette's possession? That she was alive and had something to do with Dylan's abduction?

No, that was too dreadful to contemplate. But what else could it be?

"Okay, Dylan. Have your breakfast now, and we'll talk about this later."

After Dylan had finished eating, Sawyer got him settled in his room and called the detective in charge of the investigation. Bigelow was very interested in this new development and said he'd be over within the hour.

"Do you think I should see if I can arrange to have Dylan's therapist here?" Sawyer asked.

"That's your call, but I plan to bring someone from Victim Services to help. The person I'm thinking of, if she's available, specializes in working with kids in these types of situations."

"Okay. Good." Sawyer felt relieved, since he doubted Dr. Gleason would've been available on such short notice. If he saw any adverse reaction from Dylan, he'd just bring the discussion to an end.

Just as Sawyer concluded the call, Dylan wandered back out of his room, Joey under his arm. Sawyer turned on the television for him. Then he called Shannon.

"Thanks again for last night," he began. Just the sound of her voice lifted his spirits.

"Thank *you*," she said. "How's Dylan this morning?"

"We've had a...development."

"What's wrong?"

Sawyer explained about the locket.

"Are you certain he didn't find it somewhere? In your house? Under a bed perhaps?"

Sawyer let out a strangled laugh. "I wish I could say he had. That would make a lot more sense." Sawyer glanced over at Dylan, who was hugging Joey tightly while he watched *Finding Nemo*. He was rocking back and forth, which he hadn't done for days now. "I called Detective Bigelow. He and a person from Victim Services are on their way. Is there any chance you could be here with us?" He hadn't realized how much he wanted her to be there, until the words tumbled out of his mouth. "As a friend. Not in an official capacity," he added, to avoid any misunderstanding.

"Oh, Sawyer, yes, if I can, but I'm working today. I'll ask Logan."

Sawyer dragged his fingers through his hair. "Sure. Let me know what he says."

After hanging up the phone, he joined Dylan on the floor in front of the television. He scooped him up onto his lap, and they watched *Finding Nemo* together until the doorbell rang.

"Please play in your room for a while, okay?" Sawyer asked.

"But the movie…"

"We'll finish it later. I promise." He gave Dylan a nudge in the direction of his room and waited until he'd gone inside before he went to answer the door. He greeted Detective Bigelow, who introduced him to his colleague, Kim Langdon.

"Kim is with Victim Services. As I mentioned, she specializes in childhood trauma."

"Ms. Langdon," Sawyer said, shaking her hand.

"Kim's fine," she said with a warm smile that went a long way to mollify him.

"Thank you both for coming." He led them into the living room. "Can I get you anything? A coffee? Water?" He wondered how he managed to be so hospitable, when all he could think about was that the nightmare they'd been living had gotten even worse.

Bigelow glanced at Kim. "We're fine, thanks."

"Where's your son?" Kim asked, looking around.

"Dylan's in his room. I wanted to speak with you first. Dylan's been under a lot of pressure." Fleetingly, he thought of Shannon and hoped she'd be able to make it.

Kim nodded. "That's understandable, and it's smart of you to talk to us first."

"Thank—" Sawyer cut himself off when the doorbell rang again. He started for the door, then stopped abruptly. "I invited Shannon Clemens to join us. That okay with you?"

Bigelow's eyes narrowed. "*Officer* Clemens?"

"Yes. But not in an official capacity."

Bigelow frowned, and Sawyer could see he'd surprised him. "That's your call."

"I'll be right back."

Sawyer hurried to the door. Shannon was in uniform, Darwin at her side.

"I thought Darwin could help keep Dylan distracted," she said when she noticed him looking at the dog.

"Thanks for that and for coming." He wanted to touch his lips to hers, but he could feel Bigelow watching them.

When she squeezed his hand, out of Bigelow's line of sight, he sighed. "Thank you," he repeated.

Shannon took Darwin into Dylan's bedroom, then joined Sawyer in the living room. She, Bigelow and Kim exchanged greetings.

"Why don't you run through what happened this morning?" Bigelow prompted Sawyer when they were all seated.

Sawyer began to summarize what had happened. When his voice faltered, Shannon touched his knee.

Bigelow be damned, Sawyer thought. He needed that contact and took her hand in his.

"There's no rush, Mr. Evans," Kim assured him. "Take all the time you need."

"I don't know what to make of it." He sent Kim a weak smile, but had to rub his eyes to ease the sting. "I wanted to explain this to you before you talk to Dylan." He briefly outlined what Dylan had told him about the locket. "Please be gentle with him."

"Understood," Bigelow said.

"We're sorry to have to put him through this, after what he's already endured." Kim smiled encouragingly.

Sawyer nodded. "I'll go get Dylan." He got up and walked out of the room.

When had his life become such a mess? he wondered. So complicated.

Dylan was sitting on the floor with a picture book in his hands, Darwin curled up beside him, the dog's head on his lap.

"There are a couple of people here who'd like to talk to you. Is that okay?"

"Can Darwin come? And Joey?"

"Sure." Sawyer took Dylan's hand and led him into the living room. The way Darwin followed his son, without being asked to, made Sawyer doubt he could've left the dog behind, even if he'd wanted to.

Sawyer's heart shattered again as he watched Dylan hold Joey tightly, doing his best to answer Kim's questions. Bigelow again showed him pictures of his mother, but Dylan was firm in saying that she wasn't the woman who'd given him the locket. When it began to sound a little too much like an interrogation, Shannon interrupted and Sawyer was immensely grateful to her.

"May I ask him a few questions?" she asked Bigelow.

Bigelow gestured for her to go ahead. She squatted in front of Dylan, stroked Joey and asked Dylan about the toy, about what he'd been doing in his room before he'd joined them. She gently eased into some of the questions Bigelow hadn't yet asked. Dylan seemed more relaxed and Sawyer couldn't help noticing that he kept one hand on Darwin. Probably a subconscious act, Sawyer mused, but it seemed to calm him.

Whatever else happened or didn't between him and Shannon, Sawyer knew he'd be eternally grateful to her for what she was doing, guiding his son through something no child should have to endure—a police interview.

When Sawyer recognized the signs of weariness—the sucking of his thumb and the rocking—he brought the questioning to a halt.

"Dylan, would you show me your room and where Joey sleeps when he's not with you?" Shannon asked.

Sawyer appreciated that she was giving him time alone with the detective. "What do you think this means?" Sawyer asked, after they'd left.

"I don't want to speculate, but it does provide a new angle to pursue."

"You think this has something to do with Jeannette?"

"As I said, I'm not going to speculate," Bigelow responded, as he and Kim both got to their feet. "Thank you for making us aware of this. I'll be in touch."

Sawyer walked them out, and leaned heavily against the door after he closed it.

How did Jeannette's locket enter into all of this? How did Jeannette?

He wanted to ask Shannon what she thought, but that would have to wait. He couldn't do it in front of Dylan and he wasn't prepared to ask him to stay in his room again today.

Sawyer tried to gather his frayed emotions as he walked to Dylan's room. He saw Shannon sitting cross-legged on the floor with Dylan in her lap and her arms snugly around his little boy. Dylan held one of his picture books, and she traced the words on the page with a fingertip as she read to him.

Thoughts of Jeannette faded from his mind for the first time since he'd seen the locket, as his heart did a slow steady roll and fell hard.

CHAPTER TWELVE

AS SHANNON DROVE back to the division, her mind kept returning to the question of whether Jeannette Evans could've had anything to do with her son's abduction. Shannon had been painfully aware that the investigation had stalled until Dylan had walked into his father's kitchen that morning with his mother's locket in his hand, presenting a fresh lead.

One of the avenues now being pursued was the possibility that Sawyer's wife was alive. Shannon knew that family members were always among the first to be considered in child-abduction cases. If Dylan's mother *was* alive, she could be behind the abduction. The SDPD with the aid of the FBI were actively looking into Jeannette Evans's disappearance again.

How did someone deal with the disappearance of a spouse—and one as deeply loved as Jeannette had obviously been? What if, over time, you reconciled yourself to her having died—and then suddenly the possibility arose that she might not be dead after all?

And if that wasn't enough, to be forced to deal with the even more devastating prospect that the woman he'd loved, the mother of his child, might be responsible for the abduction of their son?

Unfathomable. Shannon had seen the effect on Sawyer, seen that it was tearing him apart. She wondered how he managed to stay sane.

And if his wife *was* alive, where did that leave Shannon as far as her blossoming relationship with Sawyer went? The second that thought occurred to her, shame—quick and sharp—sliced through her. How could she be so selfish as to think of herself at a time like this?

She ruthlessly kept her mind from straying there again for the remainder of the trip.

She had a busy day, but managed to sit in on another briefing.

SDPD and the FBI had again questioned Juanita Sanchez, but she had no answers. She hadn't given the locket to Dylan, nor had she been aware of its existence.

Although Dylan had claimed that it wasn't his mother who'd given him the locket, they considered it inconclusive, since the pictures Sawyer had of Jeannette were three years old. She could easily have changed her appearance—at a minimum, her hair color and style.

When Shannon had finally found a minute to sit down, she booted up her computer in the hope of catching up on some reports. Waiting for it to start, she closed her eyes and thought over the events of the day.

"Hey, everything okay, Shannon?" Rick Vasquez asked.

Her eyes flew open. "What? Why?"

"You made a sound like our dogs would if they came up against something they didn't like."

"Sorry," she murmured.

Rick rose from his desk, all imposing six-feet-three-inches of him. "Let's have a chat." He jerked his head toward the conference room. Without waiting for a reply, he strode off.

Shannon felt a mild sense of unease. She indulged it for a moment by holding her head in her hands before getting up to follow him.

"Water?" he asked as he went over to the cooler and ran some into a paper cup.

She tried to clear her suddenly dry, scratchy throat. "Yes, please." Accepting the cup he'd filled for her, she took a drink.

"Sit down." She sank into the chair and took another sip of water.

Rick sat next to her. "You really have a thing for Evans, don't you?"

She eyed the cup in her hand. Honesty was always best, as far as she was concerned. "Yeah," she murmured. When Rick didn't say anything further, she lifted her eyes to meet his.

"Look, being a cop isn't easy. Relationships aren't easy. You combine the two, that just makes it all that much harder."

When she could only stare at him, he continued. "The job almost came between me and Madison. You know the story?"

She thought back to the time at The Runway, when Madison had shared it with her. "Yes."

"We had our challenges. But what you're facing with Evans? That's a whole lot more convoluted than what Madison and I had to contend with. I don't want to discourage you, but…" He waited until she made eye contact again. "I've been a cop a lot longer than you. I know you've had some hard knocks in your life, but think about what Evans is going through. What his boy is experiencing." Rick's lips formed a hard, straight line, and his eyes darkened to near black.

Rick wasn't telling her anything that hadn't been on her mind. Incessantly.

"He and his wife didn't split up," he went on. "She disappeared. Whatever the cause, it wasn't a joint decision to end the marriage. He had no say in it. From what I've heard, he loved her, and deeply."

Shannon felt a tightness in her chest. "That's correct. Since they were in high school."

Rick nodded. "Having presumed her dead doesn't mean the love died. If anything, it might have taken on a new dimension. Now... the possibility of her being alive's been raised. We'll never know what that feels like."

She nodded mutely.

"And the kid? That's another layer of complexity."

Rick fell silent while she absorbed everything he'd said. To hear someone else put into words so clearly and succinctly what had been preying on her mind really drove it home for Shannon.

Just when she'd started to believe there *could* be something between her and Sawyer... and Dylan. Because she had to admit she'd fallen for the boy, too.

She'd wondered if she could compete with the ghost of his dead wife, but now...if Jeannette was alive? What chance did she have? She wanted to resent Rick for what he'd said, but she couldn't. He was speaking the truth, as a friend and in her best interests.

Slowly, she nodded again.

Rick got up and touched her shoulder. "Tread carefully, Shannon, but know we're all here for you. Not just us, but Madison, Ariana and Jessica, too. Evans had an exceptional reputation as a DA. I got to work with him on the Donna Thompson case. He strikes me as a decent guy, a good father—but man, what he's going through has got to mess with a guy's head."

Shannon swallowed hard against the constriction that had spread from her heart to her throat.

"Madison likes you a lot, and she's a great listener. Don't hesitate to call her."

He patted her shoulder and walked out of the room, closing the door behind him.

She rested her elbows on the table and lowered her forehead to her hands.

What had she gotten herself into?

She was in love with Sawyer, whether she liked it or not.

SAWYER REALIZED THAT the discovery of Jeannette's locket meant that the investigation into Dylan's abduction was focused on the possibility of Jeannette's being alive and somehow responsible. If the police hadn't been able to find her when she first disappeared, what were the odds of finding her now?

He couldn't recall what the stats were on that.

There was one thing he couldn't comprehend, and he knew it was a sticking point for the cops, too. If it *was* Jeannette, why had she taken *three years* to go after Dylan? But the same question had been asked when they'd considered the people Sawyer had sent to jail as an assistant DA. There was no getting around it.

None of it made sense.

Was it possible that Jeannette was alive? If so, why hadn't she once tried to contact him? Would she really have tried to abduct Dylan?

Sawyer had been planning to go back to work on Monday. With this most recent development, he'd advised the dean that he'd need another week, at least.

He couldn't imagine going through the motions at work.

And something else he couldn't envision right now was a relationship with Shannon.

He'd developed feelings for her. When he'd initially realized that, it had come as a shock. This was the first time since Jeannette's disappearance that he'd met a woman with whom his emotions had become engaged. When he'd gotten used to the idea, it had made him feel hopeful about the future.

He'd been falling in love with Shannon, but

he couldn't pursue that now, no matter how much he wanted to.

He needed answers about Jeannette first.

Answers he hadn't gotten three years ago.

How could Jeannette—a woman he thought he'd known as well as he'd known himself—have betrayed him like that? Leaving him, then letting him grieve for her, believing she was dead, only to learn she might be alive and might have abducted their son?

If she was capable of that sort of deceit, how could he trust another woman again?

Shannon wasn't Jeannette. But still…

Sawyer was horrified to discover that a part of him wished Jeannette *had* died, rather than committing the act of treachery they thought she might have.

And what kind of person did that make *him*?

He'd have to curtail his relationship with Shannon, at least until he could work out the answers to those impossible questions.

And if he did sort things out, and Shannon would no longer have him?

The sense of loss that gripped him was another surprise.

Yet, he couldn't see a way around it. Not in the short term, anyway.

He was married. He could've petitioned for a divorce. His parents and Meg had urged him to do it. They had the best of intentions; they wanted him to be open to love coming into his life again. Even the possibility of a new mother for Dylan.

Sawyer had refused to do it.

Even if he had? If Jeannette was alive, the legalities wouldn't have mattered to him. In his heart, he'd still be married. Sawyer picked up the phone to call Shannon but put it down again.

He couldn't have a coherent conversation with her just now. Besides, he owed it to her to tell her in person.

He texted her and asked if she'd meet him for coffee after her shift. When she responded and said she'd come straight over after work, he'd quickly replied to suggest they meet at Starbucks on East Harbor. Her message back was a curt, Okay, after I take Darwin home. He assumed she realized this was not a date. Next, he called Meg and asked if she'd watch Dylan for him.

Sawyer left as soon as Meg arrived. He'd made it clear he wasn't in the mood for small talk. He'd have to tell her and his parents about this latest development. But not yet...

He got to the coffee shop early and nursed a cup of coffee until Shannon walked in.

She was wearing jeans and a white shirt, her

short hair a sleek golden halo around her face. The impact of seeing her hadn't dulled. The sorrow he'd been feeling since he'd made his decision became nearly unbearable.

He'd never been so conflicted in his life.

He wanted Shannon. He *cared* about her.

But he couldn't be with her.

When she noticed him, she smiled but the smile didn't reach her eyes. She was smart and she was intuitive. What he had to say to her probably wouldn't be a great surprise.

She didn't bother to get a coffee, and her smile faded as she walked toward him.

He started to rise, but she didn't give him the chance. She slid into the seat opposite him. "How's Dylan?" she asked.

That was so like her, Sawyer thought. Caring and compassionate, and asking about Dylan first. Dylan was crazy about her, too. And that gave him pause. How would Dylan take it, not being able to see Shannon anymore? Another woman he was growing attached to, torn away from him.

Sawyer swallowed the groan that wanted to escape. "He's fine." He picked up his coffee cup, sipped and coughed. The coffee had gone completely cold.

Shannon gazed at him with those steady, bright blue eyes.

He rubbed his temples. When he looked at her again, he could see the ravages of his own grief and indecision reflected on her face.

"I can't do this," he said, his voice scratchy.

"Do what?" Her voice was tense.

"Us. I can't do us. It's not you." He reached for her hand, but she was quicker and pulled it back. "You're a remarkable, beautiful and intelligent woman." He gestured vaguely with one hand. "And you're terrific with Dylan. You're more than I could have hoped for."

She angled her head, her face now an expressionless mask. "I feel a *but* coming."

"My…" He couldn't bring himself to refer to Jeannette as anything other than his wife, especially, if by some miracle, she was alive. He'd been raised to believe that marriage was everlasting. "My wife," he said feebly. Searching for words, he opened and closed his mouth several times, but he couldn't explain himself.

Shannon briefly put her hand on top of his. "You don't have to say anything more." Her eyes brimmed with tears, but her voice was steady and resigned. "You know how to get hold of me, if you want." She got up and, with her head held high and her back straight, walked away.

Sawyer watched her go and felt that something vital had been torn out of him. He wanted to rush after her and beg her to forget everything he'd just said. He rose partway out of his seat.

But an image of Jeannette cradling baby Dylan in her arms shimmered in front of him and he sat back down.

With his heart aching, he watched Shannon walk out of the coffee shop.

And more than likely out of his life.

CHAPTER THIRTEEN

SHANNON CONCENTRATED ON putting one foot in front of the other as she left the coffee shop. Everyone who knew about her relationship with Sawyer had cautioned her that it was unwise to get involved with him.

She hadn't listened—even to herself. She'd let her heart lead.

Now she'd have to deal with the fallout.

She didn't want to go home. She didn't want to be alone with her thoughts. She stopped by her parents' place, but couldn't stay there, either. It took too much energy to keep dodging her mother's probing questions.

The next day, Shannon did her best to concentrate on work, but there was an insistent ache in her chest that overrode everything else.

Shannon no longer wanted to know about the investigation into Dylan's abduction and tried not to think about what was going on.

It wasn't her business. Sawyer had made that abundantly clear.

She ignored the probing looks from Rick,

Cal and Logan, and kept her head down at her desk.

When she got home, she made herself a ham and cheese sandwich for dinner, then took Darwin for a run. If she couldn't shut her brain down, maybe she could exhaust her body sufficiently to be able to sleep.

In theory, it made sense.

In practice, it didn't work.

She spent a mostly sleepless night tossing and turning. At six the next morning, despite a steadily falling rain, she took Darwin for another long run. By the time they turned onto her street again, the rain had thinned. Persistent rays of sunshine fought their way through the lingering clouds, transforming the drops of water clinging to blades of grass and flower petals into sparkling crystals. She wanted to see the beauty in it, but she just didn't have it in her.

It was Saturday, and the two days she had off stretched endlessly ahead of her. She'd promised to attend the surprise bridal shower Jessica was throwing for Ariana on Sunday afternoon, but that was the last thing she wanted to do.

She wasn't in the mood for socializing, nor did she relish seeing the people who'd cautioned her about getting involved with Sawyer. Sure, none of them would say "I told you so," but they had every right to. Knowing that made her feel self-conscious.

She picked up the phone several times to make an excuse and get out of going. Every time, she put the phone back down for the same two reasons. First, Ariana was her friend. She wanted to be there for her, and she didn't want to let Jessica, also a friend, down. Second, if she had to pick the lesser of two evils—being alone with her thoughts or forcing herself to be social—visiting with people won hands down over sitting alone at home.

In the end, Shannon went to the shower. Seeing the genuine smile on Jessica's face when she opened the door made Shannon grateful that she had.

"It's great to see you." Jess embraced Shannon warmly. "Let me help you with that," she said reaching for one of the large gift bags Shannon had brought with her.

Shannon's spontaneous burst of laughter obviously startled her. She pulled the bags out of Jessica's reach. "Absolutely not! You're pregnant and you're *not* lifting anything heavy." She took a minute to greet Scout, Cal's search-and-rescue dog, before following Jessica down the hall. She glanced around the crowded living room as they entered. "Is Ariana here yet?"

"No." Jessica checked her watch and chuckled. "We'll soon find out if we pulled off the surprise. Logan should be bringing her here in the next ten minutes or so, on the pretense of me needing help rearranging some things in the baby's room."

Shannon put the gifts she'd brought on the table with the rest of the presents. She didn't know too many people in the room, so she played it safe and sat next to Madison.

When Ariana arrived a few minutes later, there was no question that Jessica had succeeded in surprising her.

Ariana's eyes were as big as saucers and she clasped her hands over her mouth. Shannon smiled at the cool, collected and totally professional Ariana babbling with excitement and disbelief. She was hugged a second time that day when Ariana circled the room. "Shannon, I'm so happy you're here," she said, and her words rang with sincerity.

Shannon's spirits lifted as the afternoon progressed. If Sawyer wasn't interested in her, she'd move on with her life. Yes, she could feel sorry for him, sympathize with what he was going through, but that was where it would end.

She had family and she had friends. Three

of her friends happened to be in the room with her right now. She'd focus on family and friends, and she'd be okay.

"Did you and Sawyer have a fight?" Madison asked Shannon.

She looked up. "What?"

"You had an argument. I can see it in your eyes."

"No, we didn't." It occurred to Shannon that the situation might have been easier to accept if they did *have* a fight, rather than their civilized parting of the ways.

Madison scrutinized her face. "But there's something wrong."

She made a slight snorting sound. "You could say that."

"Are you in love with him?"

"What?" she said a second time, and felt foolish.

"You love him," Madison stated rather than asked.

Shannon's immediate reaction was to laugh it off. Pretend it wasn't true. But she couldn't lie to Madison any more than she could lie to herself.

"That obvious, is it?"

Madison patted her hand. "Only to someone who's still riding the wave of that exhilarating new love."

Shannon laughed. "New love? You and Rick have been together now, for what? A year and a half? You've been married for three months and—talk about working fast—you have a baby on the way."

Madison nodded with a grin. "Like I said, exhilarating and new, when we have our whole lives to look forward to." Her expression turned serious. "From what Rick's told me, Sawyer's a great guy, but I worry about a relationship between the two of you right now." Madison settled a hand on her still-flat stomach. "I don't know how Sawyer could think or feel anything other than what's happening with his son. I can see you're hurting. It's written all over your face." She moved her hand to place it on Shannon's. "Usually, I'd be the first to tell you to dive in. My personal motto is if you don't risk, you won't love. In this case, I have to say please be careful with your heart."

Sawyer wasn't the first man Shannon had been interested in, although the number of men she'd dated seriously was in the single digits. But she'd never felt about any of the others the way she did about Sawyer. She took a furtive glance around. Everyone's attention seemed to be elsewhere, and she and Madison were alone at their end of the room. "Relationships have never been easy for me," Shannon confessed. "The men I've dated have always had a tough time with my profession."

"Logan had job issues with his relationships, too," Madison murmured.

"Sorry?"

"Oh, that's a story for another day. You were saying about the men you've dated..."

"Well, for one reason or another, my job just didn't sit well with them. Then there's Sawyer. He's strong and confident. He values what I do, and he has a greater appreciation of it because of his time in the DA's office. Still, your advice is sound," she said with a sigh. "I've worked really hard to get where I am. To be good enough. To be better than the rest. You'd know from Rick how much competition there is to get into the K-9 Unit. With Sawyer, I thought maybe—"

Shannon held up a hand when Madison was about to say something. "I know the timing is all wrong. I can imagine how muddled his emotions must be if mine aren't straightforward."

One of Ariana's friends came around with a tray of mimosas. Madison declined because of her pregnancy, but Shannon accepted a glass.

"Go on," Madison said with an encouraging look when the woman was gone.

Shannon shrugged self-consciously. "I can't

even be one hundred percent certain of my own feelings. Is this about Sawyer and, of course, Dylan, but I've begun to wonder again if my feelings are somehow tangled up with Charlie, my little brother? But that's a moot point, since it's not up to me. Sawyer's made it clear that he doesn't want… No, that he *can't* have a relationship at present."

"Only you can answer the question about your own feelings. As for Sawyer, he's bound to experience a lot of mood swings. There's no harm in taking it slow," Madison advised. "Your hearts will know if and when it's right."

Sawyer sat hunched on a glider in the backyard of his parents' home. Dylan perched on a swing while Meghan pushed him. It hadn't been easy telling his family about the latest development.

"Sawyer," his mother said and sat down next to him. "There has to be something your father and I can do to help."

"Mom, I wish there was."

"Son, you have to snap out of this," Sawyer's father interjected as he came to stand on the deck beside them. "If not for you, then for Dylan. Look at him, Sawyer."

Sawyer recognized that his father was trying "tough love" on him, since all else had failed. His son looked as morose as he felt. Boy, did his father hit a bull's-eye. "I know, Dad. I know."

A moment later, Dylan hopped off the swing, and he and Meg joined them on the deck.

He saw the look that passed between his mother and sister, and knew it didn't bode well for him. His mother put on a bright smile. "How about we go inside, Dylan, and have some ice cream?"

"Okay," Dylan said without any obvious enthusiasm.

"Come on, Frank. You can have ice cream, too."

His father still had enough humor in him to roll his eyes at Sawyer. "Enjoy your chat." He patted his expanding belly. "I know your mother wants me out of the way, but I'm not going to be getting much ice cream." He briefly rested a hand on Sawyer's shoulder.

When Dylan and their parents were gone, Meg took their mother's spot on the glider. They watched a hummingbird flit around a potted bougainvillea. When it darted away, Meg turned to him.

"Have you thought about a therapist?"

"Dylan still sees Dr. Gleason for an hour every week."

Meg's eyes were sad. "I didn't mean for Dylan. I meant for you."

"You can't be serious."

"Actually, I am." She tucked a leg under her and shifted to face him. "You need to do something, Sawyer. You can't keep going on like this."

"I'll get through it."

"I know it's hard on you," she persisted. "Not knowing if Jeannette's alive. And if she is, well…the whole slew of other questions that would raise. But you have to be realistic. Whatever the answers are, going back to what you and Jeannette had is not a possibility."

Sawyer lowered his head and rubbed the back of his neck.

"Sawyer, what you and Jeannette had was special. I thought the world of her, too. She was one of my closest friends. But you can't delude yourself that you can have it back. No matter what, it won't happen. You *cannot* go back."

Meg was right; he couldn't deny it. He'd concluded the same thing. Intellectually. But emotionally, he couldn't get beyond his fear and confusion.

"What happened to the police officer you were seeing?"

He raised his head and glared at his sister. "How did you even know I was seeing her?"

She glanced at the French doors that led to the kitchen. "Dylan told me. He won't stop talking about her and her dog—and the dog you're getting him." She gave him a quick smile. "He really seems to have developed an attachment to her. Shutting her out of his life could cause more trauma."

"Don't do this, Meg," Sawyer warned. "Don't make me feel guiltier about ending a relationship I shouldn't have started in the first place. Don't bring Dylan into it."

"I'm not bringing Dylan into it. He's *already* in it." She laid a hand on his arm. "Don't throw away what might be a good thing for you and for Dylan," she said more emphatically.

Sawyer had let Meghan say her piece, knowing she had his best interests at heart, but now he had to draw the line. "It's over," he said curtly.

"Why?"

He frowned at Meg. "Because I ended it."

"Please tell me it's not because of Jeannette."

He felt the anger build again…and the longing for Shannon. "I can't let go of Jeannette if there's a chance they'll find her," he said in a defeated voice.

"Is that really smart, Sawyer?" she asked, and had him wondering again about the wisdom of what he was doing.

If Jeannette was alive, there was a good chance she'd taken Dylan.

CHAPTER FOURTEEN

L ATE M ONDAY AFTERNOON at the office, Rick brought a large bouquet of flowers over to Shannon.

"I saw this at the front desk for you. Must be getting serious with Evans," he said with an easy smile.

Shannon eyed the flowers warily. Rick obviously wasn't aware of her conversation with Madison. That was a true test of a friend. Madison had listened to her, supported her, but respected the confidence, not even sharing it with her husband. It reminded her how important friends were, and that she was fortunate to have some very special ones.

Murmuring an indistinct thanks, she accepted the flowers and took them to the kitchen. Fortunately the room was empty, so she had some privacy. She removed the cellophane and tissue paper to find a beautiful mass of vivid-colored tropical flowers, but they did nothing to brighten her spirits. She pulled the

card that accompanied the flowers from its
envelope.

I'm sorry.
Will you forgive me?
Can we be friends?
Sawyer and Dylan
P.S. Dylan would like a dog and we need
your help.

"Seriously?" The word slipped out before
Shannon could stop it. She quickly glanced
around to make sure she was still alone.

Sawyer wanted to be friends? Those kisses
they'd exchanged implied more than friendship. But signing the card from him *and* Dylan
sent a very clear message. Friendship and
family.

Nothing more.

She was tempted to leave the flowers on the
table in the kitchen knowing that looking at
them would only aggravate the pain. She went
as far as positioning the vase in the middle of
the table.

But she couldn't do it.

She scooped up the vase and took it to her
desk, where she placed it on the far-right corner. Then she angled her computer, her chair
and herself in the opposite direction.

She scrolled through a report on her screen, trying to find where she'd left off, but her gaze continued to be drawn to the flowers. Memories of her times with Sawyer flashed through her mind. A walk on a pier under a sickle-shaped slice of moon. The two of them watching Dylan wrestle with Darwin. His lips brushing over hers with the scent of gardenia and frangipani surrounding them.

"Let's go get a coffee. Better yet, how about a beer?" She nearly jumped out of her chair at the sound of Cal's voice. "You're more than an hour after shift."

"Uh, thanks for the offer, but I can't. I have to finish this report."

"Yeah? What report?"

Shannon glanced at her computer screen, then down at the papers on her desk because— quite frankly—she couldn't remember what she'd been working on.

Cal leaned against the side of her desk and smirked. "Hmm. That important, huh?"

Shannon could feel the heat rising to her cheeks and turned away.

He reached down and flipped the file folder closed. "The report can wait until tomorrow. From what I've seen, you weren't making much progress anyway. I'll buy."

Shannon cocked an eyebrow at him. To

the best of her recollection, it was her turn to buy. She was about to decline but realized she wasn't being productive anyway. "Okay." Seeing that Cal was already in plain clothes, she added, "I'll go change and be right back."

She changed into a pair of jeans and a light blouse she had in her locker. They left their dogs at the division and drove separately to Buster's Beach House Bar. Choosing a table on the patio, they each ordered a beer.

"What's going on with you and Sawyer?" Cal asked once they had their drinks.

"Why does everyone ask me that?"

"Because I've been in the early stages of a relationship that was a little rocky and I recognize it in others. So, talk to me."

Shannon shook her head. "I should've listened to Jessica. You're married to a wise woman."

"I know it, and it's just one of the many reasons I consider myself incredibly lucky to be with her. But are you trying to change the subject or does that comment relate to my question about you and Sawyer?"

Shannon lifted her bottle and sipped. "Jess told me to be careful about falling for Sawyer. She said to take it slow, if at all. Truth be told, Madison and Ariana said more or less the same thing."

Cal gave her a gentle smile. "Rick, Logan and I are fortunate to have fallen in love with the women we did. We had our differences at the start, but no relationship is problem-free and it's turned out great for us." He searched her face. "I thought things were heading in the right direction for you and Sawyer, too, since his son was returned to him. In large part thanks to you."

Shannon gazed out over the water. "I thought so, too. Until all the questions about whether his wife's still alive and, if so, did she have anything to do with Dylan's abduction." She looked back at Cal. "You heard about that?"

He nodded. "I have. That's hard to fathom."

Shannon sighed. "Yeah, and it's made him pull back. I can't blame him for wanting to end things. I blame myself for letting my feelings get involved to begin with. As you said, relationships aren't problem-free at the best of times, and we had everything stacked against us from day one. How could I expect anything to work out between us?" She stared down at her bottle. "It was irresponsible and insensitive of me to start anything with Sawyer."

"Hey, stop that!"

Shannon's gaze shot up to meet Cal's.

"There's no benefit in beating yourself up over it. I've learned that a heart can have a will of its own and can be quite insistent about having its way…and that it often knows best."

Shannon couldn't resist a chuckle at Cal's romantic turn of phrase.

"I'm guessing that humongous mass of flowers on your desk is from Sawyer," he continued, "because I don't see either of you as the type who'd move on so quickly."

"Good guess."

"And I'll bet he's sorry and wants to see you, but you're not prepared to forgive him yet, not to mention forgive yourself."

Shannon grinned. "You'll make detective someday," she said, realizing how much she'd needed to get out, have a laugh.

"I know you said that our significant others cautioned you to be careful and take it slow. I can't disagree, but if you factor in everything Evans has gone through and is still going through, you should cut him some slack. If you really care about the guy, hang in there. You can't expect him to be rational and focused on his own needs at a time like this." Cal picked up his bottle and took a drink. "Trust me. When my daughter, Haley, was out of my life—and at least I knew she was safe and well-cared for by my ex—I wasn't my normal charming self. The last thing I wanted was a relationship. Jess can vouch for that, but she didn't write me off. If you believe in Sawyer, give him a chance," Cal repeated.

Shannon thought about what Cal had said as she swung by the division to pick up Darwin and her flowers, and all the way home.

She reminded herself again that in her twenty-eight years, she'd never felt about anyone the way she did about Sawyer. She'd try being his friend, and see if, over time, they could recapture what had begun to develop between them.

When she arrived home, she was feeling distinctly better and she'd decided it was worth a try. If she backed away from his offer of friendship, what sort of person would she be? And what if, by taking a short-term view, she missed out on the opportunity of a lifetime?

She took Darwin for a quick jog around the block before retrieving the flowers and duffel bag from her Explorer and letting herself into the house. She set the vase on the hall table, kicked off her shoes and put her duffel in the bottom of the hall closet. She glanced down at Darwin, who was watching her expectantly. "Are you hungry?" she asked. When his whole body wriggled and he woofed enthusiastically, she ran her hand over his head. "Okay, then. Go get your bowl."

He streaked into the kitchen and by the time

she'd joined him, he had his dog dish clamped in his mouth, tail wagging feverishly.

"Good boy!" she praised him. "Bring it here," she said, going to the cupboard where she kept his kibble. Taking the bowl from Darwin, she poured a generous cup of food into the dish, then placed it on the mat next to the cupboard. Darwin promptly plopped down, his tail whooshing on the floor. "Okay," she said—the command that signaled he could start eating.

Shannon pulled a Coke out of the fridge and reached for her phone. Smiling, she sat down. They'd see how long she and Sawyer could remain just friends.

She hadn't dated a lot in her life, but that was because she'd had other priorities and she was…selective. It didn't mean she didn't know how to turn on the charm. If it was a dog he wanted, she could help him with that.

With the smile still on her face, she dialed Sawyer's number.

SHANNON SHIFTED FROM one foot to the other as she waited on Sawyer's front porch. She'd decided that helping him and Dylan pick out a rescue dog would be a stress-free and enjoyable way to reboot their relationship—whatever that relationship turned out to be.

Standing on the porch now, she wasn't so sure about the stress-free part.

When Sawyer opened the door, the pure pleasure on his face, along with the silly grin, went a long way toward easing her nerves.

"Hi," he said. His smile faded. "I'm sorry—"

She waved the apology away with one hand. "Thank you for the flowers. They're beautiful and more than enough as an apology."

"I'm glad you liked them." The smile was back and he held out his hand.

When she placed hers in it after a moment's hesitation, he raised it to his lips and brushed a kiss across her knuckles. "It's good to see you again. Rather than apologizing, let me say thank you."

At the sound of running feet, they both turned.

"You're here!" Dylan exclaimed as he came to a skidding halt next to his father. He peered around Shannon. "Where's Darwin?"

"He stayed home today."

Dylan's mouth drew into a pout and his lower lip stuck out. "But I thought he'd help us pick out my dog. You know. To make sure he thinks my dog is okay and that they'll get along and everything."

Shannon crouched down. "I'm certain Darwin will approve of your dog and they'll be pals. Darwin gave me some advice, so I'll keep that in mind when we meet the dogs. How does that sound?"

"I guess that's okay." Dylan's lower lip still wasn't quite back in place.

"Dylan," Sawyer said, "Shannon is here to help us. You should thank her, not complain that she didn't bring Darwin."

Dylan glanced up at Sawyer. "Sorry, Dad." He turned back to Shannon. "Thanks for helping." He reached for Sawyer's hand and tugged. "Can we go now?"

They drove to the San Diego Animal Rescue League facility in Sawyer's Range Rover.

"All right, champ. Let's go see what we can find," Sawyer said, as he parked near the front entrance. He released Dylan from his car seat and helped him hop out.

Dylan ran ahead to the front door of the shelter, and Sawyer and Shannon followed.

As they entered the waiting area, their presence immediately set off a cacophony of excited barking in the back. Dylan jumped up and down in an attempt to see over the counter, and Sawyer leaned toward Shannon. "I might live to regret this."

Shannon grinned at him. "Look at Dylan! You're *absolutely* doing the right thing."

A young man in torn jeans and an Animal

Rescue League T-shirt emerged from the back. "I'm Seth," he said, holding out a hand. "What can I do for you?"

"We're here to get a dog!" Dylan chimed in before Sawyer could respond.

"You've come to the right place." Seth told them. "Do you know what kind of dog you'd like?"

"A small one," Sawyer said quickly before Dylan could voice his own opinion.

Seth smiled. "If that's your only requirement, we can help you, no problem. Let me take you to the back." He gestured for them to come with him.

Shannon touched Sawyer's arm before they entered the kennel area. "Just so you know," she whispered. "Smaller dogs tend to be noisier and can be hyper, too."

"I'll take my chances with a small one," he murmured.

Shannon laughed.

"Look, Dad! Look at *all* these dogs!" Dylan shouted over the din. He ran from one kennel to the next, before turning to them again. "How am I supposed to pick *just one*?"

Sawyer gave Seth a pleading look.

"Uh, why don't I take you around and introduce you to some of our residents ready for adoption, and tell you a little bit about each one?"

Sawyer appreciated his intervention and also that Seth was guiding Dylan to the cages with smaller dogs. All the barking was starting to give him a headache, but the more dogs they saw, the more concerned Sawyer became about the animals' plight. He made a mental note to send regular donations to the shelter. He might not be able to save every dog, but he could help with their care until they found homes.

"How about this one?" he asked Dylan as they stopped at a cage housing a subdued beagle.

"He's nice," Dylan said as he considered the dog. He moved to the next cage, in which a little Jack Russell terrier was leaping and yipping with boundless energy.

Sawyer glanced at Shannon and she gave him a knowing grin. "Small dogs," she mouthed. He looked wistfully at the beagle. "What's his story?" he asked Seth.

"The beagle's already adopted," Seth told him. "He'll be going to his forever home tomorrow."

At the sound of a deep woof from a cage behind them, they glanced over at the large white, russet and black dog with floppy ears.

One of his eyes was ringed with black, the other with russet. He sat sedately, and observed them with wise, sad eyes.

Dylan skipped over to the cage and slid his fingers through the chain-link.

The big dog rose.

Sawyer had visions of the dog chomping on his son's fingers and was about to pull him back, but Seth stepped forward. "He's okay," he assured Sawyer. "You don't have to worry about Rufus. He's a gentle giant. As placid as they come."

Rufus proceeded to prove it by lumbering over to the gate, and with a huge pink tongue, slathering Dylan's fingers with dog drool.

Dylan giggled and wiggled his fingers, obviously hoping for a repeat performance.

Rufus obliged. With the tips of his fingers, Dylan rubbed the side of Rufus's snout and the dog pressed his face up against the cage door, closing his eyes and moaning in sheer bliss.

"Daddy, I want Rufus to be our dog!"

"Dylan, I thought we agreed we'd get a *small* dog."

"Nuh-uh. I never said that!" He gave Sawyer a mischievous grin.

"When did he become so clever?" Sawyer said under his breath to Shannon. "So, what do you think?"

"Well, let's see," she responded, before joining Dylan in front of Rufus's kennel.

The two of them murmured to each other as they scratched the dog through the chain-link. Dylan leaned against Shannon and she placed a hand on his shoulder. They looked so natural together—like mother and son. That thought staggered Sawyer, and he quickly focused on Dylan again.

There was no denying the boy's excitement.

Sawyer sighed. Small dog. He thought he'd been very clear about wanting a *small* dog. He sucked in a breath and reconciled himself to the inevitable. His son's happiness came before all else. "So, Seth, what's Rufus's story?"

Seth's smile flashed. "He's a terrific dog. Here, let me show you." He unlatched the gate and called Rufus to him.

It was a good sign that Rufus was obedient. He immediately started toward Seth, with just a short detour to nuzzle Dylan and accept a hug from him. When the dog reached Seth, he sat and put his paw in Seth's outstretched hand. "Good boy," Seth said, rubbing the dog's head.

Seth stepped aside to let Dylan and Shannon interact with the dog.

"He's two to three years old," Seth explained. "We think he's a cross between a Bernese mountain dog and an Australian shepherd. That would explain his size," he said with another smile. "He was found wandering the streets, without tags, collar or microchip. He was underweight and his fur was so badly matted, we figured he'd been living on the streets for a while. But he was gentle, had good manners and understood basic commands. We thought he was lost, but we never managed to track down his owners. We cleaned him up, got him back to full health, and now he's ready for adoption."

Shannon turned to Dylan. "You really like Rufus, don't you?"

"I don't think he needs any encouragement," Sawyer murmured as Dylan nodded and threw his arms around the dog's neck.

"Why hasn't he been adopted yet?" Shannon asked.

Seth shrugged. "Large dogs, especially full-grown ones, tend to be harder to place. And he's only been ready for adoption for a week, so it hasn't been that long."

Dylan still had one arm slung around Rufus and was giggling at something Shannon had said. If the dog made Dylan happy, that was what mattered most.

Twenty minutes later, with the ownership certificate in Sawyer's hand and an initial supply of dog food under his arm, they were walking Rufus to the SUV.

Sawyer noted that the dog did seem gentle, good-natured and obedient. He bounded into the back of the SUV on command and sent Sawyer what looked like a grateful grin.

Outsmarted by a dog and a kid, he thought.

They made a quick stop at a pet-food store for additional provisions. Sawyer was astonished that, by the time they added everything Shannon said they'd need and a generous number of dog toys that Dylan insisted Rufus couldn't live without, the total had exceeded five hundred dollars. A small dog wouldn't have needed so much stuff, he told himself, more for the sake of form than conviction.

At Sawyer's house, Dylan took Rufus into his bedroom, along with the dog bed they'd just bought, while Sawyer and Shannon unloaded the rest of the supplies. When he'd found places to store everything, at least temporarily, Sawyer took two Cokes out of the fridge and offered one to Shannon.

"I can't believe what you got me into," he said, holding back a smile as he leaned against the kitchen counter.

"You don't regret getting Rufus, do you?" she asked with genuine concern clouding her eyes.

He glanced meaningfully down at the white

tiles in his kitchen, already liberally sprinkled with black-and-brown fur, then shook his head. "No. To see the smile on Dylan's face? To have him so excited and energized? How could I regret giving such joy to my son?" Now he let the smile appear. "Thank you for suggesting it."

Her blue eyes warmed. He felt the punch of how beautiful she was—her large eyes dominating her face, the short, straight nose and that mouth that was so expressive with its full lower lip. The mouth he had a sudden urge to kiss again.

It took considerable willpower, but he resisted the temptation. He didn't want her to think he was completely crazy. This time he'd have to show her that he cared about her, and that he could be trusted not to keep vacillating.

"Let me thank you, Shannon, by taking you to dinner," he said and watched the emotions play across her face.

CHAPTER FIFTEEN

SHANNON WONDERED ABOUT her sanity as she held the new dress in front of her and critically assessed it in her full-length mirror.

She couldn't help being excited about having dinner with Sawyer, but nothing had been resolved. Nothing had changed.

Would he simply pull away from her again?

If so, how many of these ups and downs could she handle, when she could no longer deny that she was in love with him? And *because* she was, she hadn't been able to say no when he'd asked her out.

Well aware of the limitations of her wardrobe, she'd enlisted Madison's help to find a new dress.

Madison had been more than happy to oblige. After Shannon's indecisiveness while shopping with Madison, trying on outfit after outfit, feeling self-conscious, Madison had insisted she go with the red jersey dress. It had a scoop neck, and it ended midthigh. She'd finally capitulated.

Shannon considered the color against her skin tone and hair. She had to agree it worked. There was a rosy glow to her skin, and it wasn't just the blush of excitement.

She removed the dress from the hanger, slipped it on and gave it a few tugs. Had it really been that short in the store? She stepped into high-heeled, strappy sandals, another new purchase. She checked herself in the mirror, turning one way, then another, and decided it would do. Glancing at her bedside clock, she saw that she was on time. Hearing the doorbell, she noted that so was Sawyer.

She left Darwin in her bedroom and walked cautiously, in deference to the heels, down the stairs to let Sawyer in.

Sawyer's brows rose the minute he laid eyes on Shannon. "You look…" He reached for her hand. "Spectacular!"

That made the financial outlay for dress and shoes worth it.

Still holding her hand, he leaned toward her and sniffed. "You smell wonderful, too."

Shannon seldom wore perfume, but today she'd not only spritzed some on, she'd slathered her skin with some sort of body lotion Madison had urged on her. Score another one for Madison, she thought as she locked the door behind them.

At the restaurant—Frisco's Steakhouse this time—Shannon was impressed once more by how smoothly they were whisked through the beautiful entry, into the dining room and to their table.

They were seated, in Shannon's opinion, at the best table in the house, next to a decorative gas fireplace. There were candles, crystal and flowers on their table and all around them.

Music, mellow and classical, flowed through the room, just loud enough to set the mood and mask conversation at other tables, but not so loud that it distracted them from their own conversation. Everything about the setting made Shannon think of romance and stirred a yearning deep within her. Would Sawyer have picked this restaurant, this table, if that *hadn't* been his intention?

Their orders were taken, the wine served— all very efficiently and unobtrusively—and the whole time she couldn't believe she was sitting there with Sawyer. She didn't know where it would lead, but for now, she wanted to live in the moment and enjoy it to the fullest—the shimmer of candlelight, the gleam of crystal, and his attentiveness and charm as they finished their appetizers and their main courses were served.

Looking at him, those forest green eyes, the

strong features, the longish dark brown hair, only intensified her yearning. She lowered her gaze to her wineglass, afraid to keep looking at Sawyer, afraid to let him see everything she was feeling reflected in her eyes. Being here with him was a huge step forward, but she didn't think he was ready to discover how deeply she felt about him. With everything he had to contend with, she didn't want to burden him…or scare him off.

She swirled the wine in her glass and thought back to when he'd kissed her on the pier after their first dinner. Feeling dreamy and contented. She wondered if he'd kiss her again tonight.

It occurred to her that she even loved the sound of his voice. When he paused, she missed the sound of it.

"Is everything okay?"

She glanced up at him. "Of course. Why?" More than okay, if she could just stay in this moment.

He gave her a half smile. "I was telling you what Rufus did yesterday, but I don't think you were listening."

"Yes, I was!" she said defensively.

He grinned. "Oh, really? What did I say he did?"

"You…uh…" She gave him a sheepish smile

of her own. "My mind might have wandered a little."

He chuckled. "Was I that boring?"

"Oh, no! Not at all. I was just…" She was mortified at being caught and even more so, especially since it had been the result of thinking about his kisses.

"I can drone on at times. Anyway, it's your turn. Tell me what you've been doing to serve and protect the citizens of San Diego this week."

While Shannon told him about some of the highlights, the waiter cleared the plates from their main course, and took their order of coffee and dessert. They passed on coffee, but decided to share a crème brûlée.

Sawyer's eyes were dark and serious, as he reached for Shannon's hand and ran his thumb across a scrape along a finger.

A little embarrassed, she tried to pull her hand away, but he held tight.

"How did this happen? In the line of duty, I bet." He looked up at her for acknowledgement.

Shannon hoped the lighting was sufficiently dim so he wouldn't see her blush.

"Your hands are strong and soft. It might seem like a contradiction, but they're capable and yet feminine. You have a tough job that most people don't appreciate nearly enough, but you haven't let it harden you."

"It's still early days yet," she replied with a chuckle.

"No. I don't think that'll change."

When Shannon's cell phone rang, she gave Sawyer an apologetic look. "It's my work phone. I'm sorry, but I have to take it."

He nodded. "Clemens," she answered.

"It's Cal. You asked me to call you, so I am. It's time! Jess and I are on our way to Ocean Crest Hospital. She's having the baby!"

"Oh, oooh! That's wonderful! How's she feeling?"

"Eager to get the delivery over and done with!" Cal responded. "You said you wanted to be there for the birth. Based on her contractions, it won't be long, so you might want to get in your SUV, put your lights on and meet us there."

"That soon? Really?"

"Problem?"

Shannon was having a wonderful time and didn't want to cut the evening short. But one of her closest friends on the police force and his wife were about to have a baby. She'd been honored when they'd asked her to be a godparent, and she didn't take the responsibly lightly. She'd been the one to insist that she wanted to be there for the birth. She couldn't very well not show up.

"I'll be there as soon as I can. Do Logan and Rick know?"

"Logan does, and Rick'll be my next call. See you shortly," he said before they hung up.

"That didn't sound like official police business," Sawyer said with a smile as she put her phone back in her clutch.

"No, it wasn't. It was Cal—Cal Palmer. You remember him?"

"The other search-and-rescue officer."

"Yes. His wife, Jessica, is about to give birth to their first child together—a brother or sister to Kayla, who is adopted, and Haley, Cal's daughter from his first marriage. I'm going to be the baby's godmother. I'm sorry to end our dinner so abruptly, but it's important to me to be there. If you wouldn't mind driving me home, I promise I'll make it up to you."

"From what I gathered listening to your end of the conversation, there's not much time. If they're heading to Ocean Crest Hospital, I can get you there in fifteen minutes. If I drive you home first, it'll take you nearly an hour."

"I hadn't thought of that. I'd really appreciate it if you could drop me off at the hospital.

Then I can take a taxi home, or have Logan or Rick drive me."

Sawyer signaled for the waiter and explained that they wouldn't have dessert after all, and asked him to bring the check.

"I'll drive you home afterward."

"You mean you'll stay with me?"

"Yes. Would that be a problem?"

"No. I don't think so. I just wouldn't have expected that you'd want to."

The waiter handed Sawyer the check. "Is something not to your satisfaction, sir?" he asked.

"Everything was great. We need to get to the hospital for a delivery."

The waiter looked at Shannon. Particularly her midsection.

She laughed and placed a hand on her belly. "No, it's definitely *not* me giving birth!"

"My apologies," the waiter mumbled, while he ran Sawyer's credit card through his handheld machine.

They made good time to the hospital. Rick, Madison and Logan were already there when they arrived. Rick had an enormous stuffed bear under his arm, and Logan was holding a bright bouquet of flowers.

Rick took one look at Shannon and whistled.

He glanced at Madison apologetically. "Sorry. It just slipped out."

"Oh, that was exactly the type of reaction I was hoping for when I helped her pick that dress!" Madison gave Shannon a hug and whispered in her ear. "I was right about the dress! It's sensational on you." Then she nodded in Sawyer's direction. "Are you going to introduce me to your date?"

"Madison, this is Sawyer Evans. Sawyer, meet Madison Vasquez. You've already met her husband, Rick Vasquez, a sergeant with the K-9 Unit."

Sawyer first shook hands with Madison. "Good to see you again," he said to Rick, as he shook his hand, too, then Logan's. "Captain, it's nice to meet you in other than a professional capacity."

"Call me Logan. No one here's on duty. Ah, there's Ariana now," he said.

More introductions were made and Ariana, too, hugged Shannon and complimented her on how she looked.

"Where are Haley and Kayla?" Ariana asked.

"They're with Jessica's parents," Madison replied. "Cal and Jess didn't want them to get impatient waiting here, but they should arrive shortly."

They chatted, drank coffee, paced among the other people in the waiting room, until finally Cal emerged from the delivery room, grinning from ear to ear. "We have a son!" he announced. "Healthy, eight pounds, three ounces. Mom and baby Ronin are both doing great!"

Rick was the first to give Cal a bear hug, followed by Logan and the others. Shannon was the last in line to offer her congratulations. Then Cal noticed Sawyer and gave Shannon a raised-brow look before turning to him.

Sawyer extended his hand. "Congratulations."

"Thanks," Cal said. "We appreciate you being here." He turned back to the others. "They were just getting Jess and Ronin comfortable. I think it's been long enough. We can go see them now."

Cal led the way to Jessica's room.

She was propped up in bed and had the baby, wrapped in a fuzzy blue blanket, snuggled against her. Shannon saw her press her lips to the top of the little bald head, as the baby made an adorable mewing sound and yawned hugely. She'd never thought of herself as maternal or terribly sentimental, but seeing Jess with her baby, and Cal now sitting on the edge of the bed, one arm around Jess's shoulders and the other tenderly stroking his son's cheek, caused something to shift inside her. Jess and Cal and Ronin were a unit. Happy and so obviously filled with love.

She felt a touch on her hand, then Sawyer laced his fingers through hers. Their gazes met and held. If she hadn't already fallen head over heels for him, seeing that he was equally moved by the tableau in front of them would have done it.

For a moment, everything around them seemed to fade away as she lost herself in his eyes.

Loud laughter pulled her out of her reverie and she glanced over at the bed, where Jessica, Cal and baby Ronin were clustered. Madison perched on the other side.

"That boy's going to take after his father, no question," Rick said with a guffaw. "He's already got hold of a beautiful woman and won't let go!"

Only then did Shannon notice that the baby had his small hand in a fist, tightly clutching a lock of Madison's long red hair.

Cal reached over and very gently opened his son's hand to free Madison's hair, before the baby clenched it again.

When the door swung open, Jess and Cal's

daughters, Haley and Kayla, ran into the room, squealing with excitement. Cal slid off the bed and gathered them both in his arms. An older couple, whom Shannon guessed to be Jessica's parents, followed. The woman was quick to rush to the bedside and hug her daughter, while the man sauntered over more slowly. He swept back his daughter's hair and dropped a kiss on her forehead. Next, he carefully pushed the blanket away from Ronin's face and stroked the tiny pink cheek.

He bent down, murmured something in his daughter's ear. When he straightened and reached out to shake Cal's hand, Shannon noticed the sheen of moisture on his face.

Despite all the activity around them, Shannon couldn't get the look on Sawyer's face out of her mind. Oddly, she didn't feel self-conscious about the fact that he continued to hold her hand in the presence of her friends and colleagues.

A nurse came in shortly after, and asked that everyone leave to allow the new mother and baby Ronin to get some well-deserved rest.

As Sawyer drove Shannon home, she kept thinking about the wonder of the evening, culminating in the connection they'd made in the hospital room. She was absolutely sure he'd felt it, too.

For the first time in her life, Shannon dreamed of a forever love and a family, and Sawyer was cast in the starring role.

CHAPTER SIXTEEN

SHANNON WAS STILL basking in the afterglow of the evening when she and Darwin entered the squad room the next morning.

"Shannon, can you come in here for a minute, please?" Logan called to her from the doorway of his office.

"Sure." She slid her duffel under her desk, and gave Darwin a "down-stay" command.

"What's up, Jagger?" she asked once she was in his office and seated.

His eyes narrowed and seemed to scrutinize her face before he spoke again. "I don't think you're going to like this. Evans will like it even less."

A cold chill crept up Shannon's spine. Her happy mood of only moments ago was no more than a memory.

"Leary believes they've located Evans's ex-wife. If it *is* her, you know it's not out of the realm of possibility for her to have abducted her own son."

Shannon felt the blood drain from her face.

"Have they found any evidence to corroborate that she was involved?"

Logan shook his head. "Not that I'm aware of, no. But we've been coming up empty with every other angle we've pursued. We have no viable suspects. If Jeannette Evans *is* alive, her abducting the boy would be the most plausible scenario we have to date. If it is her, she's living under an assumed name. That adds some weight to our supposition. People don't generally change their names on a whim. She now goes by the name Lilly Harris. Middle name Michelle. But here's the kicker. She appears to be remarried."

Shannon squeezed her lips together. She recalled that Sawyer had said he hadn't divorced her. She doubted it was possible for his wife to have gotten a divorce without his knowledge. The only coherent thought she was able to form was that Sawyer would be devastated. The FBI must not have the right person. This couldn't be happening. "If the woman *is* Jeannette Evans, surely Sawyer would've heard from her, if for no other reason than to petition for divorce. Or she would've turned up during the search three years ago."

"You know that's not necessarily the case."

"When she originally disappeared, nothing popped, but we work cold cases periodically and so does the FBI. Wouldn't there have been *some* flag along the way that she was alive? A credit card? Passport or security check? Contact with her own family, if not her husband and son?" She knew she was grasping at straws. There was a reason the legal presumption of death required seven years. People could and had turned up unexpectedly years after their disappearance.

"Not necessarily," he repeated.

"If she'd assumed an alias, that could mean all kinds of things." Her heart was breaking for Sawyer and she was desperately trying to find the least catastrophic answer.

"Yes, it could," Logan agreed. "But one of those would be possible ill intent."

Shannon's thoughts were muddled, tripping and tumbling over each other. If it was true, what would it mean for Sawyer? For Dylan?

No. She wasn't ready to accept that a mother, a woman who was loved by Sawyer, could have done something as abhorrent and traumatic as kidnapping her own child. There had to be another explanation. She sincerely hoped so, for Sawyer's and Dylan's sakes.

And on a purely selfish note, now that it could be a reality, what would that mean for her? For them? Was it just the evening before that she'd fantasized about a happy-ever-after with him?

"We'll know more once the FBI has made contact," Logan said, interrupting her thoughts. "If it's her, she's living in Wickenburg, Arizona. FBI Special Agent Gavin Leary is on his way there now."

"How did they find her?"

"They got lucky on that. Through facial recognition on social media. The FBI has been doing regular searches since Dylan was abducted. She recently set up a Facebook account, after her second child was born, apparently to provide updates on her kids."

"She has kids?"

Logan nodded. "Two. A toddler and a baby."

All Shannon could think of was how Sawyer would take *that* news. Jeannette had left him and Dylan, and now had a new family? "If she is behind the abduction, why? She has two kids. Would that have made her long for her firstborn?"

"Shannon, you're asking me questions I can't possibly answer. Why don't we let Leary do his job?"

"It would also explain why there hadn't been a ransom request. If it was her, she intended to keep Dylan and add him to her family. That would make the most sense, wouldn't it?"

"Shannon, stop speculating. Like I said, let the FBI do their work."

She paused, turning it all over in her mind. "Does Sawyer know?"

"No. Leary wants to verify that Lilly Harris is in fact Jeannette Evans, before throwing this curveball at him."

"But…"

"I understand what you're thinking. He has a right to know. Leary's fairly certain it's her. Having some time to prepare before they confirm might help him deal with it."

Shannon nodded mutely, although she wondered if there could be any way to prepare for the shock of his wife not only being alive, but married and with kids. She didn't even want to think about the abduction.

"This is against procedure." Logan sighed. "If you want to inform him, I'll take the heat from Leary, if there is any."

Shannon glanced down at her hands and noticed that she'd been squeezing them together so hard her knuckles had gone white. She relaxed her grip. How was she supposed to tell the man she was in love with that the woman *he'd* loved and still had feelings for, the mother of the child he adored, was more than likely alive and living in Arizona? And if so, that she could be responsible for having abducted his son.

Shannon had to question—if she was the messenger, would he hate her for it?

But how could she claim to care about him and not want to be the person to deliver this devastating news?

Either way, it would probably be the death knell for their relationship.

"It's not your responsibility," Logan said softly. "I wanted to give you the option, but you don't have to do it. Leary will tell him what he needs to know in due course."

Shannon sucked in a huge breath. "I want to do it. Thank you for giving me the opportunity."

Logan picked up a sheet of paper from his desk, stared at it. With a grim look on his face, he held it out to her.

She took the paper and it fluttered in her shaking hand.

It was a printout of a Facebook page. The woman was smiling broadly, a toddler leaning on her thigh and a baby cradled in her arm.

She'd seen the pictures of Jeannette in Sawyer's house. She knew this picture was of Jeannette, but in it she looked even more beautiful.

She raised her eyes to meet Logan's. "This is

Jeannette Evans." She handed the paper back to him.

"As I said, Leary's certain, too, otherwise I wouldn't have suggested you say anything to Sawyer. When you do speak to him about this, remember we deal in facts, not half-truths. Tell him only what we know."

"Understood," she said and left his office.

At her desk, she collapsed into her chair.

"Problem, Shannon?" Rick asked from behind his desk.

Shannon closed her eyes. "Why did Cal and Jess have to take *those* two weeks in July to go on vacation?"

Rick laughed. "You're begrudging Cal time off with his family?" Before she could answer, his face sobered and he continued. "Looking at you, I'm guessing something has come up in the Dylan Evans case and it's not good news."

"You got that right. Actually, it's not so much *not* good news as…I'm floored."

"Do you want to go get a coffee and talk about it?"

She shook her head. "No, I'm fine."

Rick got up, sat in Cal's chair and rolled it over to her desk. "Okay, but talking it through might help."

Maybe he had a point. "The FBI thinks they've located Sawyer's ex-wife—wife, actually, since they never got divorced… If she is alive, it's probable that she's behind the abduction."

"Huh. That's a tough one."

"Oh, yeah."

"Hey," Rick said in a cheerful voice. "I was going to grill a couple of steaks for Madison and me. You interested in coming over for dinner?"

"I appreciate the offer, but I'll take a rain check, if that's okay." She cast her eyes downward. "I need to see Sawyer."

Rick rose and pushed the chair back. "Okay, but if you want to stop by later, we'll be there. It's easy enough to toss another steak on the grill."

"Thanks," Shannon said, and watched him walk back to his own desk. A lump formed in her throat. She had wonderful colleagues. Her dream job was hers and she loved it. Maybe she just wasn't meant to have a relationship. Or at least not with Sawyer.

She felt an ache settle in her heart. Doing her best to ignore it, she reached for the phone to call Sawyer.

THAT EVENING, SHANNON parked the Explorer in Sawyer's driveway. She sat for a moment, staring at his house. She loved the look of it.

The wide porch with the comfortable chairs. The neat lawn and colorful gardens. Last night when she'd fantasized about a future for them, she'd gone as far as imagining herself in *this* house with Sawyer and Dylan. That just brought another pang of pain and regret over what might have been. They hadn't even talked about love, let alone marriage, so she'd been getting way ahead of herself.

In fact, the only time Sawyer had spoken of love, he'd been talking about Dylan…and Jeannette.

"Oh, God." How was she supposed to do this? Maybe it should've been Logan. Or she should have let normal procedure take its course, and left it to Special Agent Leary. Both Logan and the FBI agent had been the bearers of bad news too many times before, but that meant they'd know how to be sensitive. Had she made a huge mistake accepting Logan's offer to let her do it? Would her inexperience cause her to bungle it and make matters worse for Sawyer? She rubbed at her eyes.

She was thankful that when she'd called Sawyer, she'd at least had the foresight to ask him to have his sister or parents take Dylan for the evening. Sawyer had sounded hesitant but he'd agreed. That was a small blessing, since she couldn't anticipate how he'd react to her bombshell. She thought it best not to have his son within earshot.

Shannon walked slowly up the porch steps to Sawyer's front door. She wiped her damp palms on her pants before knocking. She tried to remember the words she'd settled on and had practiced on the drive over, but her memory was suddenly blank. When Sawyer opened the door, wearing jeans and a T-shirt, looking rumpled but impossibly handsome, she nearly panicked and ran.

He showed surprise at seeing her in her uniform, but leaned in and brushed his lips over hers.

She wanted to step forward and into his embrace but knew it wouldn't be right until she'd told him what she'd come to say. And the purpose of this visit was not for him to console her. Just the opposite. If there was any way he could be comforted after the information she was about to drop on him, she'd do her best.

When Rufus bounded over with surprising energy for his size, she squatted down to rub behind his ears. The big goofy smile, lolling tongue and rapidly wagging tail told her he was happy in his new home. Sawyer spontaneously stroked the dog's head, which conveyed that Rufus had won him over, too.

"There's something wrong," he said flatly.

She rose and brushed unsuccessfully at the copious amount of dog hair on her pants. Rufus was a shedder, no question. "Can we go in and sit down?"

Sawyer eased back and narrowed his eyes. "Sure," he said. "What can I get you?"

"Water would be great," she responded and followed him into the kitchen. She perched on a stool by the counter and watched him take a glass from the cupboard, fill it with ice and then water.

He passed it to her, rested his palms on the counter and leaned forward. "This isn't a social call, is it?"

"No. Could you sit down, please?"

"I'm fine standing." His words had an edge to them. He must have realized it, because his tone softened when he continued. "You ask me to get Meg to take Dylan for the evening, making me think…well, making me think. You show up on my doorstep in uniform, acting as if you've just lost your best friend, and you want me to sit down before we talk? I can put two and two together, and I know this has to do with Dylan's abduction and it's not good news. So please get on with it."

Shannon pushed her glass away and looked Sawyer straight in the eye. "The FBI believes they've found your wife."

The emotions that played across his face could have been comical except that they cut through her like a sharp knife. The expression that settled was a mixture of hope and disbelief. He groped for a stool and finally sat down. "They think Jeannette is alive?"

Shannon nodded.

"Where? How can I contact her?" His words came out in a mad rush.

Shannon hadn't known how he'd react, but she hadn't expected this hopeful eagerness. He must never have stopped loving Jeannette—even now, when she was a possible suspect in his son's abduction.

"Sawyer, you can't contact her because she's a person of interest in a police investigation. Normally, this information wouldn't be shared with you at this stage." She took a deep breath and went on in a less officious tone. "Contacting her could interfere with the investigation. Sawyer, we have to determine if she was in any way involved in Dylan's abduction."

He shook his head and jumped off the stool. "No! I can't believe that. I knew Jeannette nearly half her life. I've thought about it." His laugh was brittle. "Incessantly, since the possibility was raised. She wouldn't be capable of doing it. It's not in her makeup."

Shannon's immediate impulse was to ask if

he'd thought her capable of deserting him and Dylan the way she had, but knew there was nothing to be gained by that. "The FBI still needs to eliminate her as a suspect. For now, all I know is that they think they found her."

"What *can* you tell me?"

"She's living in Wickenburg, Arizona. Under a different name."

She watched the realization—and the pain—register on his face. Logan had said the FBI agents were of the opinion that it took some doing to establish her new identity. Sawyer would know that, too. But it wasn't relevant to their discussion and went against Logan's advice to stay with the facts. Shannon had an urge to hold him. To give him at least that much comfort. But she didn't want to blur the line. She *was* here in an official capacity. "FBI Special Agent Leary is on his way to see her now." She glanced at her watch. "He might be there already."

Sawyer stepped back, bumped into a stool, sat down. "Okay." His face had gone pale. His eyes were shadowed. "Can I see her or maybe talk to her after the FBI has?"

"I don't know. They might not want you to contact her until the investigation is over, but I'll ask."

"Can…can you tell me the name she's using?"

"Sawyer…"

"I won't try to find her or contact her. You have my word. I'm a lawyer and I know the consequences if I interfere with the investigation. Just give me a name."

Maybe she *could* give him that much. It would be her neck on the line—if he did use the information to get in touch with Jeannette, but she had to trust him. There was no guile in his eyes. Just pain. "Lilly Michelle Harris."

He rubbed his eyes with the thumb and forefinger of his right hand. "Thank you," he murmured.

And now Shannon had to deliver the hardest blow of all. She skirted the counter and sat on the stool next to his. Blurred lines be damned. She reached for his hands and felt the chill that must have invaded his whole body.

"Sawyer, she's married and has two young children."

His mouth worked as if he was gasping for air as a drowning man might. He withdrew his hands from hers and staggered to his feet. She'd seen him suffering and in grief, but she hadn't seen him cry the entire time she'd known him despite everything he'd had to bear.

Until now.

A single tear coursed down his cheek.

She closed the gap between them and wrapped her arms around him. When he held on tightly, she shed silent tears of her own.

CHAPTER SEVENTEEN

SAWYER COULDN'T BELIEVE that Jeannette had purposely left him and Dylan, and never bothered to contact him, even if only to let him know she was okay. Worse yet, instead of having the courage to say she wanted out of their marriage, she'd just disappeared, leaving him to search and mourn and finally conclude that she'd died somehow, somewhere, tragically.

And for what? To marry someone else and start another family?

Anger sparked and burned hot and intense inside him.

Sawyer released Shannon, spun away from her and strode to the glass-paned door leading to the backyard. Rufus was sitting in front of it, looking outside expectantly. When Sawyer didn't slide the door open, the dog gave a little huff and slunk away to curl up on his dog bed in a corner of the room.

Had Jeannette known the man she was with now? Had she left him to marry this man?

And if she had a new family and was happy, would she have taken Dylan?

No. Even if she was guilty of leaving him for another man in the most cowardly and insensitive manner possible, he couldn't believe Jeannette would be capable of taking their son from him like that.

But he never would have believed her capable of deserting him the way she had, either.

The fury, the recriminations, the *disbelief* were all churning inside him, threatening to explode. "I need to think all of this over."

He heard Shannon's stool scrape back. "Sawyer…"

He didn't say anything. He didn't know *what* to say.

"I'm so sorry," she whispered.

He didn't turn around until he heard the front door close behind her.

He called Meg and asked if she'd mind keeping Dylan overnight.

He got a beer from the refrigerator, popped the top, then took it and a framed picture of Jeannette and him on their wedding day outside with him.

He placed the picture on the table and took a long drink.

Why had the woman he loved left him and her child the way she had?

There were no answers. None that made sense.

He struggled even more with the thought of her kidnapping Dylan.

When he finished his beer, he went inside for another. This time he brought Rufus out with him. The dog must've been well aware of his mood, since he was reluctant to go with him at first. A large Milk-Bone provided the needed incentive, but Rufus still kept a reasonable distance between himself and Sawyer, curling up in the far corner of the deck to feast on his treat.

Now he was scaring their dog.

Sawyer rose and sat down next to Rufus. "It's okay, big guy. My mood's got nothing to do with you." He leaned back against the wall, handed the dog another treat and scratched behind his ear.

With his free hand, Sawyer reached for the bottle again. He wasn't someone who overindulged. The only times he'd been drunk in his life were at a frat party in university and the day after Jeannette had disappeared.

Tonight? Well, tonight might be the third time. How much worse could things get? Sawyer pushed off the deck and stalked to the edge of the patio, then back to the table. He lifted up the silver frame.

Jeannette was beautiful. She always had been. He'd remembered thinking she was the prettiest girl in school. But it was her heart, her compassion and decency that had truly captured him.

In the picture, she was wearing a sleek, white gown, with a lace overlay and a long flowing veil. She was gazing up at him and laughing. He remembered that heady summer day six years ago as if it was yesterday.

But looking at her picture now…he no longer felt that all-consuming love.

What if she *was* alive? Putting aside for the moment that she was married—to someone else—could they go back, he and Jeannette? Were second chances possible?

As he tried to picture marriage with Jeannette—past or future—he couldn't seem to.

Shannon kept intruding on his thoughts.

And remorse seared through him.

When the doorbell rang, Rufus gave out a machine-gunfire series of barks, and the frame slipped out of Sawyer's hand, smashing on the deck. "Great. Just great," he mumbled.

Rufus barked again, and the instant Sawyer slid the patio door open, he raced to the front hall. Sawyer followed him. Opening the door and seeing Meghan standing there, he looked around anxiously.

"Hey, Rufus! How's he doing?" she asked Sawyer, bending over to lavish the dog with attention.

"Can we talk about the dog later? Where's Dylan?" Sawyer asked, panic threatening to paralyze him.

"He's fine. I left him in my car for a moment," she said, quick to reassure him. "Nice to see you, too," she added and planted a kiss on his cheek.

"What are you doing here?" Sawyer demanded.

"Shannon called me."

"What? Why?"

"She thought you shouldn't be alone right now. But she didn't say why. Let me bring Dylan in. We'll get him settled in his room and then you can explain."

Sawyer went to get Dylan from Meg's car. Together, they got him ready for bed and left him in his room watching a show on Sawyer's iPad, Rufus by his side. Sawyer closed his bedroom door and trailed his sister down the hall. She knew her way around his kitchen and wasted no time pouring herself a glass of wine. She held the bottle toward him.

"No, thanks. I've got a beer going outside." He followed Meg again as she headed to the patio.

"So, what's got Shannon worried enough to look up my number and call me?" she asked, as she stood at the edge of the deck and leaned against the railing.

"Nothing." Everything. But he didn't think he had it in him to talk about it right then.

"Yeah?" she asked with a meaningful glance at the picture frame and shattered glass on the wooden planks.

Sawyer bent down, picked up the frame and shook off the shards of glass. He stared at the picture again. There was a long scratch down the center. How poetic that a piece of broken glass had scored the picture—directly between him and Jeannette. With a short, bitter laugh, he put it down on the table, slumped in a chair and finished off his beer.

Meg took a sip of her wine and set the glass on the table. She went back in and reemerged with a broom and dustpan. Without a word, she swept up the glass and emptied the dustpan into a garbage can in the corner of the deck.

She sat in a chair next to Sawyer and took another sip. "Now, do you want to try to convince me again that there's nothing wrong?"

He looked at the picture and sighed. "The FBI thinks they've found Jeannette."

He slid his gaze toward his sister. "I don't know, Meg. How am I supposed to deal with the possibility that Jeannette's alive? That I'm still *married*?"

Meghan pulled her chair closer to Sawyer's. "Well, as for the latter, that would be easy enough to remedy, like Mom and Dad and I have been telling you to do."

He laughed, the sound harsh to his own ears. "Oh, well. It gets better. If it *is* her, she's married to someone else and has two kids."

"What?" The word was an incredulous croak. "How is that possible?"

"I don't know how legal it is, seeing she already *had* a husband, but that's what I've been told."

"You should've gotten the divorce," Meghan grumbled. "I won't say I told you so, but…"

"I could have, yeah. But would it really have made a difference? Legally perhaps, but you know how we both feel—" He stopped midsentence, recollecting what he'd been thinking before Meg arrived. That he no longer loved Jeannette that way.

He was falling in love with Shannon.

"What?" Megan asked.

Sawyer looked up.

"You were saying something and then stopped."

He drained his bottle and nodded at her glass. "With the discussion we're about to have, I'm going to top up your wine, and you'll either spend the night here, or I'll put you in a cab."

Meghan accompanied him to the kitchen and sat down at the counter. Sawyer topped up her glass with the white wine and—deciding to switch to wine, too—poured a red for himself. He took a bag of chocolate chip cookies from a cupboard before he sat down, too.

Meghan snatched a cookie and practically inhaled it. That made him smile, which was a bit of a miracle.

"I don't know what to say to you or how I can help," she said, as she licked crumbs from her fingers. "If nothing else, I'm a good listener."

"I'd almost reconciled myself to the idea that Jeannette was dead. Rationalized that she *had* to be, because why else wouldn't I have heard from her? If not for my sake—and let me tell you that hurts one hell of a lot—then for Dylan's." He rubbed at the ache behind his temples. "How can a woman leave her child? And we're not talking about any woman. We're talking about Jeannette, a woman with a bigger heart than almost anyone I've known."

Meghan reached for his hand and held it. "I wish I had answers for you, but I don't. I knew Jeannette nearly as long as you did. I can't imagine it either. And—I'm sorry to say this—we can't discount the possibility that she's the one who's responsible for Dylan's abduction."

Sawyer raised his glass and took a gulp of his wine. "Don't think that hasn't been on my mind. If she's capable of something like that, I never knew her at—" He snapped his mouth shut when he noticed Dylan standing in the doorway. His eyes were shiny and his lower lip trembled. Rufus stood protectively by his side.

Sawyer swallowed a curse and, giving Meg a pained look, rushed to his son.

"Hey, champ. What's wrong?" he said as he crouched down in front of Dylan. When he started to lift the boy into his arms, Rufus made a rumbling sound. The bond between the boy and the dog had solidified in no time.

"I heard you yelling. Why were you yelling at Aunt Meg?"

"Oh, hey, Dylan. I wasn't yelling at Aunt Meg." He cast a glance at her, and she came to join them.

"Your dad wasn't yelling at me." She wiped away the tears under Dylan's eyes with her thumb. "Honest. We were just having a discussion. We were maybe a little louder than normal, but your dad isn't upset with me."

Dylan sniffled and wiped his face with his

own hands. "You were talking about Mommy," he said with an aggrieved sigh.

Sawyer knew that the word *mommy* was an esoteric concept to Dylan. He'd been much too young when Jeannette disappeared to remember her. To Dylan, not having a mother was something that made him different from the other kids. "Yes, we were, but I wasn't yelling at her either. We just miss her."

Meg nodded. "Why don't you have a cookie with us?" Sawyer suggested. "You can give Rufus one, too. His doggy cookies, not yours," he amended.

"'Kay."

Sawyer carried Dylan over to the counter, gave him a cookie and poured him a glass of milk. He got a couple of dog biscuits from the cupboard and handed them to Dylan, who immediately passed them to the dog. Apparently satisfied that all was well in Dylan's world again, Rufus sat and his tail began to sweep the floor. Sawyer rolled his eyes at all the fur the swishing tail stirred up.

He and Meg chatted while Dylan finished his milk and cookies. When Dylan was done, he scooted off the stool to go back to his room with Rufus.

When they were alone again, they kept their voices low.

"As far as Jeannette goes, we'll have to wait and see what the FBI comes up with." He took a moment to study his sister. "Want to know something else?"

"There's more?"

"Oh, yeah."

"Sounds like we need more wine." This time Meghan topped up their glasses.

"I think I'm falling in love."

Meg had been lifting the glass to her lips, but she put it back down and tapped her ear. "I don't believe I heard you correctly."

"You heard me. Lousy timing. Not very smart, but we can't always help when we fall in love."

"Shannon?" Meghan asked quietly.

Sawyer had been staring at the wine swirling in his glass. He raised his head. "Yeah. I think I'm in love with her."

Meg leaned back. "Okay, I'm a scientist and I'm not blind. I wonder why I didn't see it before. But timing-wise? Oh, Sawyer. How are you going to deal with that on top of everything else—and how does she feel about you?"

"I'll have to deal with it the best I can because I don't have much of a say in it. Believe me, it wasn't premeditated. It just happened. As for how she feels about me... The fact that she's hung in despite the way I've run hot and cold says a lot. I don't know much more than that. If she does have feelings for me, this development with Jeannette has got to weigh on her, too." He turned grief-stricken eyes toward his sister. "How am I supposed to pursue a relationship with Shannon when I might still have a wife in Arizona?"

"Look, I understand about loyalty and lifelong commitments as much as you do. It's how we were raised. But whether she's alive or not, Jeannette is a ghost to you and Dylan. She's been out of your lives for almost Dylan's entire life and for half the time since you married her. If she *is* alive—and that's not definite yet, is it?"

"It's probable."

Meg nodded. "All the more reason you're going to have to prepare yourself for discovering why she left. Whatever it is, you won't be happy with the answer. And if she *is* behind Dylan's abduction... Well, I don't have words for that. Don't throw away what you might be able to have with Shannon. At least don't do it for the wrong reasons. The way Dylan talks about her, there's a special attachment between them, too. Sawyer, from what I've seen and heard, she'd make a wonderful mother."

Sawyer's reflexive and immediate reaction

was to argue that it was much too soon to think about that.

But he recalled the times he'd seen Shannon with Dylan. He couldn't deny that the thought had occurred to him, too.

SPECIAL AGENT LEARY knocked on the door of the sprawling bungalow in Wickenburg, Arizona. He stuck his hands in his pockets, and looked around and down the street as he and Special Agent Anne Wilson waited for the door to open. When he heard the snick of the lock, he faced forward again.

"May I help you?" asked the young woman with lovely features, soft blue eyes and rich, auburn hair hanging nearly to her waist.

"Special Agent Leary. FBI," he said, holding up his ID. "This is my colleague, Special Agent Anne Wilson," he added as she held out her badge, too.

The woman's mouth formed an O as she examined their badges. There was no question in Leary's mind that this was the woman they were seeking, but they had to go through the motions. "We're looking for Ms. Jeannette Evans."

She shook her head. "I'm sorry. You have the wrong address. I don't know anyone by that name."

Leary watched for the slightest indication of pretense but saw none. "Might I ask who you are?"

She looked mildly uncomfortable but answered with only a brief hesitation. "I'm Lilly Harris."

At the sound of high-pitched squeals, Lilly glanced over her shoulder. "Oh, I'm sorry. Can you excuse me for a minute?"

"Of course," Leary said.

They waited until she returned with a toddler in her arms. The little girl couldn't have been more than eighteen months and was dressed in a pretty pink dress, frilly white socks and white shoes. She had an arm wrapped around Lilly's neck.

Lilly gave the girl a warm smile before turning her attention back to them. "Special Agents, what can I do for you?"

"Would you mind if we came inside?"

Leary saw the flash of doubt tinged by the first show of irritation on her face, and she tightened her arm protectively around her daughter.

"Would you like to take a closer look at our IDs? I can give you a number to call for verification, if you wish."

Her brows furrowed, but she took a step back from the doorway. "No. That's fine."

She led them into a cozy, meticulously neat living room. Scattered around the room were pictures of her, the man Leary presumed to be her husband, the little girl she was holding and a baby. She gestured to the sofa. "Please have a seat while I settle Amie down for her nap. I won't be long." She returned a few minutes later. "I apologize for keeping you waiting. Would you like some coffee? Water maybe?"

"Water would be nice. Thank you," Leary responded.

"That would be great for me, too. Thanks," Wilson said.

When she returned with three glasses of ice water, Leary took one as did Wilson. "Is your husband home, Mrs. Harris?"

"Why do you ask?" There was the fleeting look of mistrust again, but it was gone as fast as it had appeared.

"Because if he is, it might be better if he joined us."

"No. I'm sorry. He's at work. Oh—" She pressed a hand to her mouth. "Does this have something to do with Ron? With my husband?"

"No, it doesn't," Wilson assured her.

Leary could see the pulse beating at her throat. She was nervous, but he didn't think it was because she was hiding anything. Heck, even the most upstanding people tended to get nervous when talking to the FBI. He started by asking her some general questions. About herself, her family and her life.

Her responses were consistent with the information he had from the background search they'd conducted. He got no sense of deceit. Just reserve.

"To confirm, the name Jeannette Evans doesn't sound familiar to you?" he asked, for the record.

"I've already told you, no."

"How about Jeannette Warner?" he asked, using her maiden name.

She seemed to consider again, then shook her head in confusion. "No. I'm sorry. I've answered your questions. Could you tell me what this is all about and why you're asking me about people I don't know?"

Her body language and the gleam in her eyes told Leary that she was beginning to understand. "Jeannette Evans went missing from San Diego three years ago."

"And what does that have to do with me? You think…" Her voice petered out.

"Jeannette Evans went missing in March of that year. March 28, to be exact."

The tumbler she'd been holding slipped out of her hand, spilling water all over the carpet.

"Oh, gosh," she exclaimed, as she reached for napkins and tried to mop up the water.

Leary took a handkerchief out of his pocket and gave it to her, while Wilson bent down to help.

When Lilly had done the best she could, she set the empty tumbler on the table and laced her fingers together. Her face had gone paper-white and her eyes looked impossibly large in that pale face.

"Can you tell us about your life before you got married? Maybe show us some pictures of yourself from the time you were a child to, say, your late twenties?" Leary prompted.

"No, I can't," she said, so softly he barely heard her. "I...I was in an accident. Three years ago. On March 28. I don't have any possessions or remember anything from before then."

Leary didn't believe in coincidence, and it appeared Jeannette/Lilly didn't, either. She was obviously intelligent and was able to figure out why they were there. He could see that she'd accepted the undeniable.

She *was* Jeannette Evans.

Taking turns, Leary and Wilson told her about her life as Jeannette, her husband and son, but withheld the information about Dylan's abduction. Leary's instincts said she wasn't feigning memory loss. If, in fact, she had no recollection of her past or her son, she wasn't responsible for the abduction. Still, he wasn't ready to categorically clear her yet, so he wanted to continue to observe her reactions.

"You…You think I'm Jeannette Evans?"

Leary read shock rather than disbelief on her face. He could understand why she wouldn't want it to be true, any more than Evans did. Here she was in a comfortable, by all indications, happy life with a husband and two kids—and yet she had another husband and kid in San Diego.

To answer her question, Wilson pulled out a picture of Jeannette that Sawyer had given them, taken a couple of weeks before her disappearance. The woman in the photograph had her long honey-blond hair drawn back and was wearing jeans and a sweater, but there was no denying it was the same person. She handed it to Lilly.

Her gaze locked on the photo and she covered her mouth with her free hand. "Oh, my God…" she murmured.

"Could you tell us what you know about your accident?" he asked gently.

"I was found in a ditch by the side of a road," she began haltingly. "A team of paramedics found me. Someone had called 911.

They took me to the hospital, and I was diagnosed with a severe concussion that resulted in memory loss. I had no identification. Nothing other than the clothes I was wearing. The local police were unable to determine who I was. There were no matches in the local or national missing persons' databases. I stayed in the hospital for a few days for monitoring. The doctors initially hoped that my memory, or at least some of it, would return.

"It didn't." She reached for her glass and remembered that it was empty.

"Let me get you some more water," Wilson offered.

"Yes. Thank you. Tap water is fine.

"I can't explain what it's like," she continued. "Not to know anyone, not to have family or a friend to turn to, not even to know yourself."

Tears shimmered in her eyes. When Wilson returned with her water, she drank deeply.

"The one positive thing was that I met my husband while I was in the hospital. Ronald is a staff pediatrician."

A weak smile softened her face. "Ronald was incredibly kind to me. He arranged for me to stay with his mother after I left the hospital. With no identity, no money, I wouldn't have known what to do otherwise. His mother is a teacher and she helped me get a job as a teacher's assistant at the school where she works. Well, one thing led to another, and Ron and I fell in love, married six months later and the kids followed shortly after. Ron is a bit older than I am, and he was keen to get started on a family." Her smile firmed. "He's a wonderful husband and father."

Leary was convinced that none of it was an act. She really didn't have any recollection of her life from before she was found in the ditch. That was easily verifiable through hospital records. Her husband wouldn't have been involved in her care, so there'd be no question of falsified reports.

"How did you end up with the name Lilly?" he asked out of curiosity.

"Oh, that was Ron, too. He hired a lawyer and instructed him to do whatever was required to establish an identity for me. And the name? After I met Ron, he brought me flowers every day at the hospital." She smiled again, and Leary understood how easy it would be for someone to fall in love with her. "Lilies were my favorite."

He had a few more questions before turning it over to Wilson.

"Mrs. Ev...ah, Mrs. Harris, would you like

to phone your husband?" Wilson asked. "I imagine you'd like to talk to him."

Lilly grasped on to that, almost like a life-line. "Yes. Yes, I would like to phone him."

She left to make the call. When she returned, she was still pale and appeared shaky. If she was everything she seemed to be, Leary realized they'd just pulled the rug right out from under her, leaving nothing below but a gaping abyss. "We can wait with you until he gets here, if that would help," he suggested.

They left forty minutes later, after Ronald Harris got home.

They'd found Jeannette Evans. She couldn't have been responsible for her son's abduction, Leary was quite certain. She would've had to be an Oscar-worthy actress to fake the amnesia and the reaction to discovering who she was.

They were back to square one.

CHAPTER EIGHTEEN

ON THEIR RETURN from Arizona, Special Agents Leary and Wilson went directly to Sawyer's home to advise him that they'd found Jeannette. He was thankful Shannon had prepared him for the possibility that Jeannette was alive. The fact that she had no recollection of their life together was another shock he had to absorb. They assured him they didn't consider her a suspect, but asked him not to contact her yet, because of the ongoing investigation.

As far as investigations went, the SDPD and FBI were again actively pursuing the case of Jeannette Evans's disappearance, but now as a result of abduction.

Despite having to grapple with the bombshell that Jeannette was alive, Sawyer was gradually easing back into a normal life. He returned to work and Dylan was back in day care during the mornings. Sawyer's mother was again watching him in the afternoons. Sawyer was also encouraged by the reports he was receiving from Dylan's therapist about the progress his son was making with his recovery.

As he began to come to terms with the fact that Jeannette was alive, he thought more and more about the discussion he'd had with Meghan the day he'd found out. He had to acknowledge that he was falling in love with Shannon.

He'd have to tell her at some point, but he wanted his life to be a *little* more normal before he told her how he felt. He couldn't blame her if she was skeptical about it. He wanted to make sure that when he told her, she understood he meant it. That it wasn't just an aberration caused by the trauma they'd experienced.

Although he was glad to be back at work, he was still playing catch-up. The downside of being back was that he missed spending time with Dylan. He welcomed the occasional day off without lectures, and took those opportunities, when he could, to stay home with his son.

They'd gone to the zoo that morning and Dylan had had a great time. Now Sawyer was having a coffee in the backyard, watching Dylan play with Rufus. His son's giggles as he rolled over the big dog made Sawyer grin. Dylan's therapist agreed that Rufus was having a huge positive impact on Dylan's recovery.

Something else he owed thanks to Shannon for.

When Sawyer's cell phone rang, he glanced at the display. His assistant's name and number appeared on the screen.

"Hi, Miranda. What's up?"

"Sawyer, I'm sorry to bother you, but with all the adjustments we've had to make to your schedule, I'm afraid I messed up. I forgot to let you know about a meeting."

"Don't worry about it. There's been a lot going on. We'll work it out."

"Except the meeting is this afternoon. In just under two hours."

Sawyer wanted to groan. The last thing he felt like doing was going to work today. "Can you reschedule?"

"I tried, but no. The meeting's with the new lawyer in the San Diego County District Attorney's office."

"Who?" Sawyer drew a blank.

"Alex Boyden. You told the district attorney when you last spoke to him that you'd be happy to mentor Alex."

"Oh, right. Thanks for reminding me. And why can't you reschedule?"

"I called the DA's office as soon as I noticed my mistake. Apparently Alex is out of the office at a meeting and would leave right from there. When I asked for her cell number, they said Alex's phone had died and a new one was on order. They tried calling the office where the meeting was. The meeting ended early and Alex had already left. Look, I'm sorry and it's my fault. I'll apologize profusely to Alex and reschedule the meeting for some time next week. How does that sound?"

Sawyer couldn't help smiling again as he watched Rufus roll onto his back, paws flailing in the air, inviting Dylan to rub his belly. He remembered what the DA had said about the new hotshot assistant DA, and why he wanted Sawyer to mentor her. Missing their first meeting would not be a good example. "My parents left for La Jolla this morning for a long weekend and Meg's at work. Let me see if I can get someone to watch Dylan. If so, I'll head right in. I might be late but that's better than being a no-show." He remembered it was Shannon's day off and she was running errands for her mother. "Give me a few minutes and I'll call you back."

SEEING SAWYER'S NAME and number on the display screen of her phone, Shannon felt a little flutter in her heart as she answered and they exchanged greetings. They had plans to spend the evening together with Dylan, and she was looking forward to seeing them both.

"Shannon, since you're not working today, would you be able to help me out this afternoon?" Sawyer asked.

"Sure, if I can."

"Miranda, my assistant, just called. She mixed up some dates in my schedule. I have to get to work for a meeting. I tried Meghan, but she can't leave the lab and my parents are gone for a few days. If you're free, would you mind watching Dylan for me?"

"I'd be happy to. When do you need me?"

"As soon as you can get over here."

She glanced at her watch. "I'm not far from your house right now. I can be there in fifteen minutes."

"Great! That's great. I'm going to take a quick shower to wash off any residual animal scents I might've picked up while we were at the zoo this morning. I'll leave a key for you under the flowerpot. Come on in when you get here. Dylan's excited about spending the afternoon with you. Hey," he said as she was about to hang up. "Thanks, Shannon. This is a huge help. I'll make dinner for us when I get back."

"Sounds good."

Shannon was glad she'd left Darwin at home. She didn't want any problems arising between Rufus and Darwin while she was alone with Dylan. Once Sawyer returned, she'd drive back home to feed and walk Darwin before dinner.

She pulled into Sawyer's driveway in under fifteen minutes, found the key and let herself into his house.

SAWYER WAS RUBBING his wet hair with a towel when he walked out of his bedroom, wearing dress pants, a white shirt and a sports jacket. He strode down the hall toward the living room—and stopped dead in his tracks.

Dylan was kneeling by the coffee table, a coloring book open in front of him. He had a crayon in his hand. The tip of his tongue was caught between his teeth, a sure sign that he was concentrating. Shannon sat cross-legged at the end of the table, her back to him. Her shorts were hiked up and her slim legs glowed with her light tan. She was leaning toward Dylan and his drawing. Rufus lay stretched out on the carpet next to them, snoring softly.

When Dylan finished what he was doing and looked up at Shannon expectantly, she gave him an encouraging rub on the back.

"That's terrific!" she told him, and Sawyer was ecstatic seeing the genuine, carefree smile that spread across his son's face. He would've fallen in love with Shannon for that alone. For the way she'd made Dylan smile, when these days those smiles were still few and far between.

"What about the pony's mane? What color are you going to use?" she asked him.

Dylan pulled at his lower lip contemplatively, as he surveyed his collection of crayons. "This one!" He picked up a yellow one and held it out to show her.

"Perfect! Do you know what color mane he'll have if you use that crayon?"

Dylan thought about it for a moment. "He'll have a blond mane."

"That's right. Just a little darker than the color of your hair," she said and gave a strand of his hair a light tug. "And he'll look very handsome."

Dylan concentrated on his coloring again, and Shannon gave him her undivided attention.

When he declared that he was finished, Shannon clapped her hands. "You did such a nice job. Wait until your dad sees it."

"Thanks for helping me," Dylan said, hugging Shannon. As she turned to wrap her arms around Dylan, her gaze met Sawyer's over the top of his son's head.

Not wanting to say anything to break the

magic of the moment, he smiled at her, passed the towel from his right hand to his left and tapped his hand over his heart, trying to convey how much what she was doing meant to him.

When Dylan pulled back, Shannon pointed to Sawyer. "There's your dad now. Why don't you show him your picture?"

"What have you got there?" Sawyer asked, as he strolled over to them.

Dylan excitedly showed Sawyer not only the picture he'd just finished coloring but a couple of others, too.

"Shannon helped me," he said and reached for her hand.

Sawyer couldn't deny it anymore. He knew he'd been falling in love with Shannon. But now? It was a done deal.

Sawyer cleared his throat. "I'd better get going."

He said goodbye to Dylan and they left him coloring while Shannon walked him to his Range Rover.

"Thanks again for doing this," he said, and gave her a quick kiss before he climbed into the SUV.

SMILING, SHANNON WAVED as she watched Sawyer back out of his driveway. When she turned to the house, her smile widened. Dylan was standing in the doorway, his arm slung around Rufus.

"Hey, Dylan," she said as she walked up the steps to the front door. "I brought you guys something." She reached into her handbag, which she'd left in the hall.

"What is it?" Dylan asked, bouncing on the toes of his sneakers.

Shannon handed him the red, jumbo-size Kong. Rufus immediately leaned closer to sniff it. Dylan stuck a finger in the opening at one end. "It has a hole in the middle."

"Yes. You can slide a rope through there," she said, pointing to the hole. "And if you tie it, you can throw it farther. Or, you can put treats in it. We use these to train police dogs."

Dylan looked up at her with wide eyes. "This is what you used to train Darwin?"

"Yup! But it's a toy, too. That's why the dogs do what we ask, because they know they'll get to play later. Why don't we go to the backyard and you can try it with Rufus?"

"'Kay!"

She locked the front door and they walked through the house, Rufus scampering along beside them. She didn't know if she'd fallen more in love with the little boy or his father, but there was no question that her heart was invested in both. It wasn't a hardship to spend time with Dylan. Not in the least.

"Dylan, would you like some apple juice?" she asked when they got to the kitchen.

"Yes, please."

Shannon filled his sippy cup and gave it to him. He took a drink and handed it back to her. "Thanks. Can I play with Rufus now?"

"Sure." She opened the door to the backyard and Rufus darted out.

She called Rufus back and gestured for him to sit. "Throw the Kong for him and let's see if he'll fetch it and bring it back to you."

She stood back to watch. Dylan's first attempt didn't go more than a couple of feet, but Rufus was a good sport about it. He retrieved the Kong and dropped it at Dylan's feet. Assuming a sitting position, the dog waited patiently, tongue lolling, until Dylan threw the Kong again. This time, Dylan sent it flying. The kid had a good arm, especially for his age. With a happy woof, Rufus tore after it, trotted back to Dylan and spat the toy at his feet.

"Look at that!" Dylan squealed. "I taught Rufus how to fetch."

"You sure did!"

Shannon sat on a deck chair and watched the boy play with the dog. She couldn't imagine a kid not having a dog. The joy Rufus brought

Dylan was worth more than all the kibble the dog would eat in his lifetime.

She smirked a little, remembering Sawyer hadn't been all that keen on getting a dog at first. But when he'd realized how much it meant to Dylan, there'd been no hesitation. He did what he considered best for his son. And they'd ended up with a *big* dog, not the small one Sawyer had been determined to get.

Yes, he was a good father. A good person.

And he'd stolen her heart.

She sat forward in her deck chair, narrowing her eyes. Dylan had thrown the Kong into the sandbox, and Rufus dived in after it.

She sensed what was going to happen before it did. At the sound of Rufus's high-pitched screams, she shot out of the chair and ran over to where the dog had skidded in Dylan's sandbox. Sand coated Rufus's face and had obviously gotten in his eyes. He was squealing and pawing at them.

Seeing the dog in distress, Dylan burst into tears. "Fix him. Fix Rufus!" he wailed.

"I will. I just need to take him into the kitchen and flush out his eyes with water."

"Is Rufus going to be okay?"

Dylan's hysterics were agitating Rufus even further. "Dylan, calm down please. Let's get Rufus inside and I'll take care of him."

She grabbed the whining dog by his collar and had to nearly drag him up the four steps to the deck and in through the kitchen door. Time was critical because she didn't want the particles of sand to scratch his cornea, nor did she want him to harm himself with his insistent attempts to scratch at his eyes.

Shannon fought the eighty-pound dog, who didn't want to budge.

She got the dog in and let the water run to warm it up before she started to flush his eyes. It must have helped, because his whining turned into quiet whimpers, and even those gradually subsided.

"Okay. You're okay. You're going to be just fine," she told the dog, in soothing tones. His face was sopping wet, but she was fairly confident that disaster had been averted. She turned the water off so Dylan could hear her. "Dylan, would you please get me…" Her voice trailed off as she looked around the kitchen, empty except for her and Rufus.

The patio door was still open, but she no longer heard Dylan crying.

"Wait," she instructed Rufus, reinforcing her command with a hand signal as she rushed to the doorway.

The backyard was empty, too, the wooden gate swinging on its hinges.

The adrenaline surge nearly brought her to her knees. The back gate had definitely been latched when they'd first come out.

And the latch was too high for Dylan to reach.

"Dylan?" she shouted, as she ran to the gate and through it. Scanning the street in both directions, she saw no sign of the boy.

She berated herself for having left Darwin at home. The dog would've been able to locate Dylan in no time, since he'd been gone for only a couple of minutes at most.

She dashed back into the kitchen and got her cell phone from her handbag. "Wait, Rufus. Wait," she said, and closed the door behind her as she hurried out to the patio.

She ran down the stairs and sprinted to the gate. Looking frantically up and down the street but there was no Dylan anywhere. She stepped out onto the sidewalk. She shouted for Dylan again, as loudly as she could.

She paused, listened and tried again. When Sawyer's neighbor came out of her house, Shannon quickly explained what had happened, and the neighbor thankfully offered to drive up and down the street on the off chance that Dylan had simply wandered away.

Shannon took another frantic look around the backyard, hoping that maybe Dylan had hidden somewhere, afraid he'd get into trouble because Rufus was hurt.

No. The backyard was empty and silent. Dylan's toys were right where they'd been, but the little boy was not.

Damn, damn, damn.

She had to call Sawyer.

First, she'd call Logan. What were the odds of Dylan having been abducted again? But then, what were the odds of him being able to unlatch the gate and getting out? She was tempted to go back into the house and search it, but that made no sense. The open latch on the gate told her Dylan had exited that way. Plus, she'd been in the kitchen and would've seen him if he'd gone inside, despite her preoccupation with Rufus.

Logan assured her that Cal would be there with Scout in half an hour.

Half an hour?

How far could a little boy get in half an hour, even if he was wandering around on his own? And this time he had shoes on.

What about Joey?

She remembered that Joey the kangaroo had been with Dylan when he was abducted. Shannon wasn't sure why, but she needed to know if Joey was with him now.

The cold dread intensified when she found

Joey perched in the middle of Dylan's bed. Was that good news or bad?

Would Dylan have wandered off on his own without his beloved Joey?

Without Darwin, there wasn't much she could do but wait for Cal and pray that Dylan would come back on his own, as unlikely as she considered that to be.

She'd procrastinated enough.

She had to call Sawyer.

SAWYER MADE GOOD time and arrived at Thomas Jefferson School of Law before Alex Boyden did. It gave him a chance to review Alex's resume. He remembered the brief discussion he'd had with the DA about the new hire. Top marks, brilliant, articulate, driven. He remembered that the DA had said that if there was a negative, it was that she was too self-assured. Alex's heart was in the right place as she could've gotten a job with any of the top law firms, but she'd chosen the DA's office. She obviously wanted to make a difference. Sawyer had to applaud that. After all, that was what had motivated him to work for the DA's office, too.

Alex's résumé was impressive, both professionally and as far as volunteer work went.

Miranda tapped on his doorframe and he glanced up.

"Alex Boyden is here to see you. Are you all set?"

"Sure. Yeah. I just finished reviewing her résumé."

Miranda smiled. "Great. I'll bring Alex right in."

Might as well look professional for the DA's new hotshot prosecutor, Sawyer thought. He shrugged into his sports jacket, as Miranda reentered his office. "Sawyer, I'd like to introduce you to Alex Boyden."

In addition to being intelligent, Alex was very attractive. Dense ebony hair cascading down past her shoulders and a thick fringe of bangs riding just above her eyebrows. Smooth, brown skin and a wide, generous mouth. Intense near-black eyes that might cause a defendant to squirm. She had a shapely physique that was obvious despite the professional pantsuit. Sawyer went over, thanked Miranda and extended a hand to Alex. "It's a pleasure to meet you. Congratulations on your appointment."

From the self-confident smile on her face, he surmised the DA had called her overconfidence correctly. Sawyer could see it in her demeanor, the sparkle in her eyes and the firmness of her handshake.

"Thank you," she said. "I understand you're the best the DA's office has had to date."

Sawyer didn't miss the emphasis on *to date*. "Well, I don't know about that, but thanks."

"I intend to change that," she said.

Sawyer's laugher burst out. Yeah, the self-confidence was definitely there. Some might call it arrogance, but she said it so smoothly, almost as if joking, that he couldn't take offense. "I bet you will," he said, as he gestured toward his meeting table.

"I need your help to do it, though," she said, inclining her head. "I appreciate your meeting with me."

"My pleasure," he said and realized he meant it. There was some humility in her, after all.

By the time Sawyer finished his meeting with Alex, he was even more impressed. True, she had an abundance of confidence, but it wasn't without cause. She was smart, quick to comprehend and eager to learn. He'd agreed to act as a mentor for her, but when she suggested they discuss it over drinks, he drew the line. Mentor, yes. A personal relationship, absolutely not. It was highly inappropriate, for one thing. Besides, there was only one woman he was interested in.

He checked his watch. Time to head home. He didn't want to miss a moment with Dylan... and Shannon.

As he was climbing into his Range Rover, his cell phone rang. He felt real pleasure when he saw Shannon's name and number on the call display.

"I'm on my way now," he said when he answered the phone. "I'm looking forward to seeing you."

"Sawyer, are you driving?"

"No. Not yet. I was about to start the engine. Why?"

"Wait. I don't know how to tell you this, other than straight out. Dylan is missing."

"*Missing*? What do you mean missing?"

CHAPTER NINETEEN

WHEN SHANNON REACHED Sawyer on his cell phone and told him what had happened, she'd heard him suck in his breath, followed by a lengthy silence.

"I'll be home as soon as I can. I'm leaving right now."

Sawyer's voice had sounded cold. Accusatory?

And why shouldn't it? Dylan was missing a second time. But *this* time, it was on her watch.

She called Cal next. Holding back the tears with enormous effort, she explained to him what had happened and asked how long he'd be.

"I'm fifteen minutes out," he told her.

Walking through the gate again, she took another long look at both ends of the street.

Nothing.

All she could do was wait.

Cal and Scout arrived first, along with Logan. They immediately started the search for Dylan. Sawyer arrived shortly after.

His rage was palpable, and Shannon took it personally. It exacerbated the self-reproach she was already feeling.

"Why was Dylan alone outside?" he asked.

"I… It was only a moment. I thought he followed me in. Rufus needed—"

"Are you saying it was because of the dog that this happened? The dog was more important than my son?"

"I—"

Sawyer shoved his hair back with both hands in an agitated motion. "Sorry. That was out of line." When he noticed Rufus cowering in the corner of the room, he squatted down and reassured him, too.

"The stats… The likelihood of a child being abducted a second time is—" Shannon stammered.

"This is *my son* we're talking about." He cut her off, but there was no heat in his voice. Only pain and distress. "It hardly matters to me what the statistics are."

He slumped heavily into a chair and cradled his head in his hands. When he heard the knock shortly after, he sprang up again. He was at the door in a heartbeat, yanking it open. Shannon rose, too, and could see that it was Cal and Logan. Looking at their faces, she knew the answer before Sawyer could ask the question.

"Did you find Dylan? Do you have anything?"

Logan shook his head. "I'm sorry. Can we come in?"

Without a word, Sawyer turned and strode away, leaving the door open for the men to follow.

Shannon caught Logan's questioning look and gave a slight shake of her head to indicate both that Sawyer wasn't doing well, and there'd been no contact from anyone about Dylan.

"Can we please sit and talk?" Logan asked Sawyer. "Detective Bigelow and Special Agent Leary are on their way."

At the next knock, Shannon got up, and Sawyer stayed with Logan and Cal. When she opened the door, Meghan stood in front of her, eyes red-rimmed and swollen, skin blotchy, her lower lip trembling. Shannon had only known Meg to be calm and collected and seeing her obvious distress made the grief well up inside her, too. She wasn't sure who initiated it, but suddenly they had their arms wrapped around each other, rocking gently.

"I can guess how Sawyer is. How are you holding up?" Meg asked, once they'd both stepped back.

She appreciated that someone would ask about *her*, especially under the circumstances, and sighed. "I'm not the one to worry about right now, but thanks. Come in."

After all the questions had been asked, the law enforcement officers excused themselves and headed back to the division, except Cal, who went out to search again. Shannon swung by her home to pick up Darwin, in case they were needed. She left him in his kennel at the division and met the others in the conference room.

"How could this have happened?" Bigelow demanded.

Shannon tried to be thankful for small mercies, in that he didn't ask how *she* could've let it happen. Sawyer hadn't used those words, either—to her great amazement and relief—but she knew everyone there *had* to be thinking it was her fault.

It was all she could think about.

But who would've expected Dylan to be abducted again? "I was just inside for a minute when he disappeared," she said feebly for the umpteenth time. "The gate was latched, the…"

"We've been through all that. What I want to know is—" Bigelow cut himself off in midsentence when Cal walked in. "Anything?" he asked.

Cal shook his head. "No. The boy was put

in a vehicle maybe twenty yards from the gate. The vehicle drove down the road to Hacienda Drive and turned left. We followed the scent to the freeway ramp." Looking tired and defeated, Cal sank into a chair. "You know as well as I do that our chances of following the trail on a freeway are negligible."

"Are there any surveillance cameras along the route?" Shannon asked, desperate to find any clue.

"We're checking," Logan replied.

The door opened again and FBI Special Agents Leary and Wilson walked in.

Most of those in the room had already attended a briefing about their interview with Jeannette Evans—now Lilly Harris—and the subsequent investigation. "I'll summarize it again, in view of the second abduction," Bigelow suggested.

"The same evening that she disappeared from her health club over three years ago, she was found in a ditch by the side of a road in Arizona. 911 had been alerted from a prepaid cell phone that was purchased from a convenience store farther down the freeway. It had been paid for with cash. That was the only call made from the phone, and all they'd been able to get from the video footage of the store's cameras was that it was bought by a woman.

The external camera was inoperable, so they didn't get anything on the vehicle." Leary ran through the rest of what they'd learned from Lilly Harris. "She has no recollection of anything that preceded waking up in the hospital," Leary concluded. "She has no knowledge of how she got there. No memory of Evans or her son, even when we showed her the pictures."

"How did she react to learning that she has another husband and a child?" Shannon asked before she could stop herself.

Anne Wilson shrugged. "Much as you'd expect. We didn't reveal their identities, but showed her pictures to see if we could jog her memory." She paused. "It couldn't have been an easy discussion with her husband. Husband number two, that is. He seems to be a smart and astute person, and they appear to be genuinely in love. I hope they'll be able to work through this."

Leary looked around the room. "Bottom line? Based on our interview with Harris, my personal judgment and factoring in the time of the first abduction, I don't believe she was involved. Nor do I suspect she would've been behind the second abduction. Finally, we showed her picture to Juanita Sanchez and she didn't recognize her. Can we move on?"

When no one objected, he turned to Shannon. His initial questions were similar to Logan's. There was nothing in his demeanor that implied he was blaming her. But it didn't matter to Shannon, because she was too busy blaming herself.

When they finished the meeting, she checked her personal cell phone, hoping and dreading in equal measure that Sawyer had called or texted her.

There was no call. No text.

Regret? Relief?

She was so shaken and conflicted, she was unsure of what she was feeling.

When she let Darwin out of his pen, quickly ascertaining that they were alone in the kennel area, she sank to her knees and wrapped her arms around the dog. He rested his head on her shoulder and leaned against her, making gentle whining noises. It was as if Darwin was giving her a hug back.

When she felt steadier, she rose. With Darwin at her heels, she left the division and headed to her Explorer.

On the drive home, she decided it was up to her to call Sawyer, regardless of how awkward that would be. She'd do that after she walked Darwin.

She wouldn't take the coward's way out by avoiding him.

By the time she parked in her driveway, she'd already changed her mind.

Not about taking the initiative, but her method of contact. She needed to have the discussion in person.

She fed and walked Darwin, chugged down a Coke and ate an apple. Not much for dinner, but her stomach would likely have revolted if she tried to force more. She changed into a pair of khakis and a light blue sweater. Finally, she gave Darwin a chew toy to keep him occupied while she was gone. It was already late evening, but she didn't doubt for an instant that Sawyer would be up.

When Shannon pulled up in front of Sawyer's house, she wished she'd called first. His driveway was full of cars. She recognized Bigelow's and Leary's police-issue vehicles. The other two belonged to Sawyer's sister and parents. He must've called them and told them what had happened, and they'd driven straight back from La Jolla. As for Bigelow and Leary, she should've realized they'd come straight over here after the briefing.

It was Meghan who opened the door and led her into the living room. Everyone looked at her, but it was Sawyer's gaze she held.

His expression was inscrutable.

CHAPTER TWENTY

SAWYER STARED AT Detective Bigelow. He couldn't believe they had no leads and nothing to go on. After he'd heard that, it was as if Bigelow was speaking in a foreign language. Or through some sort of dense liquid. He could see his mouth move, hear him, but it was beyond him to comprehend. He'd wanted his parents there and his sister. Shannon, too, and he was relieved when she showed up because he hadn't had a chance to call her. What had happened wasn't her fault, but he hadn't been rational and couldn't contain his despair when he'd first learned about it.

Sawyer turned frantic, bewildered eyes on those in the room, wanting to hear something that would give him hope.

All he saw on their faces was the same range of emotions that were churning inside him, threatening to tear him apart. He groped blindly for his mother's hand. His father, on his other side, placed a shaking arm around his shoulders.

Sawyer desperately wanted what he'd heard not to be true. Once again, they had no leads in the search for his son or his son's abductors. His emotions were in such turmoil, he could barely function. The only thing that kept him going was the belief that they *would* find Dylan again.

He focused on something he could control. He wanted to see Jeannette. He rationalized that he wanted to look into her eyes and satisfy himself that she had nothing to do with this. And she *was* Dylan's mother, whether she remembered him or not. The FBI hadn't told her yet what had happened to Dylan—either the first abduction or what happened today—but she needed to know. If they wouldn't tell her, he would. He'd reconciled himself to the fact that his feelings for Jeannette were not what they'd once been. Knowing that she had amnesia changed the grief and anger he'd been living with to a different kind of sadness. It softened the blow of her desertion—if that was what it had been. How she'd ended up in that ditch in Arizona was still a mystery. He'd been elated to learn that she was alive, for her own sake and for Dylan's.

And Shannon? If not for all the other people in the room, he would've wanted to lose himself in her arms.

Oddly, it was the silence when the detective stopped speaking that drew Sawyer's attention back to him.

"When can I see her?" he asked, his voice hoarse and unfamiliar to him.

"Sorry?" Bigelow asked.

"When can I see my wife?"

A noise—more of a gasp—had him turning to Shannon, and from the look in her eyes, he knew she was hurting, too. But he needed to see Jeannette, needed to do it to bring some form of closure.

Bigelow glanced at Leary who nodded almost imperceptibly. "She said she'd be willing to meet with you."

Sawyer ran his tongue over parchment-dry lips. "Okay. Good."

"But she insisted that her husband be there with her."

"*I'm* her husband!" Sawyer met Shannon's gaze again and saw the shimmer of tears and flinched. He hadn't meant *husband* in an emotional sense; he'd meant legally. But Jeannette had another husband and two children now. Sawyer got to his feet. Shoving his fists in his pants pockets, he stalked to the window and stared out.

He was going to lose his mind. He was sure of it. He was surprised he hadn't already.

Parents were supposed to protect their children. Keep them safe. And now he'd failed to do that for Dylan. *Twice!* It seemed he'd failed his wife, too, in that regard.

He stalked back to stand in front of the detective.

"I want to see Jeannette, whatever her conditions."

When his eyes met Shannon's, he could see the conflict there—and the pain. He understood that she didn't know where this left them. Heck, *he* didn't either. And he'd admitted to himself that he'd fallen in love with her. Perhaps against his better judgment, given the situation, but he hadn't been able to help himself.

He had to deal with his past and present before he could think of the future.

He wrenched his gaze away, turned it on Bigelow again.

"Arrange the meeting, please. As for finding Dylan, what's the plan?"

After Bigelow and Leary went through all the same points they'd discussed earlier, Shannon left Sawyer's home, along with everyone else. Sawyer understood the unasked question in the deep-blue pool of her eyes, but he couldn't do anything about it right then. He was completely drained and empty. He had nothing left to give. Not to her. Not to his family.

The police had no clear plan, as far as finding Dylan was concerned, and he felt entirely useless. There was nothing he could do other than assure himself that Jeannette didn't have anything to do with the kidnapping.

Bigelow and Leary were considering everyone they'd already looked at and eliminated. Futile maybe, but that's all they had. It would probably mean more questions for him, too. As they were leaving, he was asked to think hard about whether there was anyone else they hadn't yet considered.

Regardless of how many possibilities he pondered, he kept returning to the same conclusion. It had to be someone he'd put in jail, most likely for a long time. The cops had debated again whether it could have been a random abduction, but the chances of that were negligible, and even more so, factoring in the second abduction.

It had to be about him. The self-reproach associated with that cut through him like a scorching hot blade.

Sawyer pulled a soda out of the fridge and popped it open. He took a long drink, then rolled the cold can across his burning forehead.

And thought of Jeannette. Alive?

He'd searched his heart. His soul.

He was no longer in love with her. Oh, sure, he'd always *love* her—assuming she didn't have anything to do with Dylan's abduction—because she was the mother of his child. But not with the all-consuming love he'd had for her when they were together.

Shannon, on the other hand... He *was* in love with Shannon.

He sat on the couch and laid his head back against the cushion. What kind of father was he? What kind of human being? Thinking of himself during a time of crisis. Thinking about a personal relationship when he didn't know where his son was or what he was experiencing.

He had to take comfort in knowing that Dylan hadn't been harmed the first time.

He *had* to trust that he wouldn't be this time, either. He thought about calling Shannon, but he struggled with what to say to her. He had to take one step at a time.

He had to trust that the police were doing everything they could, and—if Bigelow came through as he'd promised—Sawyer would fly to Arizona as soon as possible to see Jeannette.

BIGELOW HAD ARRANGED the meeting. At Jeannette's request, Sawyer was meeting her and her husband at a quiet restaurant not far from her home.

Because of the flight Sawyer had booked, he'd arrived nearly half an hour early. Then, he didn't know what to do with himself. Suddenly, he couldn't remember what Jeannette looked like. Her hair had been a dark blond. He'd been told that now it was a reddish brown. But her eyes? Were they blue or gray? Were they almond-shaped?

Had he finally lost his mind?

He yanked out his iPhone and almost manically scrolled through his pictures.

Did he have pictures going three years back? Had he had the same phone?

He reached for his glass of water and drained it.

When he came across a series of shots of Jeannette, Dylan and him on the beach at El Coronado, he exhaled heavily.

And the memories came flooding back. Vivid and intense.

Jeannette sitting on their blanket on the sand, laughing up at him, Dylan held tenderly against her chest. She looked happy. And in love. He ran a finger across the screen. Down her cheek.

He remembered the love he'd felt for her, a faint echo now. A memory.

The loss saddened him.

He closed his eyes and tried to steady his breathing.

When he opened his eyes again and saw Jeannette walking toward him, he thought he was imagining her.

Somehow, she looked the same but different. How was that possible?

The same long, straight hair. The lithe build. Her eyes. They were blue-gray.

But, as he already knew, her hair was a different color and parted on the wrong side. And she was wearing lipstick…and high heels. Something she'd rarely done when they were married.

Her face was expressionless, but her movements were stilted. Tense.

His attention shifted to the man walking behind her. He had a proprietary hand on her elbow.

Sawyer felt a stab of jealousy. Unreasonable though it was, it shot through him. Then he read a similar emotion on the other man's face.

He wanted a confrontation, did he? Immediately, Sawyer felt contrite. Regardless of how it had happened, Jeannette was no longer his wife.

And the man? How must he feel learning

that his wife had another, earlier husband and a child he hadn't known about?

Detective Bigelow had told him the man's name was Ronald.

Sawyer rose as they reached the table.

What did you do when you met your wife three years later? Your wife who was now a different person… Hug her? Shake her hand?

He settled on the latter.

He'd wondered what he'd feel when she laid her hand in his.

Regret. That was it. For what was and what could have been.

Ronald's hand, when he shook it, was rigid, stiff. Was he threatened by Sawyer? He had no reason to be. He was Jeannette's present; Sawyer was her past.

Should he make small talk? he wondered. He was at a loss as to how to start. It felt awkward all around.

"This is awkward." Jeannette voiced his thought. "I'm sorry about that." Her voice broke and her husband—Ron, he'd said, not Ronald—slid a protective arm around her shoulders. She glanced at him gratefully.

They loved each other, Sawyer realized. The look that passed between them left no doubt. She'd moved on, and that simple gesture of her husband's told him he cared about her.

When the waitress stopped by, they ordered coffees, as well.

"Your son…um, our son, is missing?" she said, once they were alone again, with a quaver in her voice. "The FBI special agents didn't tell me that when we met, but the detective who called me about meeting you said he thought I should know."

"Yes."

"He said that he's been abducted again. I'm not sure how that could happen, but…I'm so sorry…"

"Thank you." Sawyer didn't know what else to say. It felt as if he was discussing Dylan's abduction with a sympathetic stranger.

"Do you…" She turned to her husband, and he squeezed her shoulder. She looked back at Sawyer. "Do you have a picture of him? Of Dylan? The FBI agents showed me one, but they didn't leave it with me."

"Of course." Sawyer ached for her as he got his phone again. The picture of the three of them on the beach was still on the screen.

No. That wasn't right, to show her a picture of them together. He scrolled through his photographs and found a recent one of Dylan. He offered her the phone.

She took it in both hands and stared at the picture. Ron peered at it, too. Her eyes shone when she passed the phone back to Sawyer with trembling hands.

"He's a beautiful boy. He looks happy."

"He is," Sawyer said, feeling thoroughly discomfited. "He was. Happy, that is…before…"

She nodded and clasped her husband's hand.

Sawyer took a quick look at Dylan's picture before he stuck his phone back in his pocket. "I was told a little about you, but I'd like to hear your side of it. Of what happened," he said.

Jeannette—Lilly, he reminded himself that he had to think of her as Lilly now—went on to explain what Sawyer had mostly known. But she made it personal and his heart broke for her, for them…and for what they'd lost, he and Jeannette. When she *was* Jeannette.

"I had some bruises and abrasions, but the worst of it was the memory loss. At first, the doctors thought it would come back."

"Lilly…" Ron said gently. "You don't have to do this."

She nodded slowly. "Yes. Yes, I do." She held Sawyer's gaze. "It's the least I can do."

"Thank you," Sawyer said again.

"I have permanent memory loss. The doctors ran test after test and concluded that the chances of regaining my memory are virtually nonexistent. Ron works at the hospital." She sent him a smile. "He was there for me every step of the way. We fell in love. I'm sorry if that hurts you, but that's what happened. I had no recollection of you or of anything prior to my accident. Ron proposed to me almost six months after I got out of the hospital." She smiled at her husband warmly. "I accepted, on one condition."

Sawyer raised an eyebrow.

Ron picked up the story. "The condition was that we not get married for another six months. As unlikely as it was, she wanted to take that time to see if her memory would return. We tried to do everything we could to find out who Lilly was and where she'd come from. The police checked the missing persons' databases. The fact that, unknown to us, she'd crossed state boundaries worked against us. We've made some inquiries since the special agents came to see us as to why there was no connection made. We don't have an answer to that yet."

"We tried. We really did…" Lilly said.

Sawyer could see how unsettling this was for her, too. "And I didn't get my memory back," she went on. "We didn't discover anything that would have helped me find out who I was."

Sawyer nodded. Through his pain, all he could think of was that waiting, in case any information came to light, had been decent of them.

"We married and I got pregnant almost right away. We have two children, Amie and Christopher."

Sawyer couldn't imagine her having two children but no memory of Dylan.

"Your hair? Why did you dye it?" It seemed like an inconsequential question, but when he'd first learned of it, he'd wondered if it was because she'd been hiding.

Lilly touched a hand to her scalp. "I'm not entirely sure. Not remembering my past, it might have been a way of distancing myself from it. I used to stand in front of the mirror for long periods, staring at my own reflection, hoping that I'd remember who I was."

Sawyer didn't trust himself to speak, so he nodded.

"Can I ask *you* a question now?" she asked.

Sawyer shrugged. "Go ahead."

"My family? Other than you and Dylan," she added in a rush. "Can you tell me anything about my family?"

Sawyer told her as much as he could. Finally, at a loss for anything else to add, he asked to see a picture of their children. Two tousle-haired kids stared back at him from the screen of Jeannette's...uh, Lilly's phone. The baby was dark blond, as Jeannette was naturally. The older child, slightly darker haired, like her father. They resembled Dylan. No surprise, perhaps, because they were his half-siblings.

Lilly put her phone back in her purse and took Ron's hand. "Honey, could you give Sawyer and me a moment alone?"

"I'll wait in the car for you," he responded, then rose. He touched her briefly on the shoulder and, with another nod at Sawyer, walked out of the restaurant.

Lilly took her napkin and started shredding it, while her eyes held Sawyer's. "I want to be very clear with you about something, and I asked Ron to leave because I want you to know that I'm not just saying this for his benefit. I can't put into words how terrible I feel about everything that's happened. I can't begin to imagine what *you* must be feeling, and I am very, very sorry for that." She took a deep breath. "But I need you to understand that my life is with Ron and our children. If I had the power to undo what happened to me three years ago, I wouldn't."

Sawyer clenched his hands under the table.

"I'm sorry," Lilly repeated. "I'm sure you're a wonderful person and I must've loved you to have married you, but now—to me—you're a stranger. I love Ron and our children, and I have no desire to return to a life I can't remember, even if it was possible for me to do so." She shook her head and her eyes were sad. "I'm not saying this to hurt you, but to help you move forward with your life, too. I'd like to meet Dylan, if you think that would be all right... When he's back home with you," she added haltingly. "Hopefully we can establish a relationship." She rose gracefully and extended a hand to Sawyer. "I hope the police find him soon, and for Dylan's sake, I hope you and I can be friends."

Sawyer watched her walk away. Once she was gone, he signaled to the waitress to refill his coffee. The whole experience had been surreal, and he wanted to take a few minutes before he drove the rental car back to the airport.

Jeannette...Lilly...was no longer his wife. That was clear. She was a different person with a different life. She'd cut him to the bone with her declaration that she wouldn't go back even if she could, but he had to respect her for it. And hadn't he concluded that he felt the same way?

He'd watched her carefully when they spoke about Dylan, and he'd shown her a picture of her son. He'd wondered whether a mother's love for her child could somehow transcend memory loss. But there'd been nothing evident beyond a stranger's concern for the plight of a child. She'd said the right things. Had expressed interest in meeting Dylan—when he was found.

Sawyer hoped he could give her that opportunity...

CHAPTER TWENTY-ONE

THE PLANE TRIP HOME was excruciating for Sawyer. All he could think of was Dylan. When he tried to force his thoughts in another direction, it was either Jeannette or Shannon who came to mind. For two very different reasons.

When his plane landed at San Diego International Airport, he first checked his phone. With no news from the police about Dylan, and with Rufus visiting with his parents for the day, there was no point in going home. There was only one person he wanted to see. Shannon.

He wanted to assure her that Jeannette was in his past. And that he hoped Shannon would be his future.

He'd been relieved to learn that Jeannette— Lilly, now—was alive and well, but that had to do with caring about her as someone he'd loved and as the mother of his child.

He called Shannon on her personal cell. It went to voice mail, so he tried her at the division. The dispatcher told him she wasn't answering and wasn't sure if she was on shift. He'd asked whether anyone could tell him if she was working, and Dispatch put him through to the K-9 Unit's admin, Beth.

Beth told him that Shannon had finished her shift and was at the division's fitness center.

He asked if he'd be able to get into the center as a civilian. Beth said it shouldn't be a problem. She said she'd get Logan to authorize it.

Sawyer went to the division straight from the airport and found her in the fitness center's swimming pool.

On her own in the pool, Shannon sliced through the water like a seal. She was wearing a dark blue one-piece, her hair slicked back with the water, and wet, it looked more brown than the golden-blond he was used to seeing. Her arms and feet broke the water with minimal disturbance.

Sawyer knew that that meant her strokes and kicks were as efficient as they could be, all energy spent on forward motion rather than splashing about.

When she reached the end of the pool, she did a clean, crisp racing turn, hardly making a ripple as she dived and surfaced a good fifteen feet from the wall.

He watched her do six lengths before she made another turn and simply glided to a halt and floated. Her arms were ahead of her but spread out, her face in the water.

Sawyer felt his nerves jump. What was she doing? Had she worn herself out completely?

He paced the edge of the pool, not daring to take his eyes off her. He counted the seconds to see how long she was floating like that, facedown. He tried to remember how long you could hold your breath. What was it? Two or two and a half minutes, max? He called to her, but there was no response.

"Damn it all," he muttered, yanked off his shoes, tugged off his jacket and dived in. Before he could reach her, she surged out of the water, gasping. She pushed her wet hair back from her face and stared at him.

"Is there news about Dylan?" she asked.

"No. Unfortunately not."

"What are you doing here, then? And why did you jump into the water with your clothes on?"

He gestured toward her. "You were floating facedown. I thought… I thought you might need help."

She narrowed her eyes. "You thought I was drowning?"

His fear for her well-being was being crowded out by embarrassment. "Well, yeah. You were swimming and then you just stopped and were lying there with your face in the water. So I…"

"Have you ever seen anyone drown?"

He shook his head.

"They certainly don't lie still. They thrash around—until they can't anymore."

"Then what were you doing?"

"Holding my breath." Her tone softened. "For search and rescue, we sometimes have to go into water. We can't wait for divers if someone's life might be at risk. To expand my lungs, I practice holding my breath. I do it after strenuous exercise, the way it would generally be in a real-life situation. After swimming for a while, having to dive down to save someone." The corners of her lips curved up. "I was also resting." She checked her watch. "I'd been swimming for over twenty minutes."

They started to make their way toward the ladder. "You were swimming at that speed for twenty minutes?" he asked, impressed.

She hung on to the metal bars, pulled herself up and out of the water, and glanced back. "Yeah."

The sleek one-piece bathing suit didn't hide much from Sawyer's view as he followed her out of the water. Shannon was lithe and subtly muscled. It horrified him that he'd even notice, when all he had on his mind was Dylan.

She wrapped a towel around herself, reached for another and handed it to him.

"Thanks." He tried to squeeze the water out of his clothes, then used the towel to dry off his face and hair.

"So, what brought you here?"

"You."

"I don't understand."

"I just got back from meeting with Jeannette and I wanted to see you."

Shannon gave him a guarded look. "How did it go?"

"Okay. Good. I'll tell you about it. Are you finished here? Can you leave?"

She stared at him with clear blue eyes.

SHANNON DIDN'T KNOW what to make of Sawyer's showing up at the division. And right after he'd seen his wife. She wanted to believe it was a positive sign, but she couldn't trust it. One of the reasons she'd decided on strenuous exercise at the end of her shift was to give herself a chance to think and to try making sense of her thoughts.

The conclusion she'd come to was that she couldn't do the emotional roller coaster anymore. Everyone who'd warned her had been correct.

It wasn't Sawyer's fault. It was the situation. And she couldn't function the way things were.

"Yes, I'm done here for the day," she said cautiously.

"Can you get changed? Meet me at my place?"

Suddenly, she began to shiver. She took another towel and draped it around her shoulders. "Sawyer, I'm sorry, but this isn't good."

"Would you rather go home and change first?"

She lowered her head and shook it. "That's not what I meant. I think I need to go home right now."

At his protracted silence, she glanced up again.

He was watching her with hooded eyes. When she didn't say anything either, he nodded.

"Okay. Well…I apologize for interrupting your swimming."

He picked up his shoes and jacket. With a final long look, he turned and walked toward the change rooms.

Shannon kept her eyes on the direction he'd gone, even when he'd left and closed the door behind him.

THE POLICE WERE no closer to finding Dylan, determining who was responsible or even figuring out how he could've gotten the locket that had belonged to Jeannette. That meant Sawyer, Jeannette, their families, as well as Shannon, were left to deal with the reality of the situation.

Leary had interviewed Juanita Sanchez again. She continued to be highly cooperative and obviously felt a great deal of blame over what had happened to Dylan. Other than poor judgment, she couldn't be accused of much, since she'd done her best to take care of him. Shannon had been glad to hear that she'd found a job as a nanny with a professional family who had three young children.

Shannon and Sawyer were both painfully aware of the statistics with respect to abducted children. The police began to consider the possibility that the perpetrator wasn't necessarily—or not only—associated with Sawyer, but might have a connection to his wife. As a former social worker, Jeannette would've had exposure to a dangerous element of society, as well. With no workable leads and the factor of the necklace, they couldn't ignore that possibility.

Shannon felt the strain between her and Sawyer acutely. Although he'd never suggested it either by word or by action, Shannon firmly believed he held her responsible for Dylan's second abduction.

Shannon, for her part, struggled with a feeling of failure and began reexamining her decision to be a police officer.

Was she fit for the job?

She contemplated quitting the force. If she did that, she *would* be admitting failure and giving up on her life's calling. And what would she do instead?

As for Dylan, four days had passed and again there was no ransom note or any other hint of the motive for the abduction or who might have done it. Quickly eliminating Jeannette's network of contacts from before her disappearance, the SDPD and FBI went back to the people Sawyer would've had conflicts with.

Shannon needed to do what she could to help return Dylan to his home again. Logan had okayed her to go with Leary and Bigelow when they questioned Stewart Rankin, the drunk driver, once more. She was restricted to observing through the one-way mirror.

Rankin was handcuffed and looked weak and repentant as he was escorted into the room. Leary signaled to the guard to uncuff him.

As soon as his wrists were free, he rubbed at the red abrasions left by the cuffs.

"Have a seat." Leary motioned to the chair on the other side of the table.

Rankin slid into it and slouched down. His gaze moved hesitantly from Leary to Bigelow and back again. Shannon saw no arrogance. No deception. She saw a broken young man who looked years older than he was.

"We'd like to ask you some questions," Bigelow began.

Rankin's head jerked. "Is it about the boy again? Is he still missing?"

Shannon read the horror on his face but saw no guilt or gloating.

"Yes," Bigelow replied, without elaborating that this was the second time.

"I told you before that I didn't have anything to do with it," Rankin mumbled in a defeated voice. "I wouldn't hurt a child…" His voice drifted off; he must have remembered that two of the people he'd killed had been under sixteen. "Not intentionally," he amended. "I just want out of here as early as I can manage. Why would I jeopardize that?"

He sounded sincere to Shannon…and seemed cowed.

"Then help us go through it again." Bigelow gave Rankin a steely stare. "To make sure we have all the facts."

Bigelow and Leary took Rankin through all the same questions they'd asked before, looking for inconsistencies or contradictions. Shannon had read the reports. She knew Rankin was being consistent in his answers. There were no signs as far as she could see that he was lying or keeping anything back. The stress was taking a toll on him, but he didn't falter in his responses. When they were approaching nearly an hour of questioning, Rankin finally broke down. His body started to shake and he covered his face with his hands. When he lowered them again, his cheeks were wet and his lips were twisted in a grimace.

Shannon tensed.

"Look, I did something dreadful. I killed five people. I didn't intend to do it, but I was stupid and it happened. I'm in here for maybe twelve years, but even worse, I have to *live* with what I did for the rest of my life! You might not care. You might not understand. But I suffer through each day with the knowledge of what I did.

"Do you really think I'd add to that by some-how being responsible for harming a child? What kind of monster do you think I am? Don't answer that. I *am* a monster for driving drunk, but…" He covered his face again as sobs racked his body. "You have to believe me! I wouldn't have…knowingly…hurt those people and…I wouldn't do anything…to a child," he managed haltingly.

If not for the fact that Rankin had killed those people, Shannon might've felt sorry for him at that moment.

"Haven't I paid the price already?" he pleaded. He rested his head in his hands. "No, no, that's wrong. I can never pay the price for what I did. But I'm in here, my family's virtually disowned me and Elaine couldn't end things fast enough after the sentencing. I have no life, no job, no family, nothing. Why would I want to make matters worse by doing what you think I did?"

Bigelow signaled the guard, and he and Leary rose to leave.

Shannon watched a few minutes longer as Rankin cried uncontrollably. No, he wouldn't have had anything to do with the abduction, she thought. Still no answers.

Frustrated, she spun away from the one-way glass.

She met Bigelow and Leary in the corridor outside the interrogation room. They'd arranged for a private office at the detention center for their use to debrief and went there now. Leary poured three cups of coffee and took them to the meeting table. Before they could begin, there was a knock at the door and Logan came in.

He greeted everyone present, got a cup of coffee for himself and sat down next to Shannon.

"How did it go?" he asked.

"He's not our perp," Leary said, confirming Shannon's own assessment.

Logan turned to Bigelow, who nodded in agreement. "So where do we go from here?"

Shannon could practically see the exasperation rippling off all three men. She understood it, because she felt it, too. "Who's Elaine?" she blurted out. "Who was she to Rankin?"

Leary turned tired eyes on her. "Elaine Brant. Rankin's ex-fiancée."

Right. That made sense, since Rankin had said she'd left him.

"Have you spoken to her?"

"We had a brief conversation when we were looking at Rankin's family. She hung around for the trial, but once the sentence was handed down, as Rankin said, she hightailed it out of there and away from him as fast as she could. The family hasn't heard from her since. She moved on with a new guy in no time at all. We get the sense she wasn't overly invested in her relationship with Rankin. My guess is it was about his family's money."

And if it *was* about the money and she *was* involved in the abduction, you could bet there would've been a ransom demand right away.

Shannon had to agree that Rankin, his family and his ex-fiancée seemed like a dead end. "What about that guy Sawyer sent to jail, the one who embezzled the money from his company?"

"No. We cleared him."

"Didn't his wife take it poorly? Had a meltdown in the courtroom?"

"Yeah. Amanda Blackstone. We've spoken to her, too. We've cleared all of them once, but we'll have another look."

"Time is not on our side," Logan added quietly. "If you need more resources, let me know. I'll pull whatever strings I need to."

SHANNON WAS GLAD her days were full, because it kept her mind off Sawyer and Dylan. Having just finished an assignment—finding a young girl who'd decided to run away from home when her mother had insisted she play outside instead of watch television—the first thing Shannon did when she got in her Explorer was check her phone. She had a number of messages. Two from Beth and one from Logan. All three reminded her of a unit meeting at eleven. Checking the time, she realized she'd have to hustle. Fortunately, traffic cooperated and she made it on time.

After parking, she rushed into the division

building, Darwin loping along beside her. Logan wanted everyone in attendance at the meeting. That meant it was something significant.

She reached the conference room with hardly a minute to spare. Darwin was with her, whether Logan liked it or not, since she hadn't had time to put him in his kennel. She bumped into Rick as she entered. He steadied her and gave her an encouraging smile. All the seats in the conference room were taken, so they stood near the door. "I heard about you finding the runaway child today. Great work—"

Before he could finish, Logan called the meeting to order.

It was only then that Shannon noticed there was a stranger in the room. He was leaning against the side counter. He looked dangerous, a jagged scar on his chin. If she'd seen him on the street, she'd wager he was involved in the drug trade. One of the cartels, perhaps, that Rick worked so hard to break.

Easily, he had to be over six feet tall. He had jet-black hair and eyes just as dark. His gaze met hers, and he insolently slid it from her eyes down to her feet and back up again.

Shannon was not one to intimidate easily, but she felt decidedly uncomfortable under his scrutiny.

Who the heck was he anyway, and what was he doing in their unit meeting?

"I have some news to share with you," Logan announced, drawing Shannon's attention away from the stranger. "First, I'd like to introduce you to Quinn Langdon."

The stranger pushed off from the counter and gave a little salute to the room.

"I'd like you to join me in welcoming Quinn to our unit. He comes to us with considerable experience, having worked with Harbor Patrol for ten years. Quinn brings with him his canine partner, Cyrus. Quinn and Cyrus are being reassigned to the SDPD from Harbor Patrol on the first of next month."

There were murmurs of welcome. Those standing closest to Quinn shook his hand or slapped his back.

"Despite being multipurpose, Cyrus does have a particular skill in cadaver detection."

The room fell silent at this declaration. They'd never had a cadaver dog before.

Changing times, she thought, and not in a positive way.

"The reason Quinn's joining us is because there are some other changes I want to share with you." He scanned the faces, took their measure. Shannon knew that Logan had high emotional intelligence and could judge his audience accurately. She sensed, from his demeanor, that whatever he had to say would not be well-received.

"I'm pleased to announce that Cal Palmer, after eight years of service in the unit, is being promoted to sergeant."

Shannon glance at Rick, who was still standing next to her. What was happening with him then? Their unit wasn't large enough for two sergeants.

She didn't have to wait long to find out.

"To address the question I know most of you have, Rick is being promoted to captain of the K-9 Unit."

She heard a couple of immediate murmurs, but then the room fell eerily silent. She was certain everyone had the same question in mind. What did that mean for Logan?

"And if you're wondering," Logan continued. He seemed flustered all of a sudden. An unusual state for Jagger. "I'll be moving into the role of Assistant Chief."

Shannon heard more surprised murmurs before a raucous round of applause burst out across the room. Back-slapping, handshakes and bear hugs followed.

When it was Shannon's turn, she stuck out her hand. "Congratulations, Logan. That's terrific. So well deserved," she said.

He looked deep into her eyes. "But?" he asked.

"Damn it all. I'm going to miss you. You gave me this opportunity. You were instrumental in my training. Don't get me wrong. I think the world of Rick. It's just that.... It's just that I'll miss you," she repeated, before she gave him a hug, too.

He patted her back. "You'll do fine. Rick's going to be a great captain. He deserves the promotion."

"So do you," she said. She stepped back and to her immense embarrassment, felt the sting of tears in her eyes. She must be overtired if her emotions were getting the better of her so frequently. She turned away from Logan, and her gaze collided with Quinn's.

She was irritated to see his brows rise and his lips curve.

She was okay with having Rick as her new captain and certainly Cal as her sergeant, but something told her she wouldn't be so comfortable with the new officer.

Having had enough surprises for one day, she called Darwin. As soon as she could do so politely, she left the conference room.

Turning the corner into the squad room, she came to an abrupt halt. Lying not three feet from her desk was the most gorgeous German shepherd she'd ever seen. He was alert and had expressive, intelligent eyes. His leash was lying next to him, but he was holding what she was certain had been a "down-stay" command.

He must be Quinn's dog, she concluded. She took several steps forward, then realized that the dog was so close to her desk she couldn't get to it without her and Darwin passing right by him.

She needed to establish her dominance from the start and took a couple of slower steps toward him.

"You can approach him," a deep male voice said from behind her. "He'll be fine with your dog, too. At ease, Cyrus," he added for the benefit of the dog as she glanced over her shoulder.

"Thanks," she said. Instructing Darwin to "sit-stay," she closed the gap between her and Cyrus. She held out a hand for him to scent. She crouched down and rubbed him behind his ears. "He's beautiful." Whatever she thought of the new cop, she couldn't deny that his dog was a beauty. "How old is he?"

"He'll be five next month. He'll probably be up for retirement soon."

She looked over at Quinn. "That's early, even for a police dog."

Quinn shrugged. "We've been through a lot together. He's earned it."

The tone of his voice was incongruous with his appearance. Especially talking about his dog, he sounded gentle. Caring. Even the lines on his face had softened from what he'd looked like in the conference room. His smile was warm, maybe a little melancholy.

A vague memory stirred about a Harbor Patrol officer who'd taken a bullet for his dog. If that was Quinn and he loved his dog as much as he seemed to, he couldn't be all bad.

Before she could say anything else, Logan called to her.

"You're needed," he told her from the doorway of his office.

"Welcome to the unit," she said to Quinn as she rose. "What's the situation?" she asked Logan when she and Darwin reached him.

"There's been a development. Bigelow and Leary have asked for your assistance."

She felt a sudden tightness in her belly.

"Rankin's outburst and mention of his fiancée, Elaine Brant, followed by your question, got them to take a closer look at her. Brant hadn't been noteworthy originally when they considered the people connected to Rankin, as you know. They want your help to check

Brant's apartment. See if there's any indication Dylan might have been there."

"Sure. Of course." Shannon's heart rate kicked up a notch. "What have they got?" She heard the hope in her own voice.

"Nothing substantive, but they don't want to leave any stone unturned. They verified that Brant broke off the engagement to Rankin as soon as he was sentenced, and she married someone else shortly thereafter. A dentist. What is of interest—and you know I don't believe in coincidence—is that she'd taken a sudden leave of absence from her job as a nutritionist the day Dylan was abducted the second time. Leary and Bigelow checked with the building manager of her apartment, and he hasn't seen her for a while. He suspects that her apartment has been unoccupied for a few days.

"Brant's family hasn't been in contact with her, either, but they told Leary and Bigelow that her marriage ended. They talked to the estranged husband, as well, who corroborated the family's story. He has no information regarding her whereabouts, either. According to him, the split had been brewing for some time, and they had a major blowup about six months ago. She stormed out. After that, she used her credit card and took cash out of ATMs regularly—until he froze their joint account—so he wasn't worried that any harm had befallen her. She seemed to have moved around after their split, staying with friends or short-term rentals, and taking odd jobs advising on nutrition and overall health."

"So, she's not likely either," Shannon concluded.

"Not any more or less than the others on our radar screen, but worth looking at and eliminating. As a start, to gain entry to her apartment, you and Darwin will have to provide probable cause for a search warrant. Especially with the passage of time, you're our best bet to determine whether Dylan was in that unit or not."

He handed her a piece of paper. "This is the address. Bigelow and Leary are on their way. They'll be waiting for you when you get there."

Shannon slipped the sheet of paper into her shirt pocket. She grabbed her duffel from under her desk and on her way to the parking lot, she stopped by the evidence room to retrieve Dylan's clothing, which they still held, thankful that the airtight bag it was sealed in would have retained his scent.

Once on the road, she was tempted to call Sawyer. Tell him what was going on. But she didn't know how solid a lead it was. They were acting on a hunch. Since this was an on-going investigation, it would have been another breach of protocol. In addition, as much as she wanted to lift Sawyer's spirits, it would be far more harmful to raise his hopes if nothing panned out.

Shannon saw the SDPD and FBI vehicles parked in front of the apartment block as she pulled up. She left her Explorer by the curb, too. When she'd let Darwin out of the back, they jogged to the entrance of the building, where Bigelow and Leary were waiting.

"We've spoken to the building manager again," Bigelow said. "Are you ready to go in?"

Shannon nodded and had Darwin sniff Dylan's shirt, while Bigelow punched in a four-digit code on the keypad by the door.

"Yeah?" was the gruff answer.

"It's Bigelow with the SDPD. Can you let us in now and meet us at the elevators?"

"Okay."

She heard the buzzing noise and the door unlatching. They strode over to the bank of elevators. With the building manager accompanying them, they took one up to the twelfth floor. She didn't have to search for apartment 1208. Darwin led them straight to it and expressed moderate interest in the smells around the door.

"That's promising," Leary observed.

"It is," Shannon agreed. "Based on Darwin's accuracy rate, I'd say it gives us probable cause to enter."

Bigelow nodded, waited for the warrant to come through then signaled for the manager to unlock the door.

Once inside, Shannon instructed Darwin to begin his search, and prayed he'd hit on something so they'd know that Dylan had been there. It wouldn't tell them where Dylan was now, but it would be a solid lead, strongly suggesting that he was with Elaine Brant.

Shannon watched Darwin move around the room in his own predetermined pattern. He'd pause. Retrace his steps. When he'd finished the living room, there was no conclusive indication that he'd smelled Dylan. She led him to the master bedroom. With a sinking heart, she watched him execute the same behavior he had in the living room.

When he finished, she wanted to groan in frustration. If Dylan had been in those rooms, sufficient time had passed that his scent had dissipated.

As they moved toward the bathroom, Darwin perked up. Shannon saw a towel and a boy's sock on the floor in one corner. Darwin made a beeline toward them. There was no mistaking his behavior now. "He's been here," Shannon shouted. "Dylan was in this apartment!"

CHAPTER TWENTY-TWO

SHANNON RECEIVED A text from Sawyer asking if it would be okay if he stopped by to see her once she got home. Asked might not have been the most accurate word, since the message didn't give her much wiggle room. Even if it had, she couldn't have said no. She missed him. And what was most disconcerting, she still loved him. As much as she wished there could be more between them, it was an impossible situation.

Sawyer was barely inside her door when he posed his first question. "Where's Dylan and why would Elaine Brant do this?"

She'd anticipated it, but unfortunately had no answer.

Shannon led Sawyer to the living room. Darwin, sensing the tension, was more subdued than usual. After a cursory greeting for Sawyer, he curled up on his bed.

Without bothering to ask, Shannon poured Sawyer a glass of Coke. She handed it to him and sat on the sofa beside him. "I expect Bigelow told you all of this already. Elaine Brant and Dylan's whereabouts are unknown at present. So is the motive for the abduction. I'm sorry I don't know more," she added.

Sawyer set his glass on the table and surged to his feet.

"If it was to avenge her fiancé, why wait three years?" he asked, pacing restlessly. "And why do it to begin with? All indications—based on what I've been told—are that she'd moved on and her marriage was, at least for a time, a positive one." He stopped and faced her. "How does this help, then? What are Bigelow and Leary doing with this information?"

Shannon rose, too, and took two steps to stand in front of him. She touched his forearm. "On the strength of the evidence Darwin provided, it's almost certain that Dylan was in Elaine Brant's apartment. We can dig deeper now, look into her background and search for potential evidence of her whereabouts. This *is* significant. We'll find her and then, hopefully, Dylan, too."

"Okay. Okay," he murmured. Then he simply rested his forehead against hers. "I'm sorry I've been hard on you. I've just been trying to…survive."

Shannon felt the stirring of love. She told herself she should step away. Instead, she slid her arms around him and found herself burrowing her head in the hollow of his shoulder. This wasn't about a relationship between them, she tried to convince herself. It was about giving and taking comfort.

And support.

She had to believe that they'd find Dylan. If she couldn't believe it, how could Sawyer?

"HEY, CLEMENS, YOU want to join us?" Bigelow asked as he, Leary and Wilson entered the K-9 Unit squad room.

She scrutinized their faces and was reasonably satisfied that it wouldn't be bad news. "Sure." She followed them into the conference room, as did a number of other SDPD officers and FBI agents. Logan signaled to Cal to join them, too.

"We think we've located Brant," Leary stated without preamble.

He had everyone's attention. There wasn't a sound in the room.

"We tracked her to Santa Ysabel through the use of her credit card and a bank machine. We found a recent charge for a cabin rental on her credit card statement. It's located in a relatively isolated RV and cabin rental resort just outside Santa Ysabel. The timing of the rental corresponds with Dylan's disappearance."

"Why would she be foolish enough to use her credit card and bank machine card?" Shannon asked.

Leary shrugged. "My guess is complacency. We didn't catch her the first time around. She probably thinks we aren't looking at her."

"We're going to move on it as soon as we finish here." Bigelow resumed the briefing. "We've got a warrant, and the local authorities have been alerted. They'll set up surveillance until we get there. If they see the boy and have reason to suspect he might be in danger, they'll take appropriate action. Otherwise, they'll wait for us. No one wants this bungled. Without motive, we have no way of knowing what her intentions are or what she'll do if confronted. Our theory is that she's acting on her own. But we could be wrong about that, and we don't want to take any chances. Assuming Dylan's fine now, we want to keep him that way."

Leary turned to Logan. "You'd offered resources before. I'd like to take you up on that. We'd like officers Palmer and Clemens with us. Both Scout and Darwin have been invaluable in our investigation. I know that'll leave you with no search-and-rescue capability for as long as it takes us—"

Logan raised a hand. "No issue. They're

ʹyours as long as yóu need them. If you require anything else, let me know."

"All right. Let's go."

Shannon got water for herself and for Darwin. Santa Ysabel was over an hour northeast
of San Diego, and she had no intention of stop-
ping along the way. There was a small convoy
of vehicles heading out of the division parking
lot and she was part of it.

With rush hour just ending, the time of day
worked to their advantage. They pulled into
the park grounds before eleven. A park em-
ployee escorted them to the cabin in question, which had a late-model van parked in
front. One of the uniformed officers ran the
plates. They had confirmation that it belonged
to Brant.

Bigelow knocked twice, announcing himself each time.

For Shannon, the short wait stretched out
like an eternity.

When there was no answer, Bigelow gave
the signal that they were going in. He used the
key he'd obtained from the park office and unlocked the door.

Shannon wasn't among the first to enter,
but she could see the living room of the cabin
from where she stood. Bigelow called her and
Cal once they'd ascertained there wasn't any-

one inside. She gave Darwin the scent and led him in. Then she noticed the brown stuffed bear sitting on the sofa, and a child's puzzle, half-assembled on the coffee table.

Almost immediately, Darwin indicated that Dylan had been inside. Cal's dog, Scout, verified it. Still, they took the dogs through each room. The bedroom also showed evidence of a child—a boy—staying there. On a small cot in the corner of the room sat two more stuffed toys, and there was a kid's T-shirt, plus two pairs of socks neatly folded on the dresser. Small sneakers peeked out from under the cot. Darwin and Scout both confirmed that the items had Dylan's scent on them.

There appeared to be only two people staying in the cabin, Dylan and a woman, presumed to be Brant. Although they still didn't know the motive, the child was being well cared for.

"It doesn't look like she's vacated or plans to do so anytime soon," Leary noted. "Unless she does have a coconspirator, which is unlikely, it's reasonable to conclude that she and Dylan are somewhere within walking distance, since her car is here. We're assuming—once again—that the boy hasn't tried to escape because of an emotional attachment associated with Stockholm syndrome."

"We either wait here until she returns or we go looking for her," Bigelow said, and turned to Shannon and Cal. "Can you and your dogs find them?"

Shannon glanced at Cal. He gave a nearly imperceptible signal to say that she should take the lead. Uncertainty coursed through her, but it was gone as fast as it had surfaced. She laid one hand on Darwin's head. "Yes, I believe so."

Bigelow nodded. "Good. Let's find the boy. Miller, Baldwin," he called out to two of the SDPD cops who'd accompanied them. "First, get the police vehicles away from the cabin and then you two stay here. Keep out of sight in case she comes back before we find her. Clemens, lead the way."

Clipping on Darwin's lead, Shannon wiped her damp palm on her pant leg and reentered the living room. She snagged the bear from the sofa and let Darwin scent it. She was positive it was Dylan's, and it was a fresher, stronger scent than anything she had. She gave Darwin the command to "find."

Darwin headed out at a fast pace and Shannon jogged behind him. He ran into the forest but stayed on well-traveled paths that dipped and turned. She could hear Cal and Scout close behind them, and farther back, Bigelow and

Leary huffing as they tried to keep up. K-9 handlers had to stay fit for a reason.

When Darwin lunged forward, Shannon went on full alert. From the intensity of the light ahead, she knew they were approaching a clearing. She tugged on the lead and signaled Darwin to ease up. She also raised a hand to alert Cal, Bigelow and Leary, then pointed to where the trail opened onto a grassy area.

With Darwin now at her side, they moved silently forward to the mouth of the trail.

The long grass of the clearing, dotted with white daisies, swayed gracefully in the gentle breeze. The sun gilded the grass and trees with an ethereal wash of gold and made the scene feel almost dreamlike. Crouched in the middle of the field was a woman in shorts and a T-shirt, long brown hair piled on top of her head. Shannon had seen pictures of Elaine Brant. It was her.

Dylan was standing next to her, and she had an arm around his shoulders. He held a daisy in one hand and seemed to be counting as he pulled off its petals. Dylan had a small stuffed kangaroo under one arm, not quite Joey but a close enough facsimile to make Shannon think the woman had tried to replace the boy's favorite toy.

If Shannon hadn't known better, she would've thought she was watching mother and son. She leaned toward Bigelow. "Let me get Dylan, please," she whispered. "He knows me and won't be as afraid."

Bigelow nodded and ordered the others to circle around and stay alert, in case Brant made a run for it.

The element of surprise was on their side.

The instant Brant noticed their presence, she tensed, wrapped her arms around Dylan and stood there, cradling the boy against her. Her eyes darted around. Seeing the law enforcement personnel, she buried her face in the boy's hair, and the tension seemed to leave her body.

On Bigelow's signal, Shannon moved in.

CHAPTER TWENTY-THREE

SHANNON HAD DYLAN and he was safe. That was all that mattered. Everything around her was a blur of activity. Bigelow and Leary took Brant into custody, read her her rights, cuffed her and hauled her away.

Shannon lowered Dylan to the ground and squatted down in front of him. "Hey, Dylan, are you okay?" she asked.

Dylan hugged the stuffed animal tight. "Uh-huh," he replied, but his eyes were glistening with tears.

"I'm going to take you to your dad. And to Rufus," she added when she saw his bottom lip quiver and he looked toward Darwin.

That statement elicited a watery smile. "'Kay."

"Rufus has been worried about you and he'll be so happy to see you. He's missed you terribly. Would you like to walk or have me carry you?"

"Can I walk with Darwin?"

"Okay." She gave him a hug, then stood up. "Will you take my hand?"

He nodded.

Shannon presumed that one of the others had called Sawyer so he'd know they had Dylan, and he was, at least physically, unharmed.

She had one of the other SDPD officers drive her vehicle back for her, so she could sit with Dylan, as she had on the previous occasion. But this time, Dylan snuggled close to her side, his little hand still in hers. As the resort's management office came into view, she immediately noticed Sawyer pacing back and forth in front of the building. She was surprised to see him there, but obviously someone had called to tell him he should meet them at the park.

Sawyer must have recognized her vehicle pulling into the lot. He ran straight to it, looking momently confused when he realized she wasn't driving. Shannon fumbled with the seat belts—hers and Dylan's—wanting to get him out of the SUV and into his father's arms as quickly as possible.

"Go," she told him when his seat belt was unclasped. Sawyer already had the door open, lifted his son into his arms and held him tight. Shannon could see that his eyes were squeezed shut, but tears trickled out from the corners as he pressed his lips to the top of Dylan's head.

She wondered how Dylan could breathe, Sawyer was holding him so tightly, but the little boy didn't seem to mind. He had his arms wound around his father's neck.

Shannon thought she should get them both inside her Explorer and drive them home. One of the other cops could take Sawyer's car. As she took a couple of hesitant steps toward Sawyer, his eyes flew open. He closed the gap between them and with Dylan still held tight against him, flung his other arm around Shannon's shoulders.

"We have her," she whispered. "It's over."

"Thank you. Thank you so much," he murmured in her ear before pressing a kiss to her temple.

Shannon stood rigidly in his embrace. He must have been swept up in the emotion of the moment once again, she decided.

Dylan was back, safe and sound, and in his father's arms. But that didn't mean they'd have smooth sailing ahead. Sawyer still had a lot to contend with. Ensuring that Dylan received the care he needed. Sorting things out with his wife. Shannon could have gone on and on.

But it felt so darn good to be in his arms,

she'd worry about what it all meant later. She'd take this moment for herself.

She wrapped one arm around Sawyer's waist and draped the other over Dylan's shoulders, and let the feelings of love and longing take hold.

As it turned out, another SDPD officer drove Sawyer and Dylan home. Shannon was required to attend a debrief at the division. There was another meeting the next morning. When the meeting ended, Logan asked Shannon to stay behind.

"Since Leary and Bigelow's interrogation of Brant gave us some answers," he said, "I thought I'd ask if you wanted to let Sawyer know what we've learned."

Shannon was about to object, not sure if she wanted to put herself in such an emotional situation with Sawyer, but she'd been neck-deep in the investigation from the start. She might as well finish it off. "Thanks, Jagger," she said with a nod. "I'll take care of it."

Shannon texted Sawyer rather than calling him. She wanted to keep this as impersonal as possible. Their relationship had been entirely professional since the day he'd sought her out at the swimming pool.

She wanted—needed—this closure, even

if it meant the end for them. Even if her heart would remain broken.

He responded almost instantly. He'd had to go into his office for a few hours to brief a colleague who'd be filling in for a couple of weeks. He'd decided to take more time off to be with Dylan. The rest of the summer semester, in fact.

He said it was fine for her to meet him at the school. Apparently, he wanted to keep things impersonal, too.

And Shannon's heart ached again at the thought of not being able to see Dylan to say goodbye.

She stayed in uniform and left Darwin in his kennel at the division. She'd go back after her meeting with Sawyer to get him.

"Hello, Shannon!" Miranda, Sawyer's assistant, rose and skirted the reception counter to give her an impulsive hug. "I'm sorry," she said, flustered. "But it's so wonderful that Sawyer has Dylan back and you caught the person responsible."

"Yes, it is." Shannon didn't know what else to say. It was hard enough trying to stay calm for her discussion with Sawyer.

"Oh, well… Sawyer's free, so let me take you right in."

Shannon followed Miranda to Sawyer's office, and did her best to contain all the emotions churning inside her.

Sawyer was sitting at his computer, tapping away at the keys, his back to her. From the look of his hair, whatever he was working on was either frustrating him or required deep concentration, since it was evident that he'd been dragging his fingers through it.

He did it again, and Shannon felt the emotions—the love—swirl up in her. She cleared her throat as Miranda knocked lightly on the door frame and left.

Sawyer's back straightened and he swung around in his chair.

She saw a mixture of feelings cross his face, before he rose and gestured to the meeting table in the corner of his office. "Thanks for coming here, Shannon. Can I get you a drink?"

She was about to decline, but thought better of it. A drink might ease the scratchiness in her throat and give her something to do with her hands. "Coffee would be nice, thanks."

Sawyer stepped out briefly. A few minutes later, Miranda brought in two mugs of coffee. She closed the door behind her when she left.

"How's Dylan?" Shannon couldn't help asking before they started.

"Good. Especially considering the Stockholm syndrome thing..." His lips compressed into a hard, straight line. "Dylan had just been getting over not seeing '*tía*'; now he keeps asking about that woman. Elaine. I understand the psychology of it intellectually, but emotionally? It's a whole different matter." He took a long drink of coffee. "So you have information for me?"

She nodded. "Elaine Brant has been charged."

"As she should be, and about time," he murmured. Shannon wondered how she could be sitting there with the man she loved, speaking to him as if they were...colleagues. Or distant acquaintances. Her own feelings might have been rioting, but she didn't sense anything like that from him. No personal connection. She thought back to the caution Madison had given her, that his feelings might not have been as invested as hers. He'd needed a lifeline to hold on to during his time of crisis. While his son was missing.

"Brant's in custody, and it didn't take long to get a confession from her." Shannon's heart twisted at the thought of what she had to tell him. "This is not going to be easy, Sawyer. I have to warn you."

His eyes narrowed. She'd never seen them as dark and hard as they were at that moment. "How could anything be worse than my son being taken from me? At least now I'll have some answers."

She sighed. "Yes, you'll have some answers, and not just about Dylan."

"What are you talking about?" His voice had an edge.

"Sawyer, Brant's obsession started years ago. Jeannette didn't leave you and Dylan of her own volition."

Sawyer's mouth opened, but no sound came out.

Whether he wanted it or not, Shannon had to comfort Sawyer before she went on. She'd do the same for anyone in this situation, wouldn't she? She placed her hand on his.

"Sawyer, Elaine Brant has wanted retribution since you prosecuted Rankin. She held you responsible for sending her fiancé to jail and, in her opinion, ruining her life. She was a nutritionist contracted by the fitness club where your wife worked out. She abducted Jeannette."

Shannon watched as Sawyer tried to process what she'd just told him. "But...that's insane."

Shannon nodded. "She might well be. Elaine had a pathological fixation on her former fiancé. She was raised in poverty, with her parents spending any available money on alcohol, so the lifestyle marriage to Rankin became an obsession. She'd been pregnant with his child at the time Rankin was sent to jail. Not only had she lost her fiancé, according to her—and the medical reports have verified this—the stress of the situation caused her to miscarry.

"When she took Jeannette, Brant wanted vengeance. She wanted to hurt you—an 'eye for an eye,' to her way of thinking. She was driven by rage and, as I said, a desire for retribution. But she hadn't thought it through, nor had she intended to keep Jeannette for long."

"But...but how is any of this possible? Jeannette was in a public place. There had to be people coming and going, security cameras..." The devastation was clearly evident on his face.

"I'm so sorry," Shannon murmured before continuing. "Although Brant wasn't consulting for Jeannette, they'd known each other in passing. Brant asked Jeannette to have coffee with her. Once she was in her car and they were some distance from the fitness center, Brant—a tall, fit woman—was able to overpower Jeannette and use chloroform on her."

Sawyer got out of the chair, shoved his hands in his pants pockets and stared out the window. "Go on," he said, his back to her, his voice low and vibrating with anger.

"As I said, Elaine hadn't known what she

intended to do with Jeannette, other than hold her for a while to make you suffer. When Jeannette unexpectedly came to from the chloroform while Elaine was driving east through Arizona, they grappled in the car. Jeannette jumped out while it was moving. Elaine tried to hold her back and all that had remained in her grasp was Jeannette's locket."

"That explains how Dylan got it."

"Yes. She'd given it to him. Elaine disposed of Jeannette's possessions—her handbag with all her identification and the gym bag she'd been carrying—but she kept the locket.

"She didn't know what happened to Jeannette after she jumped out of the car and she was too worried to go back and see for herself. Of course, we know that Jeannette landed in a ditch and suffered a concussion. Elaine claims she had no intention of hurting Jeannette, and the thought of Jeannette being injured or killed terrified her. She purchased a prepaid phone at a convenience store farther down the highway and called 911. She didn't want her to die, but she worried that if Jeannette was alive, she'd return home and identify her. After that, she kept an eye on your home—which is how she knew about Dylan. She felt guilty but still breathed a sigh of relief when she read that the SDPD presumed Jeannette was dead. Elaine believed she'd avenged what had happened to her."

Sawyer turned back and took a couple of steps toward Shannon. He looked as if he was going into shock. The color had drained from his face; even his lips had lost their tint.

"So why now? Why take Dylan after three years?" Each word was tortured. Each breath a labored wheeze.

Shannon took a sip of coffee to soothe her scratchy throat. "Elaine carried on with her life. The more time that passed, the more confident she was that her role in Jeannette's disappearance would go undiscovered. She started dating a dentist. He wasn't from a wealthy family like Rankin, but his income was solid enough to satisfy Elaine. They got married and he wanted children almost immediately, but she couldn't conceive. She was told that the miscarriage had caused irreparable harm, and she couldn't have children.

"She blamed the fact that her husband left on her inability to have children. Leary and Bigelow interviewed him. He said his leaving had nothing to do with her not being able to bear children. He said he would've been fine with adopting. He proved it, too, by showing them copies of the research he'd done. But Elaine wouldn't hear of it. She was too blinded by her anger to realize that her husband had left her not for her inability to conceive, but because it was obvious to him that she was emotionally unstable. Elaine again turned her anger and hate on you, believing that the downward spiral of her life had begun with Rankin's conviction. Wanting children and not being able to conceive, she decided it was only fair if she took *your* son. If she took Dylan."

Shannon was struggling to maintain her own composure. She wanted to weep for Sawyer, for Dylan—for what she'd hoped they could've had as a family. "Her thought was that she'd have a child—a replacement for the one she felt you'd caused her to lose— and she'd be hurting you at the same time. And she ruthlessly put her plan in effect." Sawyer walked slowly back to the window, as if his bones would shatter if he moved any faster. He stood with his back to her again.

Shannon could tell how tense he was from the rigidity of his back, the throbbing pulse in his neck.

She wanted to go to him. To hug him and try to ease the pain.

But she didn't think he'd want her to.

"Thank you for the information," he said without turning around. "If you don't mind, I'd like to be alone now."

His words confirmed her suspicion, and her stomach twisted into a hard, tight knot. No, she definitely could not survive these ups and downs.

What choice did she have other than to comply with his request? She rose and silently walked out the door.

CHAPTER TWENTY-FOUR

AT THE SOUND of the doorbell, Dylan came racing out of his room, Rufus hot on his heels. "Is that Aunt Meg?"

Sawyer was immensely grateful that Dylan seemed to be bouncing back so quickly from his ordeal "I expect it is. Would you like to let her in?"

"Yeah!"

He ran to the door, Rufus scrambling along beside him. He dutifully asked who it was, the way Sawyer had taught him. When he heard Meghan's voice, he swung the door open wide.

"How's my favorite nephew?" Meg asked as she picked Dylan up and swung him around.

"I'm your *only* nephew!" Dylan responded with a giggle.

Sawyer leaned back against the doorjamb as he watched their greeting. Their ritual done, Meghan walked over to him. She did a swift but thorough perusal.

"I'm doing okay," he said before she could say anything.

"Yeah?" she asked with a skeptical look.

"Dylan, why don't you get your sketch pad to show Aunt Meg the drawings you did this morning?"

"'Kay," he said and ran off again.

Meg waited until Dylan was out of earshot. "I can't stay long because I have to get to the lab—and yes, I know it's Saturday—but I wanted to stop by and see you. How are you really doing?"

Sawyer sighed. "Better than I was."

"Well, that's something. Have you told Dylan about Jeannette?"

Sawyer followed Meg into the living room and sat down. "Not yet."

Meg shook her head. "You'll need to do it soon, since you've agreed she can meet Dylan next weekend."

"Yeah. I know it."

Neither of them said anything more as Dylan ran back into the room. Meghan sat down next to him, and oohed and aahed over the drawings he showed her. When they'd gone through all of them, Meg encouraged him to go back to his room and draw some more.

Once they were alone again, Sawyer told her about the progress Dylan was making, according to his therapist.

"Before I go, I have one more question for

you," Meg announced. "Have you seen Shannon?"

"Don't start in on me about that."

She sighed. "We're worried about you. You can't shut yourself off from people and, if you ask me, you shouldn't shut her out."

He shook his head. "That's my business, Meg. Nobody else's."

"Don't jump down my throat. I just call them the way I see them—and I can see that you're hurting and unhappy despite having Dylan back." She gave him a kiss on the cheek. "Just think about it. Okay?" Before he could respond, she got up and started toward the door.

Sawyer had barely been able to think about anything *but* Shannon, he acknowledged after Meg left. But thinking hadn't gotten him anywhere. And this time, he hadn't been the one who'd backed away from their relationship.

Meg had made an important point, though. He'd have to tell Dylan about his mother, since he'd be meeting her in a week. It wouldn't be fair to spring it on him too suddenly.

Meg had already spoiled his mood, so he might as well get it over with now.

He walked to his son's room and looked in.

Dylan was sitting on the edge of his bed, drawing pad on his lap. Rufus sprawled on the floor and Dylan seemed to be drawing a picture of the dog.

Sawyer walked in and pulled up a chair facing Dylan. He rested his forearms on his knees and leaned forward. "Can I talk to you for a few minutes, champ?"

Dylan nodded and put his sketch pad aside.

What an incredibly sweet kid he was, Sawyer mused. He said silent thanks again for having him back home and physically unharmed.

"You remember we talked about how Mommy went to heaven?" Sawyer asked.

"Uh-huh."

"Well, Mommy *did* go away, but she didn't go to heaven."

Dylan reached for Joey. His blue eyes—so much like Jeannette's—were clouded.

"Where did she go?"

"She went to a place called Arizona."

"Is she coming home now?"

"No, she isn't."

"Doesn't she love us?"

How to answer that one? Sawyer wondered. Stay as close to the truth as possible, he decided. "When Mommy went away, she…got sick and she forgets things now."

"Like to make her bed in the morning? And brush her teeth before she goes to sleep at night?"

Sawyer burst into laughter. "I think she probably remembers those things. Mommies have to. But she forgot everything else from before she got sick."

Dylan's lower lip trembled. "She forgot us?"

Sawyer got out of the chair. Sitting on Dylan's bed, his back against the headboard, he pulled Dylan close to his side. "Unfortunately, she forgot everything."

"So she forgot us?" he persisted.

Sawyer closed his eyes and searched for the right words. "She didn't want to, and she couldn't help it. She had an accident—and hit her head very hard. You know how you have to wear a helmet when you ride your bike? So if you fall, you won't hurt your head?"

"Uh-huh."

"Well, when she hit her head, she wasn't wearing a helmet. That's what made her forget everything." He pressed his lips to his son's head. "And, yes, she forgot us."

Dylan burrowed closer to Sawyer. "That's why she hasn't come home?"

"Yeah. That's why. Here's the good news, though," Sawyer said with forced cheer. "She wants to see you."

Dylan twisted around and looked up at Sawyer. "If we see her, will she remember us?"

Sawyer brushed Dylan's hair from his forehead. He couldn't lie to him. "I don't think so, champ."

Dylan turned away.

"But we can help her make new memories of us."

Dylan looked up at Sawyer again and gave him a hesitant smile. "And she can help me make memories, too, right?"

"Yes, she can. She'd like to come see you next Saturday. Are you okay with that?"

Dylan stared down at his hands as the Mickey Mouse clock by his bed ticked away the seconds. Finally, he raised his face to Sawyer again. "I think that's okay… Will she be my mommy again?"

"She always was and always will be your mommy."

Dylan nodded thoughtfully. "But not like other kids? Their moms live with them."

"No, not like that." Sawyer wondered if he should tell Dylan now about having a half brother and sister, but chose to leave it for now. He had no way of knowing if Dylan would see it as a plus or be upset by it. He'd rather let him absorb one shock at a time.

"What would you like for lunch?" he asked to change the subject.

"Anything I want?" Dylan asked hopefully.

"Within reason," Sawyer responded with a genuine smile.

"Can I have a tuna sandwich?"

Sawyer ruffled his son's hair. "You sure can. If you want to stay here for a while, I'll prepare it in about half an hour and call you when it's ready."

"'Kay."

Dylan's spirits seemed good again, Sawyer mused as he walked out of his son's room. He was a remarkably resilient kid, and Sawyer was grateful for it. They were on their way back to normal.

Then why did Sawyer's world feel so empty and why was he so dejected?

Shannon. The answer came to him without effort.

He missed Shannon.

As Sawyer was making the sandwich, Dylan came out of his room, Rufus plastered to his side.

"It's almost ready. Are you hungry, champ?"

"Kinda. But I wanted to show you my drawing first."

"Okay." Sawyer turned to Dylan.

"I drew a picture for Shannon, Daddy."

The breath caught in his throat. "You did?"

"Uh-huh." Dylan took a rolled-up sheet of

paper from behind his back and handed it to Sawyer.

Sawyer unrolled it and felt as if he'd been hit by a thunderbolt.

Dylan had drawn a big heart in bold red crayon. Inside it was an uncanny depiction of Shannon, Dylan, Rufus, Darwin and himself. Sawyer, Dylan and Rufus were standing on one side, facing Shannon and Darwin. Sawyer had his arm extended, holding something between his fingers, obviously offering it to Shannon.

"What is all this, champ?"

Dylan looked down and scuffed the toe of his sneaker. "When we talked about Mommy, you said she wasn't coming home. But that's okay because I don't really know her. I was thinking…"

Sawyer put the sheet down on the counter and crouched in front of Dylan. "And?" he prompted.

"I was thinking I want a mommy. Like other kids have. One who *lives* with us…and tells me to make my bed in the morning and brush my teeth before I go to bed."

Through the pain, Sawyer couldn't help the smile that spread across his face.

"So… I was thinking how nice Shannon

is and how much I love Darwin, too, and I thought maybe she could be my mommy."

A heavy sigh escaped Sawyer. "That's a nice idea, Dylan, but it's not that easy."

"I know!" he said and rushed on, obviously wanting to sell his plan to Sawyer. "Aunt Meg told me all about it. You have to buy a ring and ask her and everything." He pulled his drawing off the counter. "See, that's what this is," he said, pointing to the object in Sawyer's hand. "That's the ring. And we..." He pointed to the depictions of Sawyer, himself and Rufus. "We're asking Shannon to marry us and be my mommy. And then see the heart?"

Sawyer didn't trust his voice, so he simply nodded.

"That's supposed to be a locket. Like the one you said was Mommy's. We have to get another one and put our picture inside, like in my drawing."

Dylan's eyes were luminous and glowing with hope as he stared up at Sawyer. "So, do you think Shannon would marry us?"

HOURS AFTER DYLAN went to bed, Sawyer couldn't get the thought of marrying Shannon out of his mind. It seemed his kid was smarter than he was in some ways.

He loved Shannon. He'd accepted that a

while ago, but he'd foolishly waited to tell her. Waited for the right time.

He'd waited too long.

He couldn't blame her for not being able to put up with his ups and downs, but surely she'd understand that was all behind them now.

Or would she?

Had he hurt her too much? Been inconsistent too many times?

With everything that had gone on, how could he convince her that he *did* love her? That he wanted to marry her. And that neither of those things was going to change. He wanted to make a home with her.

Sawyer's gaze landed on Dylan's drawing, and it gave him an idea.

SAWYER CALLED SHANNON early the next morning. "Dylan and I have something we'd like to give you. Any chance we could stop by after your shift this evening?"

"Oh, there's no need for you to give me anything," Shannon objected. "It's my job."

She was having a hard enough time trying to get over Sawyer and Dylan. Seeing them would only exacerbate the pain.

"It's really something from Dylan," Sawyer went on.

At least it would give her a chance to see

Dylan and say goodbye to him, although the thought of seeing Sawyer again created a burning need inside her. "Okay," she finally agreed.

When she opened her door that evening, it was only Sawyer standing on her porch.

She glanced around. "Where's Dylan?"

Sawyer stepped to the side and pointed to his Range Rover. "Right there."

Dylan sat in the passenger seat with a huge grin on his face. When he noticed her looking at him, he waved energetically.

"Will he be okay there alone? Why don't you bring him in?"

Sawyer's smile turned sheepish. "Okay, if he can play in another room with Darwin."

Shannon's instincts told her there was something going on here. "Okay," she said uncertainly.

Sawyer jogged back to his SUV, helped Dylan out and handed him a long cardboard tube that must have been on the seat beside him. Next, Sawyer let Rufus out.

Shannon raised her brows over the dog, but didn't have a chance to ask why he was there, because Dylan threw his arms around her and hugged her so hard, it was as if his life depended on it.

After Dylan hugged Darwin with equal fervor, they let the two dogs get acquainted.

They then got Dylan and the dogs settled in the kitchen.

Sawyer took Shannon's hand, held the cardboard tube with the other and led her to the living room. He placed the tube on Shannon's coffee table, tugged her down beside him and continued to hold her hand.

The emotions rioting through her at his presence and his gentle touch threatened to overwhelm her. She wanted to yell at him, insist he give her whatever they'd come to give her and be gone, because she couldn't be with him much longer and not reveal how she felt about him.

"There's something I need to tell you before I give you what we brought."

"All right…" She wanted him to go on while she could still outwardly control her emotions.

He grasped her other hand, too. "Shannon, I haven't been able to get you out of my mind. I know it hasn't been easy and I've been all over the map, but I have to tell you…I love you."

The sound she made was more like a croak than a gasp. She tried to pull her hands free, but he held tight. "Shannon, listen to me. I *love* you."

Through the haze of tears, she tried to find her voice. "Sawyer, I…I can't do this."

His eyes had never looked brighter. Or

greener. "Can you tell me you don't love me?" he challenged.

"I do love you, damn it! I've been falling in love with you almost since the day we met. But the roller-coaster ups and downs have been destroying me. I know it's not your fault, but I just can't do this," she repeated. "Each time you backed away, it tore me apart more than the time before," she added in a whisper.

"It's different now."

"There's still so much you and Dylan have to work through. How can I trust that you won't withdraw from me again?"

"First, because now Dylan's home to stay. Thanks to you…" He stroked the length of her arm. "Second, because I've never told you before that I love you."

Shannon rose and backed away from him. These were not the circumstances under which she'd longed to hear those words from Sawyer. And if he *did* change his mind again, she wasn't certain she'd survive it. She felt his hands on her shoulders, then his lips—featherlight— against the curve of her neck, trailing kisses up to her ear.

She stepped farther away. Away from his touch. "No, Sawyer. I'm sorry, but I can't go through this again…"

Sawyer turned her to face him. "Give me

a minute. Please." He grabbed the cardboard tube and started to pull something out of it, then paused to wave toward the kitchen. Shannon glanced over her shoulder just in time to see Dylan's smiling face before he ducked behind the wall—Darwin and Rufus following him.

When she looked back at Sawyer, he had a rolled piece of paper in his hand and nudged her down on the sofa and sat next to her.

"Can we agree on one thing?" he asked with a half smile.

"Depends on what it is." Her heart was beating so fast and hard, she could feel it pounding against her rib cage.

"Can we agree that Dylan is the most important thing in the world to me, and I'd never let him down or do anything intentionally to hurt him?"

Shannon found she could smile, too. "No question about that."

He nodded and his smile spread. "Okay. Good. Do you believe that if I promised him I'd do something, I'd keep my word?"

"Yes. But, Sawyer…"

"Just wait!" He unrolled the sheet of paper and looked at it for a few seconds before handing it to her.

As she stared at the drawing, her throat

seemed to close, and tears leaked from her eyes. "I...I don't understand..."

"Dylan made this drawing. He wanted to know if you could be his mommy."

By now, the tears were flowing freely down her cheeks. She swiped at them with the back of her hand. Sawyer reached into a pocket and passed her a clean handkerchief.

"I told him that nothing would make me happier than to have you as his mommy. And as my wife." He paused. Waited for her to wipe her eyes again. "And I promised Dylan I would love you forever, and that I'd ask you to marry me. Now I'll promise you the same thing. That I'll love you forever. I don't have a ring yet. I thought we'd choose that together. But I do have this drawing." He held it out to her again, and she accepted it with trembling hands. "Shannon, I love you. Will you marry me?"

Through her tears, she managed a strangled "yes," then threw herself into his arms.

Dylan let out a whoop from the archway to the kitchen and came charging in, Darwin and Rufus at his heels.

Suddenly, Shannon was in the center of a tangle of limbs and fur...and had never been happier.

* * * * *